MY DIRTY LITTLE
BOOK OF
STOLEN TIME

MY DIRTY LITTLE BOOK OF STOLEN TIME

Liz Jensen

BLOOMSBURY

First published in Great Britain in 2006
This paperback edition published 2007

Copyright © 2006 by Liz Jensen

Illustrations copyright © 2006 by Peter Bailey

The moral right of the author has been asserted

Bloomsbury Publishing Plc
36 Soho Square
London W1D 3QY

www.lizjensen.com

A CIP catalogue record for this book
is available from the British Library

ISBN 9780747585930

10 9 8 7 6 5 4 3 2

Typeset by Hewer Text UK Ltd, Edinburgh
Printed in Great Britain by Clays Ltd, St Ives plc

All papers used by Bloomsbury Publishing are natural,
recyclable products made from wood grown in well-managed
forests. The manufacturing processes conform to the
environmental regulations of the country of origin.

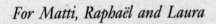

For Matti, Raphaël and Laura

Part the First: Into the Great Beyond

L ast night I dreamed I went to Østerbro again, flying towards my little quadrant of Copenhagen streets just as a fairy might, or a homing bird. I floated above my beloved city in my night-garments: not the provocative sex-shop gown of scarlet viscose I once donned for my tormentor – all tiny buttons, ribbons & teasing slits – but a chaste cotton slip, such as a child might wear. White, the colour of purity. Ah, what happy memories surged through me as I beheld the vista below. Copenhagen, with its copper domes, twisted crocodile towers, verdigris pinnacles & silver waters that glittered in the cold sunshine like an accident of spilt schnapps: Copenhagen as it was back in the old days, before the laws of time were turned on their head: Copenhagen before battery-operated dildos, Suicide Machines & mobile telephony entered my life, before the joyous hurricane of Love smashed in, & when the word winter meant something! Then, just as I spied the landmarks of Østerbro – a fringe of trees, the blue-green cupola on Holsteinsgade, & Sortedams Lake flecked with swans – I awoke & took in the dawn light, the flicker of the television, the city's electric whine, & the yowl of sirens, & my Danish dream slid away fleet as a herring.

* * *

Tick, tock: a hundred thousand clocks mimic the revolutions of the planet, & time's wheel grinds earth to earth, ash to ash. My story begins in dust and shall end in it likewise. But O, the adventures in between! Reader, you will simply not believe them, for I scarcely can myself!

The chain reaction of eerie wonders & absurd mistakes that first brought me here sparked on Classensgade in Østerbro, a suburb of Copenhagen, capital city of that mighty nation, Denmark. The year was 1897. See me there that winter: a street-girl at street level. Slush level, you would call it in today's world, but back then, cold was cold, & slush was for springtime. Shocking low the temperature was that morning. The lakes had been frozen solid for five weeks, & your breath crystallized into minuscule ice-pearls; you imagined the tinkle of them shattering on the cobbles as you walked to the bakery to buy *rundstykker*. Trot, trot, innocent little not-so-innocent. Pull your fox-trimmed bonnet down & adjust your veil over that ghost-pale face & scoot along fast, don't listen to the street-boys whistle & call out whore. Although my boots were lined with fur, my chilblained feet were already giving me all kinds of grief. Can you imagine the marrow-freezing chill of that Copenhagen air, dear reader, & the raucous-screeching seagulls that haunted the icy, sullen days which yawned into an eternal night-time of darkness? You may not credit this, but I assure you, we Danes used to virtually hibernate between November & April, back then. Pickle ourselves in aquavit & wait it out. Sometimes the clocks themselves would stop, their oiling frozen, & the bells seize up, so that even the most muscular bell-ringers would heave on the rigidified ropes to no avail, & end up seeking the warm joy of flesh on flesh instead. Money for nothing, for I took pleasure in it too, by the flickering brazier of that attic apartment on Classensgade.

It was a Wednesday, & I had eaten little since Sunday, Fru Schleswig & I having been well-nigh broke all winter due to the sudden absence of my two most lucrative clients – Herr Fabricius, jailed for fraud ('a temporary hitch, I assure you, *skat*: I will be rogering you again within the twelvemonth'), & Herr Haboe, more permanently vanished, indeed now lying one metre below ground, cause of death one bad oyster. Our shortage of ready cash, exacerbated by my recent medical indisposition & Fru Schleswig's habitual schnapps-induced torpor, meant that this morning I was in a sorry state, half hallucinating from hunger, & Lord, I do believe that I had not even applied lipstick, perfume or rouge! The snow flurried around my head like cruel confetti, & a lone crow cawed in what remained of a tree, then – mid-croak – dropped suddenly dead with a candid little thud on to the cobbles. The snow was now thickening to a white whirr, so I ran the last stretch, & burst through the door of Herr Møller's bakery, panting. The bell clanged as I entered – O, yes, the sweet smell of sugar & yeast & hot buns! – & my fate was all but sealed.

But before I pull you with me into the dizzying whirlpool of events that innocent-looking moment sucked me – ignorant! innocent! – into, let me beg a shred of your time to say an important, nay crucial word on the subject of trust. Trust, which lies at the heart of the pact we shall make together, you & I, dear (& beloved already – yes!) reader, in the sharing of these tear-stained confessions, the grubby dog-eared journal that charts the topography of my adventures. Now trust, as I discovered in what I think of as 'my travels', is a concept not limited to Denmark alone, though in the days of my naiveté I thought it was. Trust – being precious, & therefore open to abuse – brings rewards as well as its perils. The greatest of these are obvious: they involve being taken for a fool, & the many humiliating forms thereof. But the rewards – ah. Such deep satisfactions you will gain, such intimate & soulful pleasures, such profound & mind-expanding knowledge! Please remember that as I acquaint you with my tale, for what can I tell you about my extraordinary voyages without sounding like the world's most monstrous liar, or Baron Münchausen himself? Who but a trusting person – such as I most sincerely hope you are, or we are shipwrecked before we embark – would believe the depravity of my upbringing & the strange twists of Fate that led me to territories hitherto uncharted by human science or philosophy? Or indeed the cataclysm of events that was to burgeon, most inauspiciously, from a chance encounter in a humble bakery on Classens-gade?

Where, giddy from the sudden warmth of indoors, I inhaled the sweet fumes & steadied myself against the wooden counter. Spied *tebirkes* dotted with poppyseed: smelled car-away, cinnamon, honey, marzipan, & nutmeg: feasted my eyes on dainty iced buns.

'Ah, my little Charlotte!' said Herr Møller, greeting me with a broad pastry-man smile. 'Hell's bells, you look like death warmed up! Too much fornication on an empty stomach, I'll be bound!'

Well, he was jolly this morning.

I was the only customer in the shop, & it seemed that Herr Møller's wife was out in the back courtyard mulching yeast or breastfeeding her plethora of infants or whatever bakers' wives do, otherwise he would not have dared speak to me in such a familiar manner.

'Illness,' I said hoarsely, 'brought me low for a week.' I had caught an influenza through the over-frequent exposure of my naked flesh to the air of a cold attic, in the course of my professional activities – a fact which caused Herr Møller merely to shake his head in amusement. 'Such are the wages of strumpetry, my little troll! Occupational hazard, wench!'

I did not personally consider it a joke that the intimate services I offered – of which Herr Møller himself had oft enough partaken, out in the kitchen, in lieu of payment for the sweetmeats of which Fru Schleswig is so fond – brought with them certain pitfalls. The hypocrisy! But I buttoned my lip, because free pastries are free pastries, & there are times when you need them to raise a certain crone's morale. Humming the popular ballad we all had on the brain that winter ('Tragic Johanna', about a lass who took her broken heart to the banks of the Gudenå: 'deeper than Love ran that river, & deeper than Love did she drown' – O, how little Johanna could set whole tavernfuls of grown men blubbing!), Herr Møller selected a loaf for me – not quite the best, I noted, but not the worst either, & wrapped it in a page of *Berlingske Tidene*.

'Anything else, my little peach? Some of yesterday's *wienerbrød* for you & your ma? They're on the stale side, so here's two for free. Don't go getting too thin. A man likes a bit of arse. Now your ma, she's got an arse on her. There's a woman

7

knows the value of cooked dough! How much does she weigh? If you're short of money, girl, why not display her at a fair? Set up a little stall, charge them fifty øre to "guess the weight of Ogress von Flobberschmidt" or somesuch? You'd make a stack of money!'

Now, normally I was quite capable of ignoring the man's banter. Shopkeepers all run their mouths: it's part of their trade, just as certain types of talk, of the high-class pillow variety (& here I throw in the names Galileo, Rousseau, Darwin & Kierkegaard), were mine. But the mention of Fru Schleswig couldn't help but rile me. My fever had not yet subsided, & I felt my blood hotten painfully.

'Do not speak of that excruciating creature to me, Herr Møller!' I said. 'Have I not told you a thousand times, sir, that Fru Schleswig is *not my mother*? Fru Schleswig is merely a decrepit old crone whom I am generous enough to support, & were it not for the kindness of my heart she would be back in the gutter, where she came from! These are hard times, Herr Møller, & if all your suggestions about making ends meet concern weighing machines & fairgrounds, then –'

But suddenly the doorbell clanged again so despite my speech being now in full flood, I bottled it pronto, & in walked Fate. Fate, in the form of a tall, swollen-faced, accusatory-looking woman in a pompous green-tinted fur coat & matching hat, whom Herr Møller addressed most obsequiously as 'my dear Fru Krak', quite forgetting, in that instant, about the change he owed me for my *rundstykker*. The woman, who ignored my presence entirely, due to her own self-importance & sense of ladyship, then set about ordering an elaborate cake with icing & marzipan features for the delectation of Pastor Dahlberg, who was returning from a funeral in Aalborg this afternoon, she said, & needed to be greeted with something sweet. Her fancy accent grated on my ear: I recognized vowels that were born within spitting distance of the gutter, but honed & squeezed to ring aristocratic. (I had la-di-da'd myself likewise on occasion, to please those clients who harboured fantasies about lewd countesses.) But I caught a sense of genuine cash – not just ready kroner but deep, vault-&-coffer money – on the woman, & took a small step closer: close enough indeed to spot the thinness of her hair, & the dull, greying roots that belied the outer blonde.

'Ah the joys of love!' said Herr Møller, as if a lecherous pastrycook like him should know anything about it. 'So marvellous that you are finally to be wed again, Fru Krak, in your middle years, & surely at the height of your powers, after all these many sad months, nay years, of widowhood!' Then he caught sight of me pouting at being so rudely cast into the margin, & suddenly remembered my change which he handed me with a flourish.

'Upon which subject,' she said, still ignoring me completely, 'you said, Herr Møller, that you would make some enquiries for me in the neighbourhood. As you know, sadly my home is in need of attention, for grief leads to all kinds of neglect, no matter how hard one tries. And now, with my marriage to the dear Pastor on the horizon, I am in need of some reliable domestic help.'

Aha! On hearing this, I make a signal to Herr Møller: having caught his eye, I quickly sketch the vast figure of Fru Schleswig beside me in the air, then point to Lady Muck. Following my meaning at once, the baker turns to me, his face squeezed into artificial kindness.

'Well, might your ma not be a candidate, my dear Charlotte? She could do with the work, I'm sure. I imagine her to be quite a scrubber!'

At which Fru Krak wheeled round to stare at me, & I gave a curtsy, while saying quickly, lest there be misunderstanding, 'As I mentioned to you a moment ago, Herr Møller, Fru Schleswig is not my mother.' (Why would people persist in this misconception about my relationship with the embarrassing Fru Schleswig? It was a daily ordeal I endured. I should perhaps inform you at this point that my real mother was a minor princess, who was forced to abandon me as a baby.) 'But I do indeed share lodgings with the poor creature,' I continued, '& I can certainly ask her. If it's of interest to this fine lady here.'

The 'fine lady' was now looking at me in an appraising, supercilious manner.

'You are a harlot, I take it?' she said, narrowing her eyes, one of which seemed disconcertingly smaller & lower-set than the other, giving her a lopsided air. If she'd once possessed a decent physiognomy, then only the sad ruins of it remained: I could discern no jaw-line, & her puffy chin & throat were conjoined into a single feature, like the tragic thyroid of a force-fed bird.

'Yes, I do indeed walk the streets, for my sins,' I answered humbly, lowering my eyes. It could do no harm to act modest & repentant, especially if she was one of those sycophants who are keen to impress the Church. Which she would need to be if engaged to a pastor. Careful footwork would be required with this woman, if I was to profit from her. Indeed, I must out-sly her.

'So this mother of yours. Is she a harlot too?' she queried harshly.

'No, dear Fru Schleswig is a cleaner born & bred,' I lied. 'A floor-mopper & cleaner of water-closets to the very core of her being. Though she is not actually my mother.'

'Why should I care whether she is your mother or the man in the moon?' retorted Fru Krak with a strangely triumphant laugh. 'What I need to know is, can she wield a broom? Will she apply herself vigorously to a task? Is she capable of proper *scouring?*'

I assured her that Fru Schleswig was a champion scourer, & no stranger to hard graft. (Another lie, for the old creature was, & is, as idle as a sloth in an irreversible coma.) And to impress her further, I curtsied yet again, for who knows, I was thinking: might the Queen of Sheba here sometimes be in need of a personal maid, to help her dress, & be at hand to furnish her with all the necessary accoutrements of hoity-toityship such as muffs in winter & fans in summer, & prepare tea for the Pastor? Or perhaps assist the gentleman himself more directly, & in other ways? I have found the clergy, in general, to be quite a fresh bunch, & prone to guilt afterwards, which they sometimes assuage by offloading an extra krone or two on the wench who has serviced them. Such were the thoughts that flurried through my head as I respectfully suggested that Fru Schleswig & I should visit Fru Krak later that morning.

'No, come at three this afternoon,' she said, her glance flickering over my body in the same way she might look over a flank of raw beef at the butcher's, judging its worth & succulence as weighed against the contents of her purse. 'You can bring my cake along, & save me the journey. I have much to prepare, with Pastor Dahlberg's arrival this evening. I hold to very high standards,' she said, & gave me a warning glare that told me that nothing but perfection would suffice, but nor might it ever be attained, in her eyes, for it was plain to see she was a picky one.

So I complimented her on the efficiency of her thinking, & it was agreed that if all went well, Fru Schleswig could start work at Fru Krak's home on Rosenvængets Allé immediately. She had got my hackles up, though, with her sense of superiority, so as I left the bakery I lowered my veil &, beneath it, released the steam of my annoyance by pulling a comical face such as I sometimes do for the amusement of the simple-minded Fru Schleswig, who will laugh like a crazed mule at the slightest foolishness.

It was by now nine in the morning: I had a full six hours to awaken Fru Schleswig from the drunken stupor into which she had sunk the night before in our three-roomed attic, & spruce her up. As I climbed the stairs to our lodgings, I could hear her snoring from a full three flights below. There had been complaints from neighbours about these nocturnal emissions, & at times I was forced to shove a whole pillow & eiderdown over the woman's face, to silence her. I sighed as I rolled her over & surveyed her visage, as familiar to me as a winter potato, with its bulbous nose & slabby cheeks. It was hard to assess how long it would take to get her looking respectable. Reeking schnapps-fumes formed an invisible cloud around her head, & repulsive wafts of even fouler air emanated from her nether regions, fungal & glaucous. My stomach churned.

'Chop chop, Fru S!' I yelled in her ear, slapping her sweat-glazed forehead with my glove. She snorted awake & opened a glutinous eye. 'Rise & shine! I have news for you, madam! You are finally to work for a living!'

While she broke wind prodigiously, groaned & rolled around on her mattress, fighting with the dregs of sleep, I heated water on the brazier, then seized her by the arm & dragged her to the kitchen, where I poured a tepid pailful over the mass of her. She grunted like a pig.

One should begin in childhood, I suppose. Is not that the tradition, in autobiography? But forgive me, dearly beloved one (and my, you are looking well today, if I may say so!), if I skate over mine in the briefest manner possible, for the tale of my early years is simply too tragic to dwell on & I do not wish to start our tender relationship by making you cry tears of pity for me at this stage, as there will be plenty of opportunity for you to do so later. Suffice it to say that, reluctantly abandoned by my royal-blooded & beautiful young parents who were forced to flee monarchic persecution, I grew up in a nameless orphanage in the wilds of Jutland, starved of Love. The house – a gloomy, low-slung, ochre-painted building swarming with dozens of diseased brats – stood on a gaunt escarpment, lashed by whatever weather God saw fit to throw at it: wind, thunder, hail, & occasional thin shards of sun that poked through the cloud & then retreated, scared off by the barrenness of what they illuminated below. Many a little mite died of starvation & grief in that house; none thrived. It was not a place in which to blossom, or where joy might be kindled. It was home only to despair, a cankered nest to leave & to forget before it strangled your soul.

And leave it I did, before death took me.

I headed for Copenhagen. I was sixteen years old.

* * *

But just as a sheep will trail crotties stuck to its tail & hindquarters, I trailed something too. At this point I fear I must raise the subject of the human disaster Fru Fanny Schleswig, & how she became embroiled in my tale & remains a part of it, however keen I have been (for reasons you will understand, being – like me – of a refined nature) to jettison her from it altogether. Fru Schleswig had been employed as a cook (or should I say poisoner) in the orphanage in Jutland, & when I fled from that vile & dangerous place she got wind of my escape & swore to follow me, so pathetically attached was she to the young girl whom she had known from babyhood, & watched grow into the lithe & lissom young woman who was to walk into Herr Møller's bakery that winter morning & unwittingly set all hell in motion. Being of shockingly low intelligence, & barely literate, Fru Schleswig had nevertheless displayed the wiliness of a truffle-hunting pig in tracking me down in Copenhagen within hours of my arrival at the train station, insisting that whatever was my Fate, it would be hers too. To this day I cannot fathom what ugly or pitiable mix of misguided loyalty, sly opportunism & parasitic greed led her to pursue me & claim some kind of kinship. But there she was, grunting on my doorstep, & I could not turn her away.

While Fru Schleswig, who had by now opened her second eye but was not yet capable of what passed, in her terms, for human speech, fought with a bar of coal-tar soap, I descended to the florist's shop on Holsteinsgade to glean what information I could from my friend Else, with whom I used to perform in my music-hall days, before she tripped on a sausage-skin & broke her heel, & I discovered there were more lucrative activities to be pursued offstage than on it. Now that she was mistress of her own shop, Else was party to all the Østerbro gossip, & could tell me more about Fru Krak, I was sure.

'Winter-flowering cherry, tra-la-la!' she sang triumphantly as I entered. The smell of flowers & soil hit me in a soft rush & it was a moment before I saw my pretty friend, hidden as she was behind a thousand sprays of pale pink blossom, as delightful & cheerful as fresh knickers. 'All the way from the south of France,' she continued, waving a huge sprig at me. 'Here, have some.' She lowered her voice. 'But profit from it now, for it will be dead by tea-time. Blossom don't travel. I need to flog the lot today, to whatever poor fool will have it.'

Else's screaming orange hair was tied up in a most becoming though eccentric style, sitting on her head like a crouching tiger set to pounce, & pierced through with chopsticks from which several coloured beads & bells hung & jangled. Although the singing days of the Østerbo Coquettes were over, Else had never left them behind her, & seemed always to stand on a tiny stage of her own devising, upon which each of her smallest gestures was a dramatic performance. I watched her with my usual admiration as she busied herself with shears cutting laurel & catkin stalks & turning them into a deft & fiddle-de-dee arrangement. While she worked, I told her of my meeting with Lady Muck, aka Fru Krak, & she in turn told me the three facts about the woman that she had in her possession. Which were firstly that Fru Krak was a consummate bitch (which anyone, I told her, could ascertain from the distance of a furlong), she was a miser (which came as no surprise), & thirdly, that she had very probably murdered her husband, a professor of physics who was now a ghost that walked the streets of Østerbro at night, and had been seen posting letters in the box down by Sortedams Lake. Now the third piece of information did somewhat startle me, but to say that Else is prone to exaggeration is an understatement, so I did not show the level of surprise that *you*, dear one, might have done on receipt of such alarming news.

'A ghost?' I queried. 'Killed him how?'

'Well, ain't that just the mystery,' she said, now slickly weaving a length of pink ribbon into a basket of bulbs & moss. 'The poor bugger's body was never found. Which means she is a widow only in name. She never buried him. Well, you can't bury thin air, can you?'

'Curiouser & curiouser! So what happened?'

'He disappeared from the face of the earth. When Fru Krak was away taking the waters at Silkeborg. Or so she claimed, come alibi time. The Prof didn't pack no suitcase or take nothing. Odd or what? Wife's story was, he was suicidal, & must've killed himself & then got his corpse to do a vanishing trick.'

'If indeed he died,' I mused. 'An interesting case legally speaking, you might think. Since she is to remarry. If Professor Krak is actually alive enough to be seen posting letters, then does that not make the woman a bigamist?'

'Only with a bad lawyer on her side,' laughed Else, whose father was a bad lawyer: having grown up with the sound of angry clients pounding at the door asking for their money back, she knew of what she spoke. 'She got herself one who'd swear black was white, for the right dosh. And remember, the Professor ain't been seen alive in donkey's years. Except as a ghost. They said he was the *erratic* type: odd ideas, dodgy theories. Anyway, according to this lawyer, after seven years you can remarry, & *the previous alliance can be deemed by the courts null & void.*'

'And the man she's to wed? Pastor Dahlberg?'

'A widower. Interesting to see how long he lasts.' She lowered her voice & pulled a doomy face, still flicking skilfully at the pink ribbon. 'My line of work, you can never have enough wreaths laid by. Charge a king's ransom for them, you can, cos Fru Customer reckons it ain't proper to haggle, question of respect for Herr Deceased. I had an old bag in here last week –'

'But how do you know all this about the Kraks?' I interrupted, keen to steer her back to the matter in hand, for when Else runs off on a tangent, she is never guaranteed to return.

'From Gudrun Olsen. We play cards together Fridays. She's Mistress of Ironing at the laundry, fifty girls she's in charge of. That's now. Back then, though, she was the Kraks' housekeeper. Fru K gave her the sack straight after. Smells fishy in itself, I'd say. Go see her: she'll tell you more than I can, & give you some ironing tips too. What Gudrun can't teach you about steam ain't worth know—'

'But the ghost!' I interrupted again. 'Tell me, you've seen it?'

She threw up her hands. 'Blimey, how would I know if I had? I never clocked Professor Krak alive, & don't know his features. There's many a man walks in this shop who could easily be dead, to look at him. But he ain't. He's just married to the wrong woman. Dead folk walk the streets every day, Charlotte. You know it as well as me, & what's more, you roger them.'

'Such a cheery view of the world you take!'

'I merely got myself two clear eyes. Avoidance of disappointment: a little lesson I learned after my sausage-skin accident. Life's breakable, Charlotte-*pige*: crash, bang, wallop! Today's party is tomorrow's popped balloon. Just think, I could've been a star, if it weren't for that ruddy scrap of pig's intestine!'

She gave the bulb-basket a last snip, whirled round, picked up a swathe of catkins, & plonked them in a tin bucket – *voilà*! At which point the door opened & a handsome red-cravatted man walked in brandishing a cane.

'Well, mercy me,' murmured Else. 'A good client of mine.'

'Mine likewise,' I said, recognizing him, & his cane, with which he was wont to demand perverted acts be performed, on payment of an additional fee.

'Herr Swampe! What a happy surprise!' we said together, then couldn't help bursting into amused laughter – laughter which for a glittering moment transformed us back into the Østerbro Coquettes, who would flick up their petticoats & reveal their lacy stocking-tops to the roar of the steaming, thundering crowds that packed the stalls.

The same memory of our heyday was clearly awoken in Herr Swampe too, for he immediately said: 'O, gorgeous as two sea-shells from the Tropics you are, my dears. The heart fair lights up with joy. I loved that naughty stage-act of yours. Quite something, that was. You drove me wild with that tongue-kissing thing you did. Sometimes I'd get so worked up –'

Knowing Herr Swampe was likely to have cash, & quickly catching on to his fantasy, which Else & I were very used to provoking in men who saw us together, for we had indeed performed as quasi Sapphics for the titillation of men, we both egged him on most effusively & when he had finished telling us about how much our act had aroused him, I chided him that he was a wicked boy who should be spanked. (You have no idea how many men like to hear this nonsense whispered in their ear whilst in the act, for they are big babies, forever greedy for the simultaneous comfort & punishment of Mother.)

'But dear Herr Swampe, tell me honest,' said Else, not losing her business sense. 'Did you come here to reminisce about the Østerbro Coquettes, or can I tempt you with something floral?'

Ah. Yes of course. He was looking for flowers for his wife's birthday, he told Else, returning to his quotidian senses with the weary sigh of a provider. But that was perfect, Else said, for she had just the thing for his lucky wife. Blossom, all the way from romantic Toulouse, flown in this very morning by hot-air balloon! (*Hot-air balloon?* Where does she get these rodomontade ideas? I marvelled.) While winking at me, she flogged Herr Swampe the blooms that would be dead by tea-time, & after he'd paid for them through the nose, he murmured in my ear, was I free for a quick spot of how's-your-father? For if I had the time he had the money, having yesterday bet on the horses & won. And so, knowing him to be a speedy in-and-out sort of customer, I said, 'Yes, so long as you do not insist I manipulate the cane, sir, for it is too early in the day for all that nonsense, I've not yet breakfasted.' Having obtained this assurance we left together & set about our business with the minimum of undressing & thanks to some well-timed whimpering & moaning on my part, & doubtless some renewed memories of the Østerbro Coquettes on his, the deed was satisfactorily concluded in five minutes flat while Fru Schleswig, quite oblivious, chomped her way through the *rundstykker* in the kitchen. Then, with both Herr Swampe & myself feeling in a smilingly generous mood towards his marriage (a frequent side-product of such transactions), I advised him to rush home to his wife with the blossom, so she could catch the full glory of it not to mention the whiff of Toulouse, & then said goodbye to him five kroner richer. After a quick fanny-douche & a splash of rose water I went to investigate how the ancient hag was doing. I found her now working her way through the stale *wienerbrød*, chewing sideways like a ruminant beast. But I needed her cheerful so said nothing. The repulsive Fru Schleswig said nothing either, but simply continued to munch, gazing blankly at me with her big cow's eyes, & thus we looked on one another in silence for a long moment, as two prisoners shackled to one another by an invisible & unbreakable leg-clamp, for all eternity.

I had no formal education as a child, & cannot recall exactly where or how I learned the alphabet & its uses, but down in the damp cellar of the orphanage was stored a mass of mouldering tomes (the property having once belonged to a man of letters) where, by the light of a single candle, I devoured all the books I could from morn till night, thus attaining a somewhat eclectic & worm-eaten education – including knowledge of a folk tale that frightened the young wits out of me, about a Russian witch called Baba Yaga Bonylegs who lived in a house in the middle of the forest that stood on giant chicken's legs & could turn at will.

It was of this story & the childhood nightmares it engendered that I was reminded when I clapped eyes on Number Nine Rosenvængets Allé for the first time, for it was a large sombre homestead set back some distance from the road, surrounded by tall conifer trees of an exceedingly dark green that gave it an air of shadow & menace. The garden gate screamed for oil as I opened it, which deepened the sense of childish unease I had been feeling as I approached with the wheezing Fru Schleswig, whom I had forced into a reluctant vow of silence for the occasion. I rang the huge brass bell &, after a long while & much scraping of iron bolts, Fru Krak opened the creaking door. Clad in a leg-of-mutton-sleeved dress of a sickly greenish hue, she acknowledged me with no more than a haughty nod, & then turned her critical attention to Fru Schleswig. Who gives a less than heart-lifting impression at the best of times, weighing a hundred kilograms as she does, but I had furnished her with a white apron rigid with starch, & cajoled her into rolling up her sleeves to reveal the almighty hams of her forearms, each as thick as a pig's thigh; so if nothing else, she looked strong enough to lift & hurl a barrel & wrest seven sailors to the ground.

'Your confectionery package from Herr Møller, with his compliments,' I said quickly, to distract her from the sight of Fru S, & waggled the ribboned & frilled box from the baker's at her. (And what a good laugh the ancient swine & I had shared when we stopped along the way to peek at the cake inside, for it was adorned with pink marzipan hearts like the mimsy concoction of a lovesick girl.)

'You can take it to the kitchen,' the Krakster said coldly, like a creature raised in darkness and drained of blood: her flesh had the look of veal. 'Follow me, both of you.' And so we trod behind her sweeping figure into the cavernous interior of the house, crossing first an entrance hall adorned with rein-deer & elk heads, & then heading down a gloomy corridor

'Your confectionery package!'

whose plaster-flaking walls gave off an ominous whiff of toad-spore. 'The Pastor & I are to be married in February,' she announced over her shoulder. 'I had thought March, but the Pastor is keen to pursue our nuptials,' & since she did not speak of it as a joyful prospect, I could not help but glean that she was one of those who prefer the anticipation of marriage to the state itself.

When we reached the kitchen, which was hung with desiccated hams, she indicated I should put the package on the table. 'Which lands me in a difficult position vis-à-vis the cleaning of this place. It will need some intensive work,' she said, now turning her attention to the wheezing Fru Schleswig with increasing distaste. I handed the old crone (whose finger was now openly exploring the inside of her nostril) a handkerchief, & gave her a glare which told her to behave herself or face the consequences. Casting my eyes around the room, & swiftly assessing the possibilities before me, the financially exciting notion which I had been incubating since I first clapped eyes on Fru Krak in the baker's shop now hatched, shook itself, spread its little wings, & prepared to fly. For it was suddenly eminently clear to me that one, there would be jewellery, trinkets, decorative objects & even small items of furniture here that might be pilfered & sold to good effect, & two, that Fru Schleswig would be dismissed within an hour here, if left to her own devices. Nothing focuses the intellect like an empty purse.

'Might I suggest in that case that you employ the two of us?' I offered sweetly to Fru Krak. 'Fru Schleswig & I can happily work in tandem, she dealing with the heavier cleaning – I note you have a damp-rot problem, which is right up Fru Schleswig's street – while I, in turn, can see to the finer side of things such as polishing & dusting. I would not like Fru Schleswig here to break any of your −' I looked around: curtains dangling dust-laden *klunke*-bobbles, all manner of *passementerie* & overstuffed armchairs, plus myriad mirrors reflecting regiments of knick-knacks and gewgaws − 'your fragile & costly ornaments.'

At which point Fru S fog-horned at me: 'Wot do u fink I am, a bull in a chyner shoppe or wot?' Already her vow of silence was broken, as I should have guessed it would be, but I ignored her &, hoping Fru Krak would do the same, pursued my theme: which was that together Fru S & I could get the work done in half the time, so that by New Year the mansion would be as new, & a fitting abode for the Pastor & his lovely wife. Might the good lady be so kind as to show us round, to get the measure of the place?

With some reluctance, & with many warnings about how she would notice immediately if any thieving went on, for she knew the value & location of every item she owned, she led us around the rest of her dismal residence; a labyrinth of decrepit passages & small, unlikely sets of twisting stairs leading to single cells in lonely towers, or to unexpected, spider-infested bedrooms. I was minded of a honeycomb after the bees have been smoked out, & despite having a good inner compass, I had lost track of its configuration within the space of twenty doors, & realized I would need to make myself a detailed map with pen & ink, if I was to master the architecture, & turn such knowledge to my profit.

'As you see, I keep many rooms locked,' Lady Muck announced, jangling the set of keys that hung at the level of her heavy hips. 'But that is to change, for Pastor Dahlberg has much in the way of furniture. Nearly every room must be opened, aired & cleaned in preparation for his arrival.'

'*Nearly* every one, madam?' I queried.

A look of alarm crossed her face, but she suppressed it quickly.

'There are one or two that remain private,' she snapped, '& will not be of concern to you.'

'Of course,' I said. 'I am sure all houses have them.' She looked at me sharply: I saw the spasm of anxiety again. 'All the best houses must, I mean,' I said soothingly, keen to disguise the sudden sense of excitement I was feeling at having spotted a chink in that icy armour of hers. This seemed to settle her somewhat, for I was getting the measure of her by now, & guessed that she was one to be mollified by the crassest of flatteries. But I will confess to you, dear reader, that the subject of the locked rooms, & the hint of agitation she betrayed at the mention of them, filled me immediately with the most overwhelming curiosity. How could it not? Clearly there was something hidden there that she would prefer to remain a secret. And had I not read *Bluebeard*, and stories of hidden treasure? I pictured a big coffer stuffed with jewels and banknotes, such as a pirate might bury on a secret island, and mark on a map with an X. A softened bar of wax, I figured, was all it would take to make an imprint of the keys. I was quite lost in my thoughts on this subject when we stopped at the top of a staircase, which Fru Schleswig was still laboriously climbing in our wake. As I have mentioned, I had instructed the elderly hag not to blab a word, & to act entirely mute, but she had already broken this pledge several times by uttering uneducated exclamations of the type: *O pittie me poor ole legs!* & *Blimey, wot it must be lyke ratling round alone in a hows this syze!*

And *Coo, look at the tinklys on that shandyleer!* – remarks which Fru Krak had fortunately chosen to ignore.

'I am not one to be cheated,' said Lady Muck, as we waited for Fru Schleswig – still expostulating – to join us.

'Cheat you, madam? O dear, I would not dream of doing such a thing. I may be a lowly sinner, but I was raised in a charitable orphanage & know the meaning of hard work,' I lied.

'I am a stickler for high standards,' she announced. 'I am sure you can tell that I come from a very aristocratic family. The Bischen-Baschens.'

She paused to let this sink in as it should.

'Oh yes indeed, the Bischen-Baschens,' I said with an impressive show of respect, though in truth I was stifling a powerful urge to laugh aloud. 'That is evident in your speech & comportment, madam. That you are of the highest breeding, that is. Though I have not heard of the Bischen-Baschens, I confess. Per se.'

'Well, you wouldn't have done, would you?' she said, emitting that same odd, triumphant bark I had first heard in the bakery, which was her version of laughter. 'Being nothing more than an uneducated strumpet!'

At which she laughed again, as if the fact that I earned my own living, instead of sponging off a husband as she had done, in the manner of a parasite, was the most hilarious notion she could imagine.

And thus it came to pass that Fru Schleswig & I began our new life, at a rate of five kroner per day, in the employ of Fru Emilie Krak, née Bischen-Baschen.

Tick, tock: time passed, but not much, for it was on the

afternoon of the very first day of our employment that I met the mysterious Professor Krak. Not in the flesh, or indeed in ghost form, but as a darkly lustrous oil portrait labelled *Professor Frederik Krak* hanging in a back hallway of Fru Krak's grandiose home. It depicted a dark, sparse-haired man in his early middle years, whose high temples gave the face below an air of intellectuality, & a certain eccentric flair. But there was something fervent in the intensity of his gaze – a dash of the fanatic – that caused me to shiver & remember Else's story of a ghost walking to the letterbox along the lakeside, wrapped in a black cloak & half-buried in a swirl of sepia mist. I resolved in that moment that I would go & visit Gudrun Olsen, the Kraks' former housekeeper, & make enquiries as to the character of Professor Krak, & what might have transpired those seven years ago to cause the mysterious sitter of this portrait to have been wiped so suddenly but indecisively from the face of the earth. Had his wife indeed murdered him, as Else had suggested? Or might he be living still? In either chilling case, my imagination was captured.

But in the meantime, there was work to be done. Behind her aristocratic Bischen-Baschen exterior, Fru Krak was a lazy, slovenly female whose house, apart from the front room where visitors might sit & the dining room where they might eat, was in such a state of slatternliness, dilapidation & neglect that it was difficult to ascertain where to begin, but begin Fru Schleswig must, & I set about a list of heavy chores upon which she could make an immediate start, while I sorted through the cleaning materials at our disposal, which were surprisingly numerous, though decayed. Soda crystals, bleach, bicarbonate & sand-soap, ancient waxes & polishes, half-finished bottles of stripping liquids & rusty tins of scouring chemicals: harsh stuffs, which rubbed one's hands raw, or would have done, had I not had the inspired idea of keeping mine at all times in my pockets & allowing Fru Schleswig to tackle the bulk of the harder work, her temperament being more suited to it. Water-closets were far beneath me, but they were slightly above Fru S, who got stuck into them with relish, shoving her whole arm inside with a wire scouring-brush & singing sailors' shanties as she did so. The old swine was a crude being, blessed neither with intelligence, beauty nor charm. But where would beauty be if it stood alone, without ugliness beside it, as a benchmark?

As for me, well, a young woman with a feather duster can be an attractive sight, if you happen to catch a glimpse of her in a mirror as you are passing. As I very often did. The mirrors in Lady Muck's house were soon as pure & gleaming as the soul of Christ itself. Now dust is best wiped, as we all know, with a damp cloth. A feather duster, aesthetically pleasing though it is, when held to the throat like a boa, will only redistribute the problem. There was much dust at Fru Krak's house, which had been in decline for many years since the departure of her husband. Whole prairies of it beneath the beds & furniture, so that before the wiping could be commenced, one had to fair shovel the bulk into a dustpan. While Fru Schleswig was undertaking this & other of the heavier duties, I kept up the appearance of cleaning assiduously whenever Fru Krak was in the vicinity, with particular emphasis on the high polishing of ornaments, my hands clad in gloves to protect my delicate skin. But whenever Fru Krak was absent, either shopping or lying a-bed with her women's journals, complaining of colds & flu, sore throats & headaches, all of them imaginary, I was busy with other endeavours. The first of these was the pilfering of a whole multitude of neglected gewgaws, junk & diverse paraphenalia I found lurking in musty drawers & creaking chests, or in the corners of ancient, dust-belching cupboards, for despite the mistress's warnings & protestations to the contrary, it was clear she had little inkling of what an accumulation of clutter she presided over. And thus it came to pass that whole battalions of china soup tureens, silver tankards, faded linen, framed still-lives of tulips or bleeding game, Chinese parasols, ornamental fruit-platters & Cupid-studded vases made their way to the flea-market, & several tens of kroner correspondingly made their way to my purse, & then left it again in exchange for such necessities as food & schnapps, & such luxuries as a very darling new bodice & a frock, & a bar of sandalwood-scented 'Savon de Marseille' for Fru Schleswig, to stop her moaning about 'orl this bakke-brakin wurke bein thowne att me', & at the same time cast a deodorizing hint in her direction. But aside from acquiring & flogging the Krakster's unwanted goods, my main task was the drawing of an intricate archi-tectural map of the house, its scaled-down lines painstakingly copied out in pen & ink from pencil sketches I made & measurements gauged under cover of housework. So bom-bastically huge a residence! So many chambers! But what secrets lay within?

How brave, adventurous & clever I believed myself to be, as I filled in the lines of my map, & pondered this! And yet the truth was, I was no more than a foolish puppet, dancing to the pull of strings manipulated by a far more wily intelligence than my own! Had I known, O my dear one, what nightmare the ardent fulfilment of my greed & curiosity would trap me in, I would never have spent as much as a moment on that wretched map, but instead lifted my petticoats & run from that cursed house on Rosenvængets Allé like a bat from Hell.

But fool that I was, by the end of the first fortnight in Fru Krak's employ, I was most pleased that the bargain I had struck with Fru Schleswig concerning her responsibilities seemed to be working as anticipated. So well, indeed, that even our joyless Mistress Krak was reluctantly impressed by the way the house's interior had transformed from dinginess to colour, with shining mirrors, freshly sponged & white-washed walls, scrubbed floorboards & well-aired rooms. I did not think it necessary to inform Fru Krak that in the course of her cleaning, Fru Schleswig had come across five birds' nests in the attic, & an entire dead cat, which had seemingly perished of starvation in a side-room. Apart from all that I had pilfered & sold, other numerous oddities turned up in other places, beneath loose floorboards & on top of forgotten cupboards: broken jewellery, sea-shells, a set of quoits, a bag of marbles, & a huge tin of biscuits – still edible, according to the abysmal hygiene standards of Fru S, as demonstrated by her devouring of the whole lot in a single evening with a smacking sound that fair grated on my nerves, though I buttoned my lip, for I had learned at a tender age that the inhabitants of glass houses should not throw stones. But among the gallimaufry of clutter was one object, found by Fru Schleswig in a basement larder stinking of rotten fruit, and adorned with what looked like ancient animal dung, that baffled me: a shiny rectangle of metal, like a flat box, with numbers on its face, a little like a tiny sun-dial. Playing with it idly, I found that a little door at its back slid open and two oddly heavy cylinders fell out from a case containing small springs. Eventually I managed to stuff them back and slide the little door to, but the object (which I hid in a chamber pot) continued to be a source of puzzlement, & it was not until much later, when my life had undergone the most grotesque & unexpected of unheavals, that its identity became apparent.

But in the meantime, flummoxed, we continued work. Now you may be wondering, cherished companion, just how this miracle of domestic industry came about, knowing a little of old Fru S's habits & nature as you by now do. Well, I have not had the ball & chain that is Fru S attached to my ankle all these years without having devised ways & means of manipulating her simple mind, to enable our working relationship to function smoothly, so the deal – a classic carrot-&-stick arrangement – was that Fru Schleswig would strive to make herself presentable, arrive punctually, put in all the elbow grease she had, & at all times keep her trap shut in the company of Fru Krak. If she complied with these rules, she would be entitled to certain rewards, in addition to a generous quarter-share of the pay we jointly received, viz as much schnapps as she wanted as soon as we reached home, & permission to occupy the tattered & burst chaise-longue, stirring only to gorge on whatever victuals I had managed to forage in the shops that night. If she failed to comply, I would kick her out of our lodgings forthwith.

Simple, but effective – or so you would have thought, but Fru S grumbled mightily, with much railing & thunderous banging of her hammy fists, despite the fact that in the end she had no choice, for she had, as I pointed out, sponged off my goodwill for too long, for the entire twenty-five years of my life in fact, & it was time to call a halt or be out on her ear. She grumbled further, & (to infuriate me) called on her claim of kinship to me, for 'how dare I treet my owne mutha thus' & 'bludde is thicka than worter', & we descended into the usual squalid battle of words, for I have perhaps mentioned that the preposterous notion of a blood tie between us is very much an *idée fixe* of hers, which I can do nothing to dislodge in her poor deluded mind. In the end, I turned a deaf ear to her menaces, & flounced out to see Else, who insisted we go dancing, & it was a good idea for it lifted my mood, as dancing always does, & I brought a gentleman home with me by the name of Hans-Erik, & O, the rollicking fun we had on my mattress, by candle-light. There are times, dear reader, when I was happy indeed to be paid to have fun, because the fact is that for every foul-smelling old geezer there is a good-looking charmer who knows one end of a girl from the other, & that night I had such a gift in my arms, & nothing can be sweeter, & if the truth be told, I'd have performed the act for free if he'd asked me. But he did not, & so I scored on both counts.

It was the following day, as I was tidying up the pile of foolish women's journals to which Fru Krak was addicted, that something caught my notice which instantly gave me a valuable glimpse into the psyche of our employer. I had already remarked that after she had been flicking through such publications, & in particular the *Fine Lady*, Fru Krak would become even more agitated & pernickety than usual. I had assumed that this was because these insipid journals have a tendency to inspire insecurity & envy in women whose beauty will never match that of the fashion models depicted inside them – which was clearly the plight of the physically charmless Fru Krak. Yet on that day, I discovered there was something more, which confirmed my increasing suspicion that the chilly & detached appearance she mustered in public was but the thinnest of veneers, beneath which reigned the mightiest state of anxiety, confusion & turmoil. For when I settled down to leaf through that week's copy of the *Fine Lady*, I spotted that the text beneath one sign on the horoscope page had been most vigorously, nay frantically, circled & underlined in red ink.

As a Fine Aquarian Lady, you should not tolerate the insolence of subordinates. Make sure they know their place, but allow them leeway in matters that could help you privately. Wear yellow on Thursday afternoon & a bargain will come your way. In romance, tread carefully when recounting your memories to your loved one, lest he suspect you are not all that you have seemed. Remember that to retain her moral stature, the Aquarian Lady must stay on ground level or above at all times, & never descend belowstairs! So if you require something from the cellar, madam, send the maid (provided she does not share your star-sign) to fetch it!

'Don't forget to polish the silverware properly today,' said Fru Krak, swishing in wearing a vile dress of a bright yellow hue. With a sudden jab of the most pleasurable amusement, I noted that the day was Thursday. 'Fru Pedersen found a speck of what looked like blood on her fork on Wednesday when we were lunching.'

'It was probably a touch of tarnish, ma'am,' I murmured. 'Are you going shopping?' (For there were surely bargains to be had in Christensen & Jakobsen's haberdashery on a day like this, if one was clad like a canary!)

'*Tarnish?* Well, get rid of it, girl! Do you not recall that I am originally a Bischen-Baschen? Do you think it likely that a

Bischen-Baschen would *even contemplate* displaying tarnished cutlery to her guests? Yes, I am indeed on my way out, & when I return shall make a point of inspecting the silverware to ensure you have done your job adequately.'

Seeing that she was working herself into quite a lather, I made the right placatory & humble noises, & when she had left the house – with a warning that she 'would *not tolerate the insolence of subordinates, who come from depths to which I would not dream of descending*' (ha!) – I resolved to read Fru Krak's horoscope as avidly as she did, in future, in order to anticipate her crazes, anxieties & whims. When she returned by carriage two hours later with bulging bags & the smug smile of a woman who has paid a lot of money for something worthless but has not yet discovered it, I could not help but laugh gleefully to myself, for it confirmed that I had important information on my side.

And when one has that, it is never long before one finds a way of using it!

And so began our new life as servants of the sour-faced & foolishly gullible Fru Krak, a new life shaken only by a disquieting visit I made to the former housekeeper Gudrun Olsen in mid-November, in the third week of our employ, at the insistence of Else, who had played cards with her that Friday & had received, she said, 'a terrible scare' regarding the Krak household, which I must, repeat must, pay heed to. Afterwards, I wished I had not taken her advice, for when things are going well, one does not care to dwell on what might turn sour. But there is no crying over spilt milk, & in any case, if the truth be told, the things I learned that day – unsettling though they were – could not but spark my interest all the more.

I had followed Else's scatty directions to the laundry as best I could, but the waterfront was a maze & had it not been for the help of a tall, lanky-limbed man, his face entirely hidden by a balaclava, whom I found suddenly walking alongside me on Strandboulevarden, I would never have found the warehouse where Gudrun Olsen worked. Once it was within sight, my mysterious balaclava'd saviour took his leave, & I headed for a square building that stood on the edge of the reeking seafront, belching steam. One might have thought upon crossing its threshold that one was entering a kind of hot-air Hell, for as far as the eye could see were clusters of women in white, busying themselves like frenzied brides over foaming cauldrons, or staggering beneath the weight of stacked, bleached linen-bales, or lifting heavy steam-irons from the blazing fireplace & then losing themselves in clouds of vapour.

I asked a silver-haired waif who stood at the door – male or female I could not tell – where I might find the Mistress of Ironing, & it pointed to a high balcony upon which stood a dark-clad figure surveying the vast hall. Every now & then she would reach for a small trumpet-shaped device into which she would yell an order, & one of the women would look up, nod & then perform whatever special steamy task that she was bid. I mounted the spiral cast-iron staircase & found myself alongside Gudrun Olsen. So imposing she had appeared from below, but how tiny when you stood next to her! I am no large creature myself, but beside me she was a veritable flea.

'What brings you here, young woman?' She asked the question kindly enough but with an imposing authority for one so diminutive, barely turning her neat profile, & not taking her eyes off what was happening below. She looked to be in her late thirties or early forties, with a handsome nose & chin. 'Are you seeking work?'

'No,' I answered, 'for I already have it, cleaning on Rosenvængets Allé, in the home of Fru Krak.'

At the mention of this name, the whole of Frøken Olsen's small body stiffened. She said nothing for a moment, then pivoted around to look at me, thus revealing the other side of her face – the sudden sight of which immediately made me gasp, for across it a huge red scar was raggedly drawn, beginning at the outer corner of her left eye & reaching to the contour of her upper lip, marring what was otherwise (& only now could I see it) a quite beautiful face, open & pure. What tragic mutilation!

'I knew it would only be a matter of time before someone came to me & asked about the Kraks,' she said. 'But who would have thought it would be a friend of dear Else's?' A weary sadness clouded her voice.

'Tell me, if you would: what did you make of the Professor?' I asked. 'For now that I am working in that mansion, I confess to finding myself most intrigued to discover what manner of man he was, & what became of him.'

To my surprise, Gudrun Olsen smiled fondly. 'Where does one begin, when speaking of Professor Krak? Unlike his wife, he was a person of great enthusiasm & charm,' she said. 'Though I often believed him to be quite unhinged. If ever I met a man too clever for his own good, it was he. But I was attached to him, & when he disappeared I missed him greatly, despite what happened to me there. Despite . . .' she fingered her scar, 'despite *this*.'

I drew in a breath. 'I do not speak of my accident,' she said warningly. 'For I bear a measure of guilt – excruciating guilt – over what happened. But I have to warn you, Charlotte, that you are risking your life working in that place. No good will come of it. And nor I think do you want your pretty face ruined, as mine was.'

A shudder ran the length of my spine as I eyed her dreadful scar.

'By Fru Krak?' I whispered, aghast. My mind was in a whizzy: yes, Fru Krak had a whiff of madness about her, to be sure. But the thought of her lungeing at another woman's cheek with a ragged blade . . . it beggared belief that she might muster the energy.

Finally, as if guessing my train of thought, Gudrun Olsen gave a small smile & shook her head. 'Fru Krak is a lazy, vain fool, & as unpleasant a human specimen as you could wish to meet. But she is not the danger in that house, my dear girl. It is something else entirely that you must fear.'

'What?' I asked, all a-tremble suddenly, & wrapping my cloak around me more tightly.

'The thing that did this to me,' said Gudrun Olsen (& she did not need to indicate her mutilation for my eyes were still locked to it, mesmerized), 'was not of human flesh.'

It was late afternoon when, soaked through with steam, I left that place, dear reader, a more fearful & anxious young woman, so much so that I fancied, in my agitated state, that the tall balaclava'd man who had so kindly given me directions earlier was now following me in a sinister & invisible fashion, at the periphery of my vision. But he remained elusive, for although I sensed his presence, when I turned my head he was not to be seen. That night Gudrun Olsen's words crept into my dreams, where in the foul, sunken heart of that labyrinthine home on Rosenvængets Allé I imagined wizardry & toad-spore, & hooded men performing dark deeds that the day would quake to look upon, to feed the avid hunger of a vile machine whose wheels never stopped turning. I awoke shuddering & feverish & clad in a cold, cold sweat.

Perhaps, dear reader, you might argue that no young woman in her right mind would have gone near that house again after what Gudrun Olsen had said about the mysterious goings-on within it seven years ago. But Professor Krak himself was seemingly dead & gone, & only superstitious fools believe in ghosts, & without its engineer, the demonic machinery Gudrun had spoken of, whose purpose she did not know, was surely of no more harm than any abandoned object left to dilapidate. What did I actually know that was concrete, as opposed to a random jumble of oddities? This is what I had learned: that Professor Krak was an eccentric, reclusive man, prone to passionate outbursts of fury at his wife, & obsessed with the construction of a large machine in the basement. That the more strained his marriage to Fru Krak became, the more time he would spend in his workshop, & the more money his wife would spend on clothes, as though it were part of a silent bargain they had struck, that if she granted him the peace he craved to work on his inventions, then he would fund her wardrobe. That the couple did not sleep or eat meals together, & that Gudrun Olsen would set trays of food & drink outside his workshop door, & clear them away when she found the dishes emptied. That she would show desperate-looking, dark-cloaked men & women in at midnight or the small hours, folk whom she would never see emerge from a basement cellar known as the Oblivion Room, & how these people must be ushered in through a back door, & Fru Krak must not discover their presence. That Professor Krak would send Gudrun Olsen on tortuous errands to buy machinery parts – one kilo of nuts & bolts from this mechanical supplier, another half-kilo, of a different size, from that; a little cog-wheel from a particular ironmonger's in Frederiksberg, a flexible cord from a specialist india-rubber shop in Amager, a huge, heavy jar of mercury from a one-eyed woman in a brothel in Christianshavn. Once she was obliged to take a carriage all the way to Hellerup, at midnight, & knock on a door where a man handed her a heavy, squeaking, agitated box which she suspected, from the smell, contained live sewer rats. Then on other occasions she had been dispatched to the home of a widow, where she was instructed to elicit the story of her husband's gory death by arsenic poisoning, & then recuperate the handkerchief into which she had wept.

'You'd get her to cry, & bring him back the handkerchief?'

'That's right.'

'And he never told you why?'

'He never told me anything. But he paid me well.' Each time he sent her on such errands, Gudrun said, Professor Krak would give her a thick wad of banknotes, & tell her that under no circumstances should she mention his name in association with the item she had bought.

'What happened to him, in your opinion?' I asked finally.

'I have no idea. One day he was there, the next he had disappeared. But you can be sure that if Professor Krak is indeed dead,' she finished, 'Lord bless his soul, then it is thanks to his experimenting with ideas & practices that he should not have meddled with.'

So that was what I knew. Much and little, all at once – but if there was physical danger to be feared, I had protection at least in the form of the stout Fru Schleswig, who could kill a man with a single blow of her hand, & still any machine with a thunderous kick of her hoof, however out of control it may become: with such a physical force acting as one's human shield, & taking the brunt of whatever attack might be launched in one's direction, what need I fear? That was my reasoning, as I went with Fru Schleswig to work the next day, & the next, & furthered my forays into the heart of the building. But there was something else too, that drew me deeper in, despite what I had heard: a rapacious greed to know more about the locked basement room that Professor Krak used as his workshop & the dangerous mechanical device that might still lie, rusting & abandoned, within. And to witness for myself what horrors or what marvels Professor Krak had created illicit access to –

Yes, marvels. For surely there were marvels. Why else would all those people flock to the house in such a secretive & desperate manner? Why else would I feel so burning an urge to see the contents of the basement workshop that Gudrun called the Oblivion Room for myself? Yes: what drew me, magnetically, to discover more was the same impulse that had sucked others in. Adventure. Danger. And escape. Looking back I realize that even then, I was like an opium eater, drawn to the source of woe, heedless of its ill-effects, & mindful only of the brief ecstatic sweetness it might offer, whose boundaries were only those of my imagination.

Yes, O dear one: even then, Professor Krak's demonic invention had exerted its pull.

The Pastor, whom I met the second week, was a paunchy man in his middle to late years, with clattering false teeth that seemed to roam his mouth like a tribe of nomads in search of land on which to pitch camp.

'Pleased to meet you, my dear,' he said, eyeing my curves like a greasy old flesh-merchant, & somersaulting the contraption in his mouth. 'I hear that thanks to the good Fru Krak, you are in the process of reforming. I am glad to hear it. And I know that Christ is too.' (I was quickly to learn that Christ and Pastor Dahlberg were most loyally twinned, and always agreed with one another, whatever the subject might be.)

'I beg your pardon, sir?' I asked.

'Fru Krak informs me that she saved you from the streets. That you were a *harlot*, my dear young woman. But have since sought more appetizing work? Here with us? Praise be to God.'

But I could see from the Pastor's greedy porcine eyes that his thoughts were less with the Lord Almighty than with my breasts, & at that moment I envisaged the possible transmogrification of my employment quite clearly.

'Ah yes,' I said, cottoning on to the self-serving tale Fru Krak must have spun him, about her heroic role in my 'redemption'. 'I am so grateful to the good lady, indeed I am. Were it not for the bounty of your noble fiancée, I would be forced, through sheer need, to unbutton the top of my dress thus, & reveal my lacework corset to strangers.'

The Pastor gasped, went red in the face, & came close to choking on his oral prosthesis.

'And provoke the dirtiest & most shameful lusts,' I continued, undressing further: '– & reveal the exquisite bosoms & pert girlish nipples that nestle beneath my intimate underclothing – no! No touching, sir! And at the same time tweak up my petticoats so that they can see the flesh at the top of my leg, where the stocking ends, & . . .'

Yes, dear reader, I had him where I wanted him, for by now he was breathing heavily & struggling with the buttons of his tweed knickerbockers, but I told him, steady on, mister, cash first: five kroner. Such a pitch he had worked himself into just with the thought of seeing more, that by the time he had scrabbled for the money in his pocket & revealed the pale & desperate thing that poked from his breeches like a worm struggling for air, it was all over. Which was just as well, for a moment later Fru Krak swept in wearing an outfit of pomegranate pink as depicted on the cover of that week's edition of the *Fine Lady*, & I barely had time to cover the incriminating translucency on my skirts with my feather duster before greeting her demurely & receiving my orders concerning the tasks ahead of me & Fru Schleswig, while Pastor Dahlberg scurried from the room muttering something about a sermon on penitence, his face the colour of a peeled beetroot.

And thus did two sources of income open to me in the space of one week, & I was right glad for it, & pleased with myself indeed. For I knew that the Pastor's need for repentance would crop up again, it having struck me over the years that many married women, due to their husband's negligence, have never become acquainted with their own lust, & seeing nothing emerge from the act save more babies, they cry off with complaints of headaches, bunions & women's trouble, thus catapulting their frustrated menfolk into the laps of mistresses, or girls such as myself. Fru Krak, to look at her, was surely the last woman on earth capable of lifting her petticoats for any other purpose than to piss or shit, so it was clear to me that she would soon tire of the ordeal of servicing the ageing but still eager Dahlberg once she had secured him with the forthcoming nuptials. And had her horoscope not advised her, on the subject of subordinates, to *make sure they know their place, but allow them leeway in matters that could help you privately?*

Very well, I thought, my dear Pastor, & his good Lady Muck. But if it's to be, you shall pay a high price for it. Five kroner is just the beginning.

Have you ever had the experience, dear reader, of waking every morning obsessed by the same thought? A thought which nags at you all day, & will not relinquish its grip even as you drift into sleep, but worms deeper into your psyche, manifesting itself in the most disturbing dreams? Such was the tenacity of my urge to discover the mystery that lay deep in the bowels of the Krak household. Unearth it I must! And yes, as I have already remarked to you, the frightening but insubstantial facts Gudrun Olsen had imparted to me, accompanied by warnings of doom, had, far from damping my appetite, only whetted it further. But it turned out that there was more to come, unexpectedly, from another quarter. A week after my encounter with Gudrun, I had taken advantage of Fru Krak's absence at the hairdresser's to visit the apothecary for some rose water. Herr Bang was behind the counter, & we were soon chatting about some of the changes that were being wrought in the neighbourhood of Østerbro. He told me that his girls were to attend the new school run by Ingrid Jespersen, & that his wife would teach there too, & I in turn told him where Fru Schleswig & I were employed, it being not far from that very school, & at this news his face darkened.

'I know Fru Krak. She's been a regular customer of mine ever since her husband disappeared. A bad sleeper. I sell her a lot of potions for the nerves, but I have remarked that nothing seems to work. I'm not surprised she's twitchy, the things that went on there. And do still, if the rumours are to be believed. She has been trying to sell that house for years, but none will buy it, for it is said to be haunted.'

'What "things" went on?' I asked, a shudder running through me as I recalled Gudrun Olsen's talk of demonic machinery & sewer rats. But he did not answer me directly.

'I was acquainted with Professor Krak,' he said. I did not recognize the expression that came over his face, for I had never encountered it before; studying him closely, I remarked he looked uncomfortable, as though remembering something he would rather not.

'And what business had you with him, if I may ask?'

Herr Bang looked around him, as though to confirm that I was the only customer in the shop, which I was, then took out a stepladder & reached for a jar of liquid from a high shelf, which he proceeded to stir furiously with a small metal whisk. 'Dark business,' he said finally, as though that were the end of it. But I would not let him escape.

'But of what nature, pray? You cannot just say "dark business", sir, & then leave it hanging!'

He sighed, clearly excruciated, & whisked ever more

energetically, so that the liquid began to froth quite alarmingly, & generate little underwater sparks.

'I would not like my wife to hear of this,' he said. 'For she prefers me not to dwell on my unhappy past, knowing how much it pains me. But here it is. You see, I was married before, & my first wife caught tuberculosis & died, & so did our young baby, only six months old,' he said, still mixing vigorously.

Then he stopped & looked at me, & I saw tears in his eyes. 'It is a cruel disease.' We both surveyed the jar for a moment, in which the liquid – a pale green – was still swirling around, the little sparking particles glittering luminously within.

'I am sorry, Herr Bang,' I said softly. 'I did not know of this.'

'I was a very unhappy man &, to be honest, all I wanted was oblivion. I had heard on the grapevine that Professor Krak was known to offer . . . certain discreet services. To which, I will confess, I felt very much drawn at the time, in my distress. I felt so helpless without my wife & son, & would never have believed that only two years later I would meet my present darling wife & have three more children, & be as contented as I am. I thought my life was at an end.'

'What services?' I asked, picturing an unhappy brothel – until I remembered Gudrun Olsen speculating about séances. 'Did he put you in touch with the dead?'

'In a manner of speaking, yes,' he said cryptically. 'But let me just say that they were not joyful services he offered. They were for the desperate among us, & I was one of their number then. He offered what he called journeys to the Great Beyond.'

'The Great Beyond? What & where is that?'

'I never discovered. Let me just say that I looked into the

abyss down in the basement, my dear – but I feared what I saw, & pulled away.' His face had taken on a different cast, both wistful & full of pain. I knew better than to break the spell of his mournful reverie & so I waited. 'He was a likeable man, for all his oddness & eccentricity. I got the impression he was on a kind of mission. He spoke of those who used his services as "pioneers".' He chuckled. 'I'll never forget all those clocks he had everywhere,' he said, then paused in his whisking process to survey the jar of liquid, which had now turned a much lighter hue. 'Hundreds of them, all telling a different time, according to what capital city they represented.'

'What clocks?' I asked sharply, feeling a sudden chill, for I could picture not a single timepiece in the whole house.

'Ah. She'll have got rid of them then,' he said, nodding slowly. Then he squinted at the window. 'Did you see that man in the balaclava peering in just now?' he asked suddenly.

'A balaclava?' I queried. I looked out, but saw nothing. 'It seems to be quite popular head-gear this winter,' I said, remembering my guide on Strandboulevarden, but feeling a strange uneasiness as I did so.

'He seemed keen to come in, then changed his mind,' mused Herr Bang. 'He was probably after something embarrassing. They tend to loiter.'

'So tell me, what did Professor Krak offer, exactly?' I asked, not wanting him to lose the thread. Herr Bang thought for a moment.

'Well, he claimed that an invention of his – a certain machine he had built – could provide a solution whereby one's body would never be found. Whether it eliminated you or transported you elsewhere I never discovered, & I am not certain he did either. Many chose that route, even though Professor Krak warned that there were risks. But I decided against it, & do not regret delaying my journey to the Great Beyond.'

Seeming suddenly ill-at-ease, as if he felt he had said too much, Herr Bang stopped whisking, rinsed his implement, screwed the lid tightly back on the jar, mounted his little stepladder & returned it to the shelf, then reached for his waistcoat & pulled out his pocket-watch, which he flicked open & scrutinized. 'Now, my dear,' he said with finality & a firm smile. 'I must close the shop for lunch or my dear wife will worry. The joys of marriage, dear Charlotte. I cannot tell you. I wish the same for you one day, for you deserve a better life than whoring, if you don't mind my mentioning your trade. But stay away from that place, I implore you, & please, for my wife's sake, keep this conversation to yourself.'

'Did he do things with rats?' I asked, as he began pulling down the shutters & fiddle-faddling with keys. 'Did you witness wizardry?'

The fragments of the jigsaw were there, but piece them together coherently I could not. I would get no more clues from Herr Bang, though, that I could see, for he had become furiously & briskly normal, chatting as though steam-powered, about such topics as a new kind of luminescent soap imported from Geneva, the debate on human slavery, & the best temperature for the storage of horse-manure.

That night, as I lay sleepless next to the deeply snoring Herr Axel Axelsen (a client who took regular advantage of my overnight bargain – sunset to sunrise, with limitless shagging & all extras thrown in gratis), my exhausted but excited mind flitted through what I knew & what I still knew not, what I had guessed & others had surmised or hinted at, until my head was a-scuzz with disjointed images & battling thoughts. I suffered this a while, along with Herr Axelsen's snoring, which conjoined with that of Fru Schleswig in the adjacent room to create a veritable cacophony, until I realized that I would not sleep until I had done something, & that I must do what I always do when in a state of puzzlement: reach for a quill & chart my notions on paper. So I got up, lit a candle, threw on my frayed green silk kimono & sat at my writing desk where, to the sound of rival snores, with pen & ink I created a list, thus:

Clues
Fru Krak's anxiety . . . the disappearance of Professor Krak
– & others???
Séances? – contact with the dead
'Dark services' mentioned by Herr Bang, with reference to Oblivion & the Great Beyond
Sightings of the ghost of Professor Krak
Missing clocks
Sewer rats
Suspected wizardry
Gudrun Olsen's mutilation, caused by something *not of human flesh*, & involving her own 'excruciating guilt'
A machine, made of bizarre components amassed in a secretive manner

But the components did nothing but float before me, defying logic & coherence, with the word 'Machine' dancing tantalizingly as though jeering at my muddle & stupidity. And yet, I thought, if I could only clap eyes on this thing – the one object here which seemed to have more solid possibilities than the others – then might all the rest be explained? I had by now almost finished my cartography of the house's many rooms & corridors, its unlikely staircases & hidden accesses, & was ready to pinpoint the two basement chambers that Gudrun Olsen had referred to as the workshop & the Oblivion Room, though the problem of the keys, & how to get hold of them, remained, for a rigorous search of the Krakster's cupboards, closets, wardrobes & chests of drawers revealed no set of duplicates which I might steal. I was just pondering this conundrum, & felt myself to be on the brink of an ingenious solution regarding trained mice with miniature lassos (may I remind you that I was very tired), when Herr Axelsen's snoring changed & he rolled over, reaching out an arm for me, so quickly I shed my robe, blew out the candle, & slid in next to my client so we lay naked like spoons, & felt his half-sleeping member instantly twitch & then resolutely harden in the old familiar manner of men & their urges, & I gently guided him into me, where after a few hearty, somnambulant thrusts he spilled himself with a small grunt without ever waking up, which touched me deeply, for I have always loved the simple connection that exists between a man & his needs, so uncomplicated compared to a woman's tangled & contradictory skein of feelings & hopes. How I do enjoy the company of men, I mused as I sank back sleepily with my buttocks pressing against the soft pregnancy of Herr Axelsen's beer paunch, & how grateful I am for the way their physical side takes control, regularly over-ruling the well-intentioned edicts of their dear muddled brains! Were it not for that, how on earth would I make a living?

*　　*　　*

The next morn, having dispatched Herr Axelsen home a happier man, I roused Fru Schleswig & accompanied her to Number Nine Rosenvængets Allé, where Fru Krak was all a-yelling & a-bustle, for she could not locate her silk-and-pigskin umbrella. On the pretext of searching for it, I did a quick tour of the house to assure myself that the map I had fashioned was accurate. There were still some grey areas, but I deemed that the mysterious set of underground rooms were likely to be found in one of the three basements in the house – two of which I judged to be located beneath the main part of the building, & the third in the bowels of the small annexe that gave on to the garden. (NB And now before you do anything else, take a moment of your precious time to scrutinize my map carefully, my darling one, &, in the process of doing so, admire its intricacy, for it took me hours to draw!)

I found the missing umbrella among all the others stacked in the unlikely location of the elephant's-foot umbrella-stand, then waited impatiently for Fru Krak (dressed today in dull purple, & adorned with violet gems) to leave the house. I had a hunch that she would be headed for the botanical gardens later on, as I had read her horoscope in the *Fine Lady* the previous day: *As an astute Aquarian Woman, you will need to plan your finances in view of the material changes on the horizon. Remember that men do not respect a woman who is not a Lady, so those of a lesser rank pose you no threat, & indeed can work to your advantage, so you can afford to pity them. Celebrate this knowledge by wearing this week's lucky gemstone: amethyst. With Jupiter in the ascendant, now is the perfect time to commune with all that is exotic in Nature, but continue to beware of all that lurks* BELOW GROUND.

*   *   *

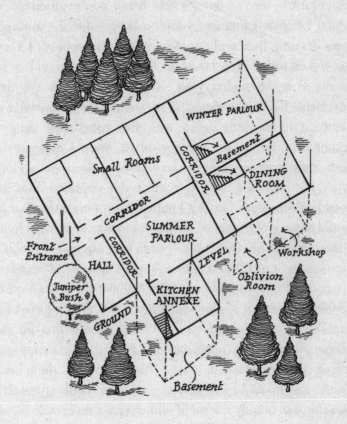

Number Nine Rosenvængets Allé – interior plan

As soon as the billowing purple cloud that was Fru Krak had swept out, smelling of violets & announcing that being of a lesser rank I posed no threat to her, & indeed she pitied me (to which I curtsied prettily), I took a lamp – for the evenings were drawing in as early as three in the afternoon, & I knew the lower part of the house to be entirely unlit unless by candle – & descended a set of stairs leading to the first basement. I had not expected to see much, & indeed was planning to do little more with this expedition than to reconnoitre, but to my great surprise, when I reached the door of the only room on this level, I found there was no lock at all, but instead a stout bolt which one operated from the outside. Emboldened by this I pulled it to, opened the door &, in the semi-gloom that filled the room like a murky cloud, almost tripped on what turned out to be a *ragnarok* of rubbish: metal rods, discarded workman's tools, pieces of smashed furniture of all constructions, styles & dimensions, & a huge & bewildering array of cogs, pendulums & other assorted in-nards from a thousand varied clocks. Could this be the graveyard of all the timepieces that Herr Bang remembered seeing in this mansion? But if so, why had they been destroyed? In any case, having made the swift assessment that this was merely a form of junk-room, a receptacle for all the out-throwings of a slovenly person who could not be bothered to dispose of their curious detritus in the normal manner, I swiftly moved back upstairs, crossed to the other wing of the house, & made my way down the staircase that led to the second basement. But no sooner had I reached the bottom of its cobwebby spiral of steps than I fancied – ah my! – that I heard a thud emanating from behind the closed door that lay at the end of the corridor before me! Immediately on my guard, I stopped in my tracks & stood motionless for a moment, as my spirit split in two, one half of it fearful, the other foolhardy. After some anxious dithering & hesitation, foolhardiness won, but it was with no little trepidation & a quaking heart that I tiptoed on towards the door.

Upon arriving at which, there came another sudden & alarming noise – this time a scuttling scrape that I knew well, & my guts contracted. I cannot abide rats, for the thought of their beady squalid eyes, oily fur & scratchy claws conjures up hideous memories of the orphanage, where they hunted in packs, & once devoured a helpless baby (I am sure of it) whose dying screams joined Baba Yaga Bonylegs as the stuff of my childhood nightmares.

But still, foolhardiness prevailed, & I urged calmness on myself, for I had not come all this way to be scared off by a rodent or two, whatever memories they evoked. Anticipating an encounter with the ghost of Professor Krak, which might turn to violence, I had taken the precaution of filling my pocket with ground pepper, so if worst came to worst, I could fling a handful of it at my attacker. I was quite sure that the door would be firmly locked, & perhaps bolted too, but I nevertheless resolved to test it, & had just grasped the knob to turn it when – OUCH! – *for Fanden!*

A sharp & painful twist forced my wrist in the other direction. I screamed, & dropped the lamp which fell to the floor, where the stuttering wick illuminated for the first time what I had missed before, hanging as it did so high up on the door.

A pair of raw, fresh pig's trotters, tied together by a piece of rough string.

I screamed again, for it seemed I had stumbled upon

evidence of a gruesome porcine ritual! Upon which ghastly realization I turned & ran forthwith, taking the stairs two at a time, stumbling over my skirts & petticoats, & rushing headlong towards the kitchen, the pepper from my pocket flying everywhere. As I turned a corner into a further corridor, I hurtled slap-bang into Fru Schleswig, who was heaving a pail of water full of soap-suds, which promptly emptied all over me, just as the doorbell rang in the most untimely manner. Still frantic, I skidded soapily to the door & flung it open – not to allow any visitors to enter so much as to escape myself – only to be greeted by the looming figure of Pastor Dahlberg whose popping eyes instantly settled themselves upon my breasts – which, being clad only in the thin film of my cotton bodice, left nothing, in their drenched state, to the imagination. I cursed myself for not going to the back door instead, but there was no time to shake him off, for he had me by the arm & was pinching tight.

'Not so fast, my dear,' he breathed, frog-marching me back inside the hall. 'You seem distressed. You must tell Papa all about it.' (*Papa!* I nearly vomited.) My heart was still banging from the shock of what I had heard from that basement room, & my breath came out in panting gasps, which (O God!) seemed to arouse 'Papa' even further, for his eyes lit up as he proceeded to enquire whether I had been a 'naughty little girl', & whether I needed to be 'severely punished' for my sins. Fru Schleswig stepped aside as we passed, & shot me a look, but I made a gesture for her to button her lip or else, for despite the shock I had suffered, & my anxiety to get out of that place, I smelled quick money on the horizon & Christmas was coming.

'I have a room upstairs I would like to show you, which is

to be my personal study in which the Lord & I can conduct our intimate conversations,' Pastor Dahlberg said, marching me up the steps with him & fair shoving me inside, where he did not waste his time undoing his breeches, & I did not waste mine – my temper & nerves being somewhat frayed by the alarming experience I had undergone only moments before – demanding with blunt insistence a fee of ten kroner & making it clear to him that I would accept no less in future, & if he wanted cheaper there was always the street. So ten kroner it was, & when I had pocketed it, he made sure I earned every ore by pressing me up against the leather-topped desk & leering at me with his clacking teeth & his chomping lips all a-guzzle, & calling me a dirty little temptress & then getting on his knees & burying his nose in my underskirts like a slobbering dog. I knew that if I did not hasten him on, he would take his horrible middle-aged time, so while he muttered & whispered & groaned on about *naughty, dirty, sexy whore* under his breath, I racked my brains for inspiration. Lord, much as my work had its delightful moments, there were times when I would have given anything to be a humble librarian in a quiet provincial town! However whilst he was huffing & puffing I finally hit upon the notion (him being a religious man) of suggesting that I was a nun being ravaged at the altar, which (praise be!) did the trick – so speedily indeed (a mere three or four more feeble pumps sufficed) that one might be forgiven for suspecting that great friend & conversational companion of the Pastor's, the Almighty himself, had intervened on my behalf.

That night, Fru Schleswig & I polished off the bottle of schnapps & I made my way to bed, drifting into slumber with pleasant fantasies of the blackmail of Pastor Dahlberg on my mind, & waking the next morn feeling optimistic, refreshed & determined to confront the ghost in the basement that very day, for there was no time like the present. And goodness gracious, why not blackmail a ghost, too, while one was at it?

Yet despite my bold plans, I will confess to you, O beloved one (& please do not think less of me for my cowardice), that as well as the curiosity I harboured about Professor Krak's basement secret, there was fear in me too, & it took all the courage I could muster to go near the place the next morning. And when I did, with the mumbling & grumbling Fru Schleswig at my side, complaining that I was making it all up & I'd 'red too mennie sillie bookes as a chylde', quite a sight met my eyes. A new bolt & huge new shiny padlock had been added to the outside of the door. Upon which, beneath the now reeking pig's trotters, hung a makeshift wooden sign covered in huge writing.

I felt the blood drain from my face & descend into my feet, which then seemed to grow a powerful & elaborate system of roots, so that I could not budge from the spot.

'You mus tel the mistris,' said Fru Schleswig eventually, for she is a slow reader & it took a full minute for her fright to catch up with mine. 'You duz not tell her then it iz me wot will. Therez sumthin not rite in this howse. There be sum kynde of eevil spirrit livin here an I duz not like it wun bit.'

And for once I agreed with her.

Still rooted there, I stared in horror at the words that had been scrawled – apparently in blood that was still fresh enough to be a glistening, scarlet red – upon the gruesome sign.

Come not near, young madam, if you value your life.

Now how would you react, O my dear one, if you were to be informed by a reliable & honest source that your dead husband was living in the basement of your home, & was making his presence alarmingly felt just weeks before your nuptials to his successor? Would you not fly into some kind of panic?

I certainly imagined that the highly-strung Fru Krak would have difficulty containing herself in the face of such news, when I conveyed it to her later that morning. I pictured her reaching for her smelling-salts, & taking to her bed, & summoning the Pastor, whom she would beg to enact an exorcism or other such hocus-pocus to calm her fluttering feminine fears, & perhaps revisiting Herr Bang at the apothecary's for some more nerve-potions, & generally making the lives of Fru Schleswig & myself as hellish as she could, with her demands & counter-demands, her fripperies, calamities & whims.

But I was quite wrong.

For instead of showing alarm, it was an expression of the foulest rage that washed over her pallid face as I told her what had happened.

'And so I came straight to you, ma'am,' I finished. 'Knowing that you would want to be aware of such a terrifying thing as an unknown inhabitant in your home.'

She looked at me in steely silence for a moment with her dead, lopsided eyes, as though measuring how much energy she could summon to answer me, & it struck me as she did so, that her face seemed even whiter than usual, indeed so bloodless that it could be mistaken for a paper mask. 'But this is no concern of mine!' she finally burst out, in a tone whose harshness grated on my ears. 'And I will thank you not to mention such absurdities again! What is more, I shall be extremely angry if you bother the Pastor with them. I am a lady, & I assure you I would never dream of descending belowstairs! Good grief, you worthless little tart! If there are rats in the basement, get rid of them. That is your job!'

'Rats who have learned the alphabet so well that they can write notices in blood, ma'am?' I queried, but she merely huffed, & accused me of intolerable insolence & the like. But I was not fooled, for her voice had betrayed her, & just afterwards when my back was turned & she thought I was not watching, I spotted her in the mirror reaching in a little leather bag around her waist & swallowing three pills in a single hasty gulp.

Keen to share the excitement of my discoveries, I made the excuse of needing to buy more soda crystals, & scurried out posthaste to the florist's shop to recount the story to Else, who by a lucky chance was playing cards with none other than Gudrun Olsen. For a moment I watched the two women seated upright as alert as two bright birds, their fingers flying like the Devil among the rose-buds & the snippings of flower-stalks on the table before them, & then, when their game seemed to come if not to a halt then to a pause of some kind, where the cards required reshuffling, I greeted them & recounted the story of the noises in the basement room, & the warning notice, & Fru Krak's unusual reaction to being told of them.

'That means he's in there!' said Gudrun, slamming the cards down on the table. 'And that he never died! He is in there, alive, & she knows it! They must have a pact.'

'But how does he come out?' asked Else.

We had to wait while Gudrun shuffled & applied her mind

to the question. Her scar looked paler today, as though coated in powder. 'There must be a secret passage,' she said after a moment. 'That house is a warren of traps & sewers & strange connections. It is like a rotted brain. He must get out at night.' She looked excited at the thought, & then I remembered in the laundry she said she had been much attached to her employer, for all his oddity.

'That's when he's been sighted,' said Else. 'Always after dark, & wrapped in a cloak with half his face hidden by a scarf or a balaclava.'

'A balaclava?' I asked sharply, remembering the incident at Herr Bang's. Was I being spied upon? And if so, was the creature stalking me a chimera, or living flesh?

'If he really is alive,' I pondered, 'then his wife cannot marry the Pastor. Perhaps that is why she would rather not know he is down there!' And my mind galloped further, for here was even more knowledge I could use to my financial gain. What might it be worth to Fru Krak to keep her supposedly dead husband's presence a secret? A hundred kroner? Two? Per month?

I much liked this idea of mine, but just as I was getting my teeth into it, Else asked: 'Why don't he just seize the house, & boot Fru Krak out? It's his property, after all, ain't it?'

'God knows,' said Gudrun. 'But again, it points to a pact.'

'And what does he do in there, do you think?'

'The same as he always did, I expect,' she replied, almost happily. 'Tinker with his engineering all day. He'd lock himself away in there for days at a stretch,' she reminisced. 'Then when there were visitors – the noises you'd hear! Noises like murder. But I'll tell you one thing. On those nights, Fru Krak always pretended she'd gone deaf. Never asked what he was up to. Didn't want to know, I suppose. She wasn't bothered how he came about his money, so long as her purse was chock-a-block when she went shopping.'

'I clapped eyes on her myself last week,' said Else. 'I sold her some holly. *For Sataan*, what a nincompoop she looked in that green-tinted fur!'

'All I know,' said Gudrun after they had played the next round, 'is that I counted folk coming in, & when I counted them leaving, there were always fewer.'

'What sort of folk?' asked Else, scowling at her cards.

'All sorts. Men & women. Children with them, sometimes. But no one ever came asking about them afterwards. I never got it. Where did they go, & why did no one care that they had disappeared?'

And so Gudrun sat dealing the cards, & Else sat advising me to discover all as soon as I could, but to apply caution, & then Gudrun counselled the opposite, but nevertheless fished in her purse for a rusty key which she said she had pilfered from the Kraks when she left, & which operated one of the back doors, though she could not recall which, & Else warned in her usual dramatic way that I would probably die in the process of uncovering the truth, & Gudrun echoed that if I valued my life, I should stay away, & throw the key in the lake, & fingered her scar in a most meaningful & disconcerting manner.

'I'll be *grief-struck* to lose you, Charlotte!' wailed Else with a tear in her eye as Gudrun dealt another set of cards. 'We've had such larks together you & me, & I'll miss your company something rotten!' And she stifled a dramatic sob while scooping up her cards, surveying her hand & doing some nifty rearranging. But O, had we only known that for once

Else had no need to exaggerate! That I would indeed die, at least in a manner of speaking, & lose all hope of seeing her dear face again!

As I watched them play on, I considered again what Herr Bang had told me, which I had promised not to disclose, & saw how it fitted in with what Gudrun had said. And then a notion struck me, clear as a pearl, & my heart went pit-a-pat, & while the aces & the kings & the queens & the numbers flew again, I watched the two women with their fast fingers & their quick flashes of argument & the red & the black, & then suddenly all hearts & diamonds, spades & clubs ranked up in groups of flushes & they laughed & cheered. And quietly I took my leave of the two of them in the candle-light, with the first scent of Christmas spices hanging in the air.

We would feast upon a tasty fat goose with apple & prune stuffing, accompanied by sugared potatoes with lashings of gravy; & then, when even Fru Schleswig thought she could eat no more, there would appear before us a palely fragrant rice pudding bloated with whipped cream & flavoured with chopped almonds, served with cherry sauce, & the prize of a marzipan pig for whichever one of us found the whole nut hidden in the pudding, followed by as much port as we could glug down. Such were the opulent temptations I described to persuade the obese one – who is not a creature of intelligence, as you will have gleaned, O precious reader – into assisting with my plan, for I told her there might be money to be had by it, & money meant a succulent Christmas meal, if she complied. Soon she was drooling, for being of a gluttonous disposition, the prospect of large quantities of fine victuals made enough of an impression to win her assistance – for what it was worth. (Though as you shall shortly see, it was worth nothing, & it was thanks to her that the whole scheme went so horribly awry.)

Fired up with a quart of schnapps, we waited until the clock chimed half past eleven, then made our way in the freezing, owl-hooting dark to the Krak residence, Fru Schleswig waddling behind me & grumbling all the while about her *pore neez*. There, thanks to the enterprising Gudrun's pilfered key, we entered quiet as church mice (or should I say quiet as one small discreet church mouse & one large clumsy ox), & descended the spiral stairs that debouched directly into the basement, where we waited for the church bell to ring midnight, for my plan was for Fru S to attack the lock just as it tolled, & time the blows of her pickaxe to coincide with their ringing, thus muffling the sound of our illicit activities. I must pride myself here on coming up with such an inspired scheme, for it worked so brilliantly that within three mighty strokes, Fru S had forced the lock open: with a sudden lurch the door swung wide like a gaping mouth, exposing a yawning darkness within. Here was what Gudrun Olsen had called the Oblivion Room.

Tick, tock.

We stood in silence for a moment, our eyes straining against the pitch dark, which the lantern barely permeated. So far, there was no sight or sound of human life. But what was I hoping for? Had I really been expecting to come face to face with Professor Krak?

Feeling both relieved & disappointed not to see the man step out in person, I shooed Fru S on to the landing & ordered her in a fierce whisper to stand guard there, in case Fru Krak awoke & came to interrupt us. Well aware that the slothful creature was capable of falling asleep at any moment (even when standing up, in the manner of a horse or cow), I instructed her to sing 'Tragic Johanna' under her breath, & in this way stay conscious while I performed my survey of the Oblivion Room. And so off she lumbered to the landing of the spiral staircase & settled herself there, mumbling incoherencies under her breath about what had she done to be so cursed with her only child, & 'howe dare any dorter boss her pore old mutha so'.

Fru Schleswig dispatched to her duties, I wielded my lamp aloft before me & stepped with some trepidation back into the room – where suddenly (and believe me, I drew in a sharp breath, O my dear one!) my eyes, growing accustomed to the gloom, fell upon the most inexplicable set of objects I had ever seen in all of my twenty-five years on this harsh earth. The first thing that struck me, for it was nearest to hand, was a most unusual-looking bicycle, whose wheels seemed quite motiveless, for the contraption was clamped to the floor by a protective casing made of metal. Its handlebars faced the corner of the room, in which, standing on a corner shelf halfway up the wall – good grief! – sat a huge glass case, that looked to contain an orange, fur-covered creature with a humanoid face & big moody eyes that seemed filled with pain & reproach. *For Fanden*, it was some kind of monkey, or my name was not Charlotte Dagmar Marie of Østerbro! I could not meet its eyes: indeed, I feared they were alive, & scrutinizing me. For some reason, the sadness in the creature's child-like face made me awash with a strange emotion I could not identify, & I felt like screaming at it tearfully: *I have done nothing! I am innocent!* Looking down, for I could not keep my

eyes on the thing a second longer, I spied below it a chair, &
next to it a small occasional table with a dainty white tablecloth, frilled with lacework, upon which stood a half-full
bottle of schnapps, another bottle, medical-looking but un-
marked, a mound of cotton wool, and a small open box,
velvet-lined. I approached, & drew a breath: inside lay a silver
scalpel. Good Lord, what bloody business went on here?
What ritual tortures & sacrifices were carried out beneath the
monkey's baleful gaze, in the name of the Great Beyond? No
wonder Gudrun had heard screams!

I felt that I had witnessed enough for one evening, but I was
not to escape so readily: turning to leave, I drew in another
sharp breath. For there in the corner, gleaming in the gloom,
squatting four-square on the floor like a huge, elaborately
carbuncled toad, was the strangest contraption I had ever
seen. Claiming a quarter of the room's space, the demonic
machine in whose construction Gudrun had colluded gave
almost a vegetal impression, sporting as it did a leathery skin,
pocked like ostrich-hide. Lord, I half expected it to sigh &
breathe! Its shape was rectangular, but with rounded corners,
& a humped roof, like the engine-carriage of a train, & at its
centre was a sliding door made of dark leather & wood, with
murky glass panes in which nothing could be seen but the
reflection of my own petrified face.

Would you have done as I did, reader, & hesitated before
opening the door & peering inside? I think you would! But
excitement & curiosity would have got the better of you, just
as they did me, & after that brief moment of doubt, you would
have slipped in there in a flash. I cast my lamp around & saw
that the interior of the machine comprised a single, small
room into which perhaps ten people might be squeezed, & in

The strangest contraption I had ever seen

contrast to the outside, all within it appeared most man-made & functional. As I stepped in, my eyes first fell upon an array of brass pulleys, wheels & cogs, parts of nickel, & parts of ivory akin to piano-keys, & adorned – in a seemingly haphazard manner – with myriad clock-faces, all telling different times. At the centre stood a red velvet chaise-longue upon which I supposed the victim must lie, & beside it, a great translucent sphere of what might have been glass, or crystal or – yes! Quartz, it seemed to be, though transparent enough to reveal that inside it lay the dregs of a pinkish liquid. The orb was in turn connected by wires to a series of dials & a metal lever which it appeared that one must push or pull, & a map of the world upon which were marked heavily the Equator & various meridians.

I was just beginning to run my hands across the cool, smooth surface of the orb when a loud, shuddering noise – a deep dragging reverberation, followed by a whistling hoot – emanated from the landing. With a lurch of panic followed swiftly by rage, I recognized it as one of Fru Schleswig's mighty snores.

Satan's underwear! More inauspicious it could not have been, that Fru Schleswig should choose this most crucial of moments to fall asleep at her duties, & flagrantly counter-mand my most precise instructions. As if to mock me, the snoring seemed then to deepen in pitch & heighten in volume, thunderously. O Lord! I had to silence it, for I knew it would be only a matter of time before the noise awoke the nervous & light-sleeping Fru Krak. So, quickly – and *whimpering* with frustration, I do assure you – I hastened out, casting only the quickest of parting glances back at the mysterious machine that I had now finally seen for myself.

66

I was mounting the spiral stairs & approaching the small landing where Fru Schleswig slept so raucously when I became conscious of a shaky light emerging direct from above, whereupon a huge quivering shadow then appeared which I knew at once to be none other than that of Fru Krak, clad in a preposterous pink balloon-shaped garment adorned with sea-horses, her head knobbled with hair-devices, hovering at the top of the stairs. There was no time to react, for only a fraction of a second later the shadow was followed by the nightgowned figure that cast it, its shaking hand brandishing what appeared to be a very ancient & rusted revolver.

'Halt right there & do not move a muscle!' my employer threatened with a shaking voice. 'Or I shall shoot your brains out!' At this, the prone Fru Schleswig changed the rhythm of her snoring & twitched mightily before rolling to one side & snorting suddenly into a confused but vengeful state of wakefulness.

'O no you duz notte!' the old creature boomed, heaving walrus-like to her feet. 'Yoo duz notte fryten me for wun minnit with yer silly gunne!'

How to keep her at bay? Then came a veritable brainwave.

'Fru Krak, remember you are not just a daughter of the esteemed Bischen-Baschen family, but a fine Aquarian Lady, too!' I called up the stairs. 'Your horoscope is forever reminding you not to descend below ground level, if you value your moral standing!' And then, to Fru Schleswig, I hissed: 'Quick! Follow me!' For I knew that if we did not instantly rush to barricade ourselves within the chamber, all was lost, for there would be no getting past Fru Krak & her pistol. Once in the Oblivion Room, I imagined we would find another exit, perhaps taking us to a secret passage which led to a room elsewhere in the mansion or even, if we were lucky, outdoors, enabling us to flee – but with Fru Krak now opening up her firearm & cramming its barrel with three brass bullets the size of marbles, there was no time to lose – a realization which finally penetrated the consciousness of Fru Schleswig, who burst into action, thundering down the stairs & storming hard on my heels into the Oblivion Room. Swiftly, I leaped into the machine, hoping to slide shut the door to the contraption & lock myself inside – but Fru Schleswig was having none of it, & fair wrestled me to the ground.

'O no you duz notte, yung lassy!' she bawled, gripping the door & preventing me from closing it. 'Do notte dreem of lokkin out yor old ma! Yu think I am goin to let yu giv me the slyppe a second tyme you ar kwite rong!'

And with that she came blundering & squeezing her way in, shoving her massive body through the wood & glass portal – bruising my ribs something terrible in the process – & crashing down on to the chaise-longue next to me, which groaned with her weight & threatened, for one terrifying split second, to topple. Frantic to right it, I put all my weight the other end, while she grabbed hold of the big brass lever to steady herself, & forced it down just as –

No!

Fru Krak's concern to protect her property had outweighed the dictates of the stars, for she had now descended the stairs, & loomed upon us in her pink sea-horse nightgown, her eyes popping from her head as she levelled the bulky weapon at my heart. Quite visible through the open doors, she was but five metres away.

The end had come.

'No!' I screamed. 'Madam, do not shoot!'

68

But it was too late.

The last thing to be heard in that life was a deafening, thunderous explosion, & the last thing I saw was the ugly, vengeful face of Fru Krak, & the last thing I smelled was sulphur. For Fru Krak had fired her murderous blunderbuss.

And of the three people in that basement, one of us was surely dead.

Part the Second: The Tin City

A nd thus did the world end.

But not as I had thought. For although I had indeed been witness, in that heart-stopping moment in which Fru Krak fired her gruesome firearm, to the destruction of a human life (viz: my own), it was not through death that I was to pass away and enter another realm. For Fate had other plans.

They say that we humans are no more than a collection of the thoughts, knowledge & memories we have accumulated through experience. If so, then what worse plight can you conjure, dear reader, than to wash up like Gulliver, on that eerie beach where all one has thought, known or remembered has no meaning? Where all the lessons of one's life are set at naught? Where one must start with nothing, like an innocent babe fresh-shot from the womb? Such was my predicament when I encountered the strange new world that lay before me, a world in which my existence was jinxed with dire danger, far beyond the compass of my courage, & worse than anything the most fevered psyche could have cooked up.

But I jump ahead of myself, for the fact was, I saw & thought nothing when I first landed, & certainly had no inkling that I was anywhere else but in the Great Beyond.

After the violent explosion from Fru Krak's gun, I felt myself flung backwards & then seemed to reel in a slow & circular way before plummeting down into a vast prairie of nothingness that was then filled with a whole confusion of images & thoughts that tumbled before my eyes, from the earliest years of my childhood: I saw the orphanage with its dark windows & peeling ochre paint; I witnessed myself wandering barefoot in the kitchen garden among the giant knobbled stalks of Brussels sprouts, winkling out woodlice to force into curled balls which I devoured like sweetmeats; I spied the mouldering books stacked in the cellar – *Great Thoughts of Great Men*, *A Jutland Housewife's Almanac* & *Fifty Favourite Folk Tales*, with the illustration of Baba Yaga Bony-legs & her chicken-leg house; I quailed as the mountain of Fru Schleswig towered above me in a broad apron, her forearms caked in flour, her shadow blackening the wooden floorboards upon which I squatted; & then I was on the train to Copenhagen, where on arrival I straightway spotted Else on the platform, pick-pocketing gentlemen, so pretty & distracting in her peach striped bonnet adorned with posies; I beheld us dreaming up & practising our act, & then performing it, with the screaming crowds cheering the sight of our petticoats in the music-hall; & then I winced at Else slipping on the sausage-skin & cracking her poor heel; & then re-encountered in a flash the first man I sold my body to & then the second, third, fourth, fifth, sixth & so on, until they whirled together in a mad confusion of faces & organs, & the pile of thrown-off breeches grew higher & higher on the floor; & then came a blurred picture of Herr Møller's bakery on Classensgade & Fru Krak's house on Rosenvængets Allé & the door of the Oblivion Room upon which hung rotting pig's trotters; & then I saw once again the machine, with the red chaise-longue & the quaking sphere of quartz, & then the furiously swollen face & lopsided eyes of Fru Krak which briefly sparked with sick triumphant relish as she aimed the antique firearm at my cleavage & pulled the trigger. Such was the sum of my life, & as I spun there in that chilly space that was surely death's antechamber, I was seized with rebellion, for I thought – no! My time has not yet come! Please, dear God, if you do indeed exist, which hitherto I will confess that I have much doubted, due to such supreme unfairness dominating this unhappy world, then grant me a little more time, for I am not finished! I am unspeakably far from done, sir! I have not yet lived, not yet loved! Only lost! I am not ready for death, you most cruel of bastards! I insist! Fie upon you, celestial torturer, *I cannot & I will not die!*

And then, as if in answer to my humble prayer, there came a ghostly hooting in my ears, & such was the discomfort of that sensation – which was much akin to an appalling ear-ache, dear one (& I felt, too, as though I had been doused in freezing brine, for I ached & shivered with cold all over) – that I was confronted with a strange feeling of recognition: pain. *Pain: life!* Life! Life after all! And I felt that I was lying on a floor. It was dark & so I could see nothing, but I knew one thing: that I existed still.

'I have come back from the brink!' I yelled aloud, & weak & cracked though my voice sounded, & terrified through and through though I was, there came a sudden warm rush in my heart when I heard my own words, for they confirmed again that my blood had not quit pumping in my veins, & that the most unexpectedly merciful Almighty had indeed listened, & that it was therefore –

No! Yes! No! –

That dear, loyal, innocent, brave, stalwart martyr Fru Schleswig who had taken the bullet that was intended for me!

At which I found myself choking, & seized by a confusion so coruscating as to nearly kill me, for much as the lugubrious creature has been a ball & chain to me & I have oft wished her dead & gone from this earth, I have been acquainted with her for as long as I can remember, & that does not count as naught. Indeed, so much did it suddenly mean that my heart knew not what to do, & had I been standing at that point, my knees would have jellified, & I might have collapsed there & then into a dead & most feminine faint.

But then, as if my thoughts had been read by the creature herself, there came from some distance to my left the all-too-familiar sound of breaking wind, followed by a deep groan, & I knew that she was yet with us, at which a morsel of me felt assuaged but then – instantaneously – another larger morsel felt another thing: a giant writhing snake of rage, for despite it being my most fervent wish to be free of Fru S, I realized that – pox & damnation! – she had yet again succeeded in forcing herself along with me!

All of which cruel psychic pain expressed itself in a single choking cry, to which some moments later Fru Schleswig (being slower on the uptake) replied with a similar cry, but deeper & less ladylike, followed by a panting & a wheezing sound, for she too had finally absorbed the painful & incontrovertible fact that we were both miraculously alive, yet still in the grip of the invisible shackles that bind us together for all eternity on this planet.

*   *   *

But what planet, precisely? What manner of place was this, that Fru S & I had spun to? I could see nothing at first, but gradually my eyes adapted themselves to the murk, which was odourless & with a greenish tinge, as though the walls, like a subterranean cave, were clad in a phosphorescent alga that cast an eerie light all of its own.

I cast my glance around in mental disarray, my heart beating like the clappers, but saw no trace of the contraption in the emerald glow of the hall in which we found ourselves. Had we been debouched & then abandoned by the mechanism that brought us here? Or had it simply catapulted us to this place, & remained *in situ* in the basement at Fru Krak's? It certainly felt I had undergone a long & unprotected journey, for my flesh & bones ached as though I had been battered ferociously by a sea-storm, my clothes seemed chilly & wet, & when I put my fingers to my hair, I realized it too was moist, & all undone & tangled around my shoulders like a hank of seaweed, with grains of sand in it: I licked my finger then, & tasted salt. Good Lord, had Fru Schleswig & I travelled the high seas unawares? Flown through the air, got too close to the ocean, & been tossed by waves en route? If so, it was even more of a miracle that we were still alive!

Gulping back my horror, I staggered weakly to my feet, whereupon the sensation of having been shaken up & bruised hit me with shocking forcefulness. In the darkness I looked around for Fru Schleswig, & found her lying on her back some three metres away from me in a pool of water, helpless as an upturned Galapagos turtle, her new apron seemingly torn to shreds & her straggled hair all dripping & unkempt. A small crab dropped from what remained of her scrazzled chignon, & scuttled away into a dark corner.

'Come, madam, we must get out of this place & hide ourselves somewhere & then work out the lie of the land!' I urged, hauling her to her feet, a strenuous & exhausting operation performed to the accompaniment of her non-stop grumbling, wheezing & moaning about her poor freezing swollen-up legs & her half-broken back, & punctuated by a further series of foul retorts from her nether sphincter.

'Shh!' I whispered. 'Restrain yourself, madam, or we are undone!' (You would not believe, dear one, what a mass of noise can emanate from a single humanoid figure under strain.) When she was finally in an upright position, & steadied there with one hand against the wall, we were able to take in our surroundings a little better, & see for the first time how unaccountably strange indeed they were, for it now appeared that we stood beneath a huge dark metal structure – Lord, a giant telescope, high above which – *for Fanden!* – hovered a dead-straight line of shimmering green light, suspended seemingly in thin air but vibrating like the wing of a frantic trapped moth. This emerald line lit up the high domed roof above itself, & did not stop at the window but shot outwards from it, & into the far distance of the night. What strange wizardry was this? A mystery enshrouded in an enigma, in turn wrapped deeply up in preposterousness & danger!

'Oi duz notte lyke it here,' muttered Fru Schleswig. 'Letz go strate bakke.' And it was then that she, too, spotted that the machine had vanished, at which she let out a loud low of anger, like a maddened bull. 'Tiz all yor forlt!' she fumed, turning on me with red-faced rage. 'Look wot u dun now! Herez anutha fyne mess u hav gotten us into, & it is thanques to u, u silly gurl. I did notte spankke u enuf wen u woz a babby! I shudve –'

But I straightway clapped my hand to her mouth, & then forced her tuberous arm sharply up behind her back to further restrain her, for I had heard a sound: the distant click & clack of a door opening & then closing, though where it emerged from I could not tell, such a strange echo was there in that dark place, that bejozzled everything around. Fru Schleswig was by now rolling her eyes at me, grunting & trying to say something in a repellently moist & spitty way, which I would not let her do, until finally she squirmed free of my grip & pointed with her sausagey finger in the direction of a side-hallway I had not seen, where appeared an extremely tall, dark, lanky-limbed man who was walking fast, nay almost running towards us & who, from the way he scarecrowed out his long arms, as if to grab or embrace us, & cried hoarsely, 'Welcome!', appeared to have been expecting us. My hand still slapped firm across Fru Schleswig's now fighting mouth ('Bite me & you're mincemeat,' I hissed in her ear), we stood rooted there as he made his gangling way towards us, & as he approached closer I saw that he was clad in the plainest & most dismal clothes imaginable, some kind of fancy dress, one might surmise, if one were to disguise oneself as a prisoner from a bygone era, or another country where they do things differently. So preoccupied was I by the bald, undecorated lines of the outfit he wore that I did not immediately take in his face. But when I did, I gasped. For there, most unmistak-able, were the high temples & bulging forehead; the dark, flashing eyes: as sure as Fru Fanny Schleswig was not my mother, it was the man whose portrait hung in the hall, Professor Frederik Krak! The artist had captured his likeness, particularly the sheen on his face which I now saw to be not an effect of oil-paint so much as good old-fashioned sweat, that dampened the man's forehead & reflected the overhead light in a streak of green luminescence which shone like a wound, as though an enraged Thor had split his head apart with a mighty hammer.

'Welcome, dear ladies! Welcome indeed!' he cried, beaming twitchily. His voice sounded most familiar. *Put a balaclava on him*, I thought suddenly, *& I would swear we have already met.* 'Another success story!' he continued, clearly – for reasons I could not fathom – quite pleased with himself. 'I am honoured to make your acquaintance formally at last!' But something nervous behind this hearty welcome hinted that his delight was matched by a sense of relief. God knows, I thought, what is going on inside that bulging brain. Best beware.

'Let us free this good woman,' he murmurs, at which he bends to forcibly unclamp my palm from Fru Schleswig's mouth (thus unleashing a torrent of expletives on her part, all directed at me), & gives a small, formal bow, introduces himself as my humble servant, Frederik Krak, Professor of Physics, & Explorer of the Unknown, & kisses the back of my hand in the manner of a Hungarian nobleman (I had one once, who liked to tickle my fanny with a goose feather), & then he takes Fru Schleswig's big greasy flipper & kisses it too, which renders her straightway all a-goggle because you can be sure she has never had her hand kissed before, nor any part of her I should imagine, & the surprise of it has the same effect as an entire cooking apple being stuffed in her gob, stuck-pig-wise, ie complete silence, which is a relief after the hellish hoo-ha she's been kicking up.

The man's a charmer, I think, as I watch Fru Schleswig's visage melt like a chunk of lard at the cheap ploy. *Watch out. A charmer & a balaclava'd spy.*

'I expect you are wondering how it is that you came here all the way from Denmark, dear ladies,' he says with a spasm of his hand, which cannot seem to sit still, & nor can any part of him indeed, for he is all a-rattle with nerves & tics & little anxious shudders.

'Came from it to where?'

'To London!' he responds brightly, as though the name of that famously moribund and depraved city, full of scheming foreigners, could be anything other than a happy surprise. At which his eyes flash & flicker again with what I am now beginning to suspect is madness, pure & simple. But although the worm of anxiety shifts within me, I resolve at that moment to show the man nothing but the haughty contempt & disdain he deserves until he has explained himself.

'But London is in England!' I scoff, picking what appears to be a whelk from my hair & letting it fall to the floor with a clatter.

'Astutely noted, young lady,' he replies apologetically. 'It is indeed, I fear. For due to circumstances beyond my control, & indeed my ken, to do with the kinetic pull of latitude & the parallel push of longitude, & the conflict between local time & universal time, exacerbated by the volatility of exotic matter,' (what on earth was he talking about? He was fair dizzying me with hypotheticality!) 'we find ourselves with a direct connection between the Greenwich Meridian upon which we now stand & Østerbro, where I discovered – & indeed invented – the Krak Time-Sucker, a rare species of cosmic fault-line found only in few parts of the world, nay the universe.'

'U did wot?' growls Fru Schleswig darkly.

'As you may already have learned from your various most enterprising researches in Rosenvængets Allé, Frøken Charlotte, I experimented a-plenty with the mechanics of such an initiative,' continues Professor Krak, ignoring her & concentrating on me, for he has swiftly ascertained that the simple organism of Fru Schleswig's brain owes more to vegetable and mineral origins than the animal. 'But alas, geographically we find ourselves limited in our time-travelling possibilities, for we are dependent on the meridian & the conjunction of this feature with a Time-Sucker phenomenon, known in modern times as a "worm-hole".'

'Whoa, there, sir!' I cried. 'One thought at a time!' But there was no stopping his fevered science, which continued at a most egregious pace: as he spoke, one fancied one saw the man's skull straining with the force of all the ideas it contained, & I wondered what a phrenologist might make of the various cranial bulges that came to the fore as he so energetically emphasized. *Too clever for his own good*, had been Gudrun Olsen's phrase, & now I could see her meaning most starkly. 'Although Copenhagen is not on the meridian, it is the original starting-point, & the machine is geared to the Greenwich Line, & points thereon,' he enthused. 'The conjunction of both meridian & Time-Sucker is to be found in only a very few locations. Now the Afric isle of Marroquinta has a species of fault-line which approximates a Krak Time-Sucker. The Basilica of Our Lady of Pilar in the Spanish city of Zaragoza is also on the Krak map. One can also visit a corner of Algeria which is either a desert, a radical mosque, or a children's emporium known as Toys 'R' Us, depending on the era in which you visit it, & an uninhabited rock off Antarctica. A charming place, if sea parrots interest you. But London, I find, is the most convenient & charming of the meridianal destinations my Time Machine has to offer, which is why so many Danes from our era find themselves coming here, & assimilating most happily.'

At which my anger bursts forth, for he must stop playing around with me, & spouting all this gibberish about Afric isles and sea parrots & 'Our Lady of Pilar', & explain why one moment the innocent Fru Schleswig & I are staring into the barrel of Fru Krak's blunderbuss, & the next – find ourselves *whisked* to a place he claims is London, quite against our will. He must account for himself properly, & forthwith! 'I demand to be told just what you think you are planning to do with us here, sir! For we insist on being returned home without further ado, do we not, Fru Schleswig? Do we not?' I repeat, kicking her in the leg & thus prompting a most vehement cry of agreement.

'Ah,' he smiles, quite unperturbed by my forcefulness. 'Even though – from what I have just gleaned – returning there would entail getting a bullet in that youthful chest?'

I gulp & feel myself blanch. 'A bullet? Are you sure?'

'Most certainly I am,' he says apologetically. 'For knowing Fru Krak as I do, she will be loitering with that gun for some time, keen to take a further pot-shot, should you return. In my opinion it would be best to wait a while, for her delicate feminine nerves to settle. Do not forget, I made the terrible mistake of being married to the woman, & know her blind furies well.'

'So why did we come here, & how in heaven's name are we to return? And when?' I accuse.

'You shall have answers to all your questions in good time,

my dear, fear not,' he retorts soothingly. But I am not to be calmed so readily, for my brain is veritably boiling. 'What's more,' he continues, 'one of these days I will be more than happy to show you round the Observatory & explain the scientific mechanism of the meridian time phenomenon & particle anti-particle annihilation in more detail' (O no, I thought, no more detail please or my addled head will implode with all the unlikeliness), 'but my concern at the moment is to get you ladies out of here & into a good clean bed where you can rest after your gruelling ordeal, for having made more than fifty of such journeys myself, I am the first to recognize the physical & psychic toll they take!'

'Wot bluddie obzervatry,' boomed Fru Schleswig for whom, despite her brain containing no more intellectual energy than a rotted pumpkin or a sack of brick dust, the øre was finally beginning to drop, & who now, seemingly recovered from having her hand kissed by a gentleman, was turning nasty, her eyes like two mistrustful currants buried deep in pastry. 'I do notte kno wot wun of them iz but I do notte lyke the sound of it, I kan tel u.'

'The Greenwich Observatory,' said the Professor with a twitching grin. 'Established by King Charles who appointed an Astronomer Royal to apply himself with the most exact care & diligence to the rectification of the tables & motions of the heavens, & the places of the fixed stars, so as to find out the so-much-desired longitude of places for perfecting the art of navigation. In other words, ladies, to establish a central & crucial here from which all the theres of this planet may be measured & charted. That green line above us is a modern laser beam, marking the Meridian Line to the exactitude of a zillimetre.'

And he spread his arm indicating we should look up above us, & follow the shimmering green line, which shot, straight as time's arrow, out of the window, & seemingly out into the heavens. I went to the window & followed the path it drew, then took in a sharp breath – *for Sataan*, there before me in the far distance squatted a kind of fairyland, all lit up with a million candles – a collection of huge, geometric monuments, their myriad lights flashing, winking & sparking bright, & it seemed we were on a hill, & this fairyland was down in the valley below, & beyond it I spied the glitter of water, & a faint hum whispered from it, as though it softly breathed, but I could see no sign of life but some oddly-moving rows of lights, it being darkish outside. O curious new world, what mass of glass & metal was this, that met my eyes?

'The Tin City!' I breathed, for such had I instantly christened it, & despite my pleas to be returned to Denmark forthwith, something in me yearned to step its streets, just once, for the adventure.

He laughed. 'Actually, Canary Wharf,' he said, smiling. 'Well, young Charlotte. You are indeed a plucky one. I have been watching your progress, & was wondering how long it would take you to come here, to the Tin City, as you call it. Though I must say you are full of surprises, for I hardly expected your mother too! She must have got in with you and activated the starting mechanism!'

But little did he know what nerve he had hit. All at once the horizon seemed to twist & uglify.

'Fru Schleswig is not my mother!' I expostulated, & then (I blush at the memory, & might not be recounting it to you, had I not taken a vow of honesty) burst into tears of pure, exhausted misery. I am not normally one to bawl my eyes out, dear precious darling reader (oh, and you are looking so attractive today, if I may say so!), but I confess that I was in that moment floored by the predicament in which I found myself. Here I was in a whole new world, & there on the horizon was Fairyland, & yet *people I did not even know* were insisting on my kinship to the hideous one! This was a far cry from what I had planned, or would have planned, had I been the architect of my own destiny!

'There there, young lady. We are a highly-strung creature, to be sure!' he said, putting his arm around my shoulder in what he may have hoped to be a fatherly way, but I shook him off roughly, & Fru Schleswig's pawing hoof too, & remained in a dignified state of silence (or 'a ryte royle sulke', as Fru S mutteringly referred to it) as Professor Krak led the way down a wide bright-lit corridor to a cupboard-like room where he picked up a bag from which he pulled two enormous red blankets of a texture I had never encountered before (which might have seduced me, had I not been in such a state, for soft as the fur on the belly of a kitten they were, & as sweetly warm!), in which we wrapped ourselves before following him out, passing through an octagonal room housing brass machines in glass cases, alongside globes & telescopes, & cogged contraptions whose purpose seemed to calibrate or trap something. 'The museum,' murmured Professor Krak distractedly, & I spotted that he seemed hurried, & glanced nervously about him all the while, as though he were trespassing & had no right there. (Which later of course I learned was indeed the case, & he had only succeeded in gaining regular entrance through bribery, blackmail & extortion.) We exited through a back door that led to what he called the Fire Escape &, once at ground level, walked some way in the oddly warm night air through a wide, tree-filled field whose floor was littered with the bobbled seed-pods of the plane tree, as found on Strandboulevarden, which I was glad to see for at least they looked familiar in this landscape, though my fur-lined boots were drenched, & they squelched with water at each step. As we made our way across the mown grass of what seemed a sloping park, the humming, roaring noise swelled out from the bright light-strings, which Professor Krak announced with pride were 'cars, moving carriages powered by a motor & fossil fuel. Welcome to the modern world, my dears, where the twenty-first century has dawned!'

The twenty-first century?! Lord, spare us! I thought, but said nothing, & merely pondered the Professor's words as we tramped on in silence through the dusk or dawn or whatever this half-light was in the shadow of the Tin City, for it seemed infected & false, & clearly bore no relation to sun, moon or stars. He had knocked me down with a feather, of course, with this talk of leaping more than a century forward in time. But on the other hand – well, although it was not entirely clear to me what manner of a place this was in which we had landed up, I was beginning to surmise that we were in a world that existed invisibly, & in another sphere to our own. Not an afterlife, so much as a side-stepping of death, a kind of cosmic cheat, or parallel, or chimera which (if Professor Krak was to be believed) was taking place far into the unthinkably distant future. Well, so be it, then! A dream it was! I would wake up soon & all would be well! And I would laugh at the whole absurd story over breakfast, & perhaps even recount some of it to Fru Schleswig & make her spray the room with *rundstykke* crumbs as she in turn guffawed. But the dream did not end, &

could not be escaped from so easily, & indeed it then most swiftly turned nightmarish, for waiting at the black wrought-iron park entrance (which we scaled with the assistance of a ladder that stood there, the gates themselves being padlocked shut) stood a shiny black carriage of iron, horseless, on four wheels, that growled like a foul-tempered hippopotamus. Professor Krak bade us enter it through a door that he swung open in its side: 'Our means of transport, ladies,' he said, & then, in a foreign tongue which I presumed to be English, commenced a rushed conversation with the driver of this vehicle, who was – Lord! I could scarcely believe my eyes! – as black as a coal-scuttle, just like in the illustrations of man-eating cannibals I had seen in the cellar at the orphanage! But before I could scream in terror & make my escape, the machine roared to life with a smooth lurch & we sped into the pellucid gloaming which in that place seemed to pass for night.

The journey was punctuated by the frequent halts we were compelled to make in order that Fru Schleswig & myself – who, having found ourselves unaccountably hungry, had quickly devoured between us the cylindrical packet of choc-olate biscuits proffered by Krak – could vomit, which we both did copiously, arousing the wrath of the cannibal driver, whose white-teethed fury scared the wits from me, for I had visions of him tearing us limb from limb & munching on our bones, just as they do in the godless realms of Afric, or shrinking our heads to wear as tasteless jewellery. 'Fear not, ladies,' said Professor Krak. 'I have told him you have been to a fancy-dress party, & become merry, & I will tip him well for his pains.'

Us? Fancy dress? Merry? Kidnapped, more like! The nerve

of it! But I could say naught, so sick & discombobulated was I feeling, & so anxious about the cannibal, whom I prayed had assuaged his hunger with a good meal earlier, though his fearsome mood would indicate the opposite. London was first of all to me a land of seasickness. First the driving-machine made us sick, & then as soon as we were free of the enraged blackamoor (what dizzy relief!) we were led (– dragged! Screaming!) into a building bedazzled with lights (all up the front steps, embedded in the pathway, & shining from above, & from the sides, & all directions – never had I seen so much light at evening-time) & then bundled into a box whose door closed on all three of us. Professor Krak pressed a button & all at once we were scooped vertically upwards, leaving our stomachs at floor-level. My brain heaved, & had Fru Schleswig not caught me, I would have fallen to the floor & smithereened my skull there & then. Finally, the box's motion ceased, the door slid open (do not ask me how, & what is more I care not to know!) & we exited, veering wildly as two bagatelle balls along a brightly lit corridor, where Professor Krak pointed us onward until we came to a door which he unlocked not with a key, but seemingly with a small piece of dull-looking ivory which he inserted in a hole until an odd noise sounded & a small red light winked.

There he led us to a pale room with slatted blinds & two plain beds of birchwood & a quiet woven rug on the floor. Lord, it was a relief to see something familiar at last, that had the patina of home!

'It's all from Ikea,' he said, as though we should have heard of such a land, & then: 'Drink that down, dear ladies, each of you. It will put you in a state of drowsiness, & help you sleep. I will bring you fresh nightwear – I have quite a supply of clothes for just such arrivals as yours – & run a bath. We have all the modern conveniences which, I assure you, you will be most impressed by.'

'I will be forced into a bath over my own dead body,' I said defiantly, for I had heard of people taking baths, & drowning in them like Tragic Johanna, & I had seen the one in Fru Krak's house, a deep enamelled tub that required much scrubbing from Fru Schleswig. The creature, too, weighed in at this point, just as negatively & vociferously as I, for she has her own annual midsummer washing ritual, dear reader, the details of which I will spare you, save to tell you they involve her stripping naked, rubbing her flesh with chicken fat, and exposing herself to the dogs of the neighbourhood who lick her clean with their slobbering tongues amid much giggling on the part of the townsfolk, and much revulsion on mine. There are times when I praise God we are not related! Anyway on the issue of bathing Fru S & I were so united & adamant that Professor Krak sighingly agreed that we might simply wash & change for now, & showed us to what he called the bathroom, so white & luminous that it looked like a porcelain Heaven, with hot water – he demonstrated – that gushed from neat little taps, & liquid soap that foamed most prettily, & lights so bright that in the mirror you saw your face in more detail than you had ever done before, & had occasion to feel mighty pleased with your appearance, despite the misery of your situation. Professor Krak indicated on a chair two unadorned white nightdresses of soft cotton, one a normal size & the other gigantic, & then pointed out the water-closet, & showed how one must press a button to make the water whirlpool through its system after one had sat on it & done one's private business & dabbed at one's *tissekone* with the very soft white paper that hung in an interminably long roll next to it. With many grunts, Fru Schleswig proceeded to show great interest in the throne, so different from our own bucketed facilities, or the porcelain receptacle at Fru Krak's, & investigated in detail, & by the time we had succeeded in freeing her thick arm from the pipe Professor Krak called 'the U-bend', the sleeping potion had begun to take sudden & dramatic effect, & I felt the urgent need to get into my nightdress & horizontalize.

At which juncture it is possible that I parted with consciousness, for I have no memory of changing, walking back to the bedroom, & lying on the softest bed I ever felt beneath my bones, or falling into a deep & dreamless slumber, such as a baby might enjoy in its cot in the very earliest days of its entry to the world.

And I was such a baby, of course, dear reader, in terms of innocence. But I was not to remain in that happy state for long. The next morning I awoke to find myself still in the future: it seemed that whatever dream my sleep had conjured was proving most tenacious. And I might have carried on believing in it still, were it not for those small things that made me know that, as a part of me had suspected & feared, what I saw & felt was indeed a waking reality. The snoring of Fru Schleswig was real. I pinched myself & the pain of it was real. I looked in the mirror (the mirror being so often my solace, dear one, & my means of cheering myself – I need not explain further, as being beautiful too, I am sure you have the same experience!) & knew that my face was real, & when my heart groaned (not at my appearance – on the contrary – but at my situation), that, too, was real.

Returning to the bedroom where Fru Schleswig was just beginning to utter the first expletives of wakefulness, I saw that across a chair next to her Herr Krak had now spread a huge plain shirt, & a giant skirt, & some monstrously big white undergarments in a stretchy fabric I had never encountered before. On my own bed lay a pair of men's trousers & a shapeless man's shirt, alongside a pair of hideous bulging shoes of a soft texture, a woollen long-sleeved shift & a pair of socks. There was underwear, too: a pair of white knickers with very little lace, & a gusseted contraption, also lacking in adornment, that I presumed, from its dual concaves, that one strapped to one's bazookas. My clients would have laughed their heads off if they had seen me attempting to get into it, & I would not have blamed them, but the result was comfortable & flattered the cleavage, though it could never, to my mind, compete with the aesthetics of a corset.

'I hope I furnished you with the correct, er, *size*,' said Professor Krak who knocked & opened the door just as I had finished dressing in my mannish garb, looked me up & down, & gave me a hesitant smile. 'I have quite a collection of clothes for such occasions, as you can imagine, what with all the pioneers arriving over the years. I figured you as a 36D.' On which baffling note he said he would leave me to coax Fru S to life, & then join him, if I would be so good, for a 'hearty English breakfast'.

As Fru Schleswig struggled into her modern-day clothes, I averted my eyes & sought refuge in the view from the window, only to be rewarded with instant vertigo. We were high, high, perched upon a teetering platform. Outside, the Tin City stood in the distance, silver & grey – unlit now, except by the sun, which bounced off its flat planes & made it glitter in a harsher way than when I first saw it last night – but still I was mesmerized by its scale & its presumption. How many people must there be in this world, to live in such a place? Why, you could fit all the folk of Denmark into just a scatter of its buildings! The thought made my whole mind tilt to the perpendicular. I had never found myself higher from ground level than the top of the spiral church-tower of Christianshavn, before, but now –

Outside, there were leaves on the trees, & the sun shone bright, & it seemed to be summer.

'A tour of the apartment, ladies,' announced Professor Krak, dressed today in ecclesiastical-looking garments he introduced as 'classic contemporary leisurewear', & we followed him through the various corridors & rooms. From most of the windows one could glimpse a sickening view of the metropolis that he still claimed to be London, spread before us, with its tall blank-faced towers planted cheek by jowl, its silver snaking river, & only a very few familiar-looking buildings to rest one's gaze on amidst the relentless metal & sheets of brilliant glass, those flat façades, & the incessant hum of vehicles far below.

'Today's lady is a lucky one,' Professor Krak was proclaiming. 'See all these labour-saving devices?' he said, directing his hand towards various white cupboards in the corner of the room he called the kitchen, though it contained no trace of either victuals nor human toil. In one such cold-breathing cupboard sat many jars of indefinable substances, brightly coloured as poison, & I felt instantly hungry, for if Professor Krak were to be believed, I calculated that apart from the chocolate biscuits we had vomited up last night, we had not eaten in over a hundred years, & Fru Schleswig clearly felt a similar imperative, for she made a sudden lunge to grab a raw potato which she sank her teeth into, while Professor Krak, who merely raised an eyebrow, pointed to a small box he called a microwave, which he said was 'very popular with the English, who do not so much cook food, as heat it through'.

A habit he proceeded to demonstrate as he prepared our first breakfast.

Dear reader, beloved one: belonging as you do to the future, none of the domestic novelties we encountered for the first time that day would be of any bafflement to you, but to me and Fru Schleswig they were magic indeed. 'Believe me, you will become used to such things in a jiffy,' assured Professor Krak, upon which the machine made a sudden 'ping!'. Startled, Fru Schleswig flinched as though stung by a bee.

'Iz it broke?' she asked Professor Krak. Who in reply merely handed her a bowl of steaming porridge, which she attacked with gusto, & continued: 'Let me explain to you the rudiments of time-travel, such as I have become aware of them.' He was now spooning fragrant ground coffee into the mouth of a tall metal box, then pressing a button which provoked a whizzy hum. 'Time has certain rules. It continues to run at the normal rate in the past, just as it does here in the future. One second per second, as it were. But while it is possible to travel both back & forth in time, because of the constraints of the machine or perhaps our own bodies, it is not possible, as far as I can configure, to change the past.'

'How so?' I asked, curious despite myself.

'If only I knew the answer to that, you would see before you a contented scientist. However, I hope to get to the bottom of it someday, & either confirm the theory or prove it wrong. In the meantime, we have the Grandmother Paradox. This is one crucial question that all time-travellers must ask themselves: if I went back in time and killed my own grandmother, would I exist now?' (Oh Lord, I was feeling most disarranged & queasiatious, & was already regretting my query. Fru Schleswig, on the other hand, was in eating mode, & therefore oblivious, for she goes deaf when she masticates.) 'So you will never meet your past or future self in such a way as to alter what has already been or is about to be. Which to my belief is just as well, for confusion would then abound.' (As if it doesn't already! I thought, most vexed.) 'The machine can only make leaps – at present – of a hundred years or more,' he continued, whilst I placed my bowl of oatmeal in the micro-wave machine & turned the knob as he had done. 'I myself have gone as far back as a thousand years (to Mali, a most distressing experience which I care not to repeat) & forward three hundred, to France, which was even more so. I came to the sad conclusion that anyone living in this particular here & now (by which I mean the twenty-first century of course) would be foolish to hope for grandchildren.'

'You mean the world will end?'

'Oh, the earth will still revolve around the sun much as it does now,' he replied airily, reaching for cups. 'But the future is a sorry land, with all that is bright and exciting quite extinguished. All I saw on my visit were multi-storeyed pig farms that reached to the sky, plains of beetroot that stretched to the horizon, & buzzing between them, huge clouds of malaria-bearing mosquitoes. The people there are moody & dejected, & wheeze much due to breathing trouble. I shall not be going back. Now would you prefer cappuccino, which is light & frothy, or espresso which is rich & dark? Isn't this part of the future stupendous? You will come to admire its nerve, I do assure you.'

And so it went, & we met more so-called 'marvellous contraptions', including the *television*, whose nauseously flickering images instantly gave me a vivid headache, & the *telephone*, which for a reason I could not fathom looked familiar to me, & I gazed at it a long time before it struck me that I had indeed seen such a thing before, unearthed by Fru Schleswig in the home of Fru Krak. I had hidden it in a chamber pot.

'There are mobile varieties, too,' Professor Krak enthused, clearly most keen to impress us. He cracked his knuckles. 'Cordless! Is that not the bee's knees?' I promise you, dear ladies, that as soon as you have learned English, you will be making much use of this device!'

'And whom, pray, do you expect us to communicate with?' I snapped, determined not to be seduced by his eccentric enthusiasms. 'For I can assure you, sir, we shall not be staying here long enough to bother speaking to strangers in their local languages!'

At which he merely smiled, & chuckled, & hummed 'Tragic Johanna', as though he knew something we did not.

Whoever said *nothing troubles me more than time & space; & yet nothing troubles me less, as I never think about them* I recall not, but I knew that I had felt the same way until now. When not only did they begin to puzzle me enormously, they fair gave me a headache to boot. The great philosophers, who never minded headaches, & indeed made a living by engendering them in others, have speculated endlessly about time; this much I remember from all my mouldering books. Philosopher X says this & Philosopher Y says that – but when you try to translate their fine words into human discourse, the like of which a simple rustic being like Fru Schleswig might understand, then all evaporates as fleet as steam into airy persiflage & you find that, much as you may wish to express their high & mighty thoughts, you are struck dumb.

But back to what I hesitantly call the 'here & now': I learned quickly that more than anything else, Professor Krak liked to brag, though why I could not fathom, for the Time Machine of which he was so proud had done far more harm than good, from what I could see, & enticing though the Tin City was, I still wished to be returned to my own place & time, Fru Krak's waiting pistol or no. But I would get nowhere without information, so I let him speak. I am used to listening to the prattle of men, & I confess I do it well, for lending a sympathetic ear is part of the service one is paid for as a whore, & sometimes the most crucial aspect of the transaction. (You would not believe, O precious one, how many of those wives are right, when they complain that their husband is a crushing bore!)

But Professor Krak was not a bore: he was more of a very convincing lunatic, or so I thought at first while he explained himself, as I had demanded that he do, I for my part merely nodding & asking the occasional question & sifting the information he came out with in my mind, wondering all the while how much was fantasy & how best to make use of what was not. And as this was going on, Fru Schleswig poked & nosed her way through the apartment, pressing every button & twisting every knob she could see, thus setting all manner of electrical appliances in motion, & unleashing gas. She then discovered the nozzled creature called a *vacuum cleaner*, for which she instantly developed a most unhealthy attachment, from then on dragging it with her everywhere, plugging it into this socket or that, & starting up its motor so that it could suck at the floor, the walls and the furniture like an insatiable flatfish.

All the while I was listening to Professor Krak's story.

I learned the Time Machine took years to make, & even longer to perfect, & that some of the principles by which it worked, Fru Schleswig might be interested to know, bore parallels with the vacuum cleaner, in that Bernouilli's Principle concerning air-speed & pressure ratios applied to time-sucking as much as they did to the aspiration of dust. That he had devised a means – involving a 'secret catalysing liquid' one poured into the quartz orb – which ensured it could not be set in motion without his foreknowledge. I learned that Professor Krak had then decided to advertise discreetly in *Politiken* for people 'seeking adventure in the Great Beyond'. His contraption became known among the intimate circle that then developed, & widened by word of mouth, as the Suicide Machine, for those who entered never returned. Until one day, quite unexpectedly, a woman called Rigmor popped up, who had taken her leave a twelvemonth before, being pregnant & destitute. She had visited Greenwich in the future, she claimed, & had her baby there, abandoned it outside a charity shop & then returned to 'the past' by accident, when visiting the Observatory out of a nostalgic interest, for this was where she had first found herself.

'By pure luck, she stood under the green laser beam of the Greenwich Meridian, whose field of epistemological longitude had swept her into the Krak Time-Sucker fault-line, forcing her molecules to obey the Magnetic Memory Imperative – by which means she was catapulted back to the Copenhagen she had left a year before!' he declared. 'A stroke of luck if ever there was one!'

On Rigmor's unexpected arrival in the Krak basement, she told him she wanted to return to the future as soon as she could, for she had learned English now, & had found thriving employment in a 'nail bar'.

'So these people knew not what awaited them?'

'Desperation bends the mind to consider awful things.'

'And how long before you tried it on yourself?' I asked indignantly.

'You do not understand, my dear. Being the architect of the machine, & having sole knowledge of its inner workings, I was too valuable to go myself. I had to send envoys. No one has complained.'

'How many have been in a position to? How many never returned?'

He smiled condescendingly. 'That is hardly the point. These brave folk wanted an exit from the life they led. I provided it – no questions asked. They knew the risk they were running.'

'But *I* did not ask to come here,' I expostulated furiously. 'And nor did Fru Schleswig!' Who was at that moment using the dust-sucking contraption beneath the chair on which I sat, in a most irritating manner, so I pulled the plug from its socket, unleashing a bitter little spark which much matched my mood, & snapped at her to clean somewhere else, or I would push her into the River Thames, & cheer as her fat carcass pickled in its waters.

'Ah,' he said, with that twitchy smile of his. 'Now we are

getting to the nub of it. For I think you did ask to come here. Indeed you did. I am not speaking of your good mother, whose arrival was something of an *imprévu*, but of you personally, my little Charlotte. Were you not intrigued, dear young woman, by the thought of another life? Admit it! And were you not drawn to the machine in my cellar, despite the fact that I warned you off? You cannot deny it! *Come not near, young madam, if you value your life* were the words I wrote, as I recall. But still you came. You were curious about another life, one that might elevate you further & do that clever-minx brain of yours, & those pretty looks, more justice than the one you led on the streets of Østerbro & in the service of my charming, joyful & thankfully erstwhile wife.'

I do not normally blush, for we harlots have learned shamelessness, but just then, as I gulped, I felt my face redden furiously. For was there not a tiny grain of truth in what he said? Had I not harboured secret dreams of a better life, & other things? Had I not thought of exchanging what I was for what I might yet become? And then, a split second later, it dawned on me that Professor Krak had been clever – oh so very clever, so much cleverer than I! For he had been playing me all along! He had lured me to the machine, & my own cursed curiosity had done the rest!

But why?

The answer came that night. Professor Krak announced that he was going out, having called a meeting of what he called his 'Scandinavian flock', to tell them of our safe arrival, & to organize a welcome party for myself & 'the unexpected bonus that is Fru Schleswig'.

'But don't worry: I will be home before midnight, & in the

meantime young Franz Poppersen Muhl is coming to keep you company.'

Our companion was a weedy-looking young man of fragile sensibilities, clad in strange mud-green garments he called *combat gear*, covered with pockets & clever metal fastenings with tiny teeth. He sat at the table & drew from a voluminous bag a huge scrapbook which he opened out in front of us. 'I have been keeping a journal,' he announced. 'I call it *Journey into the Unknown.*' The pages were covered in tiny spiderish writing, & here & there coloured papers and what looked like tickets had been stuck, while other scraps fluttered out like the wings of butterflies as he leafed through. It seemed that he had come here planning to work on it, so while he glued a few cards in, & furnished written explanations for them, I asked him how he had fetched up in London. At which he proclaimed most vehemently that he was a victim of circumstance, & were it not for his fear of his parents' wrath, he would return forthwith to Copenhagen & resume his philosophy studies. Or would have done, had that opportunity not been lately blocked.

'The opportunity to return blocked?' I asked in panic, my arms laden with frozen bricks of something called 'lasagne' I had just removed from the freeze-box. My fingers grew numb as I awaited his answer. But he just looked moody. 'Explain, I beg you! Blocked how?'

'By the wife of Professor Krak, I believe,' he said finally, pushing back from the table & fiddling with the metal fastenings I later knew as zips. 'Fru Krak is to remarry, & is turning Number Nine Rosenvængets Allé upside-down with a view to finally selling the property, so our link to that world shall soon be lost, for the machine is housed there, &

will most probably be broken into a thousand pieces or sold for scrap. So far Professor Krak has held her off by making the place look haunted, but now . . .' he trailed off. 'It looks like we are done for, & we are stuck here for ever. Unless –'

'Unless what?'

He looked puzzled. 'Well, that is why you are here, Frøken Charlotte. Surely you realized? That's why everyone is so excited about your arrival. You & Fru Schleswig are Professor Krak's last hope.'

Professor Krak's last hope? I did not like the sound of this at all, but it explained a great deal, all of a sudden: Professor Krak's nervousness, & the fact that he seemed to have been expecting me (though not Fru Schleswig) all along. But how on earth had he known I would discover the machine, & enter it? Had the whole thing been a trap? Over a microwaved 'meal for two' (a hideous mish-mash of pulpy flour-paste & red-tinted offal), I questioned Franz further while Fru Schleswig polished off her own plateful & then set to thawing out more icy boxes, pausing only to squint at the gastronomic horrors depicted on their wrappings, seemingly oblivious to our conversation & the impact it might have upon her future.

'Have you ever thought of becoming a police interrogator?' the weedy Franz asked me when I had finished my questioning, & amassed much supplementary knowledge on the subject of the Time Machine & the Kraks. 'For you have squeezed me dry as a lemon & my poor brain is aching.' But he had furnished me with much to ponder.

After Franz had asked me & Fru Schleswig to pose for a photograph, which we duly did (Fru Schleswig insisted on wielding the vacuum cleaner), he showed us the picture he had taken on a screen incorporated into the tiny silver camera, & said he would 'make us each a print'. Then while he continued work on his journal, & Fru Schleswig crashed around loading plates into the crockery-whirler, I tried to summarize what I'd learned from Franz. According to him, during the seven years since he staged his own death, Professor Krak had managed to import & export himself between London & Østerbro, & make a pretty penny out of it by offering 'eternal escape' to those Danes who wished for it. Which is how Franz & others like him – the forlorn, the desperate & the plain criminal – came to London to seek a new life. The fee was a hundred kroner, but in return for this preposterous sum, Professor Krak promised them they need never return or be discovered, & tempted them with pictures of the Great Beyond, as he called London, & with stories of the technological marvels that awaited them there.

'But how did he keep Fru Krak from discovering him, & his activities?' I had asked Franz. 'Surely she had an inkling?'

'I believe she did indeed,' he'd replied. 'But somehow he has always managed to keep her at arm's length.'

I thought of her reluctance to listen to me when I told her there was a creature living in the basement of her house, and how flustered she had been when I had insisted. Ha! And what had Herr Bang said, about the place being rumoured as haunted? No wonder she had been unable to sell it. Was this also part of Professor Krak's plan? I resolved to ask him this, & all the other questions that continued to crowd my mind thereafter. I gathered from Franz that as a result of Professor Krak's recruitments, the part of London known as Greenwich – along with its sister districts of Lewisham, Deptford, Mudchute, Blackheath & the Isle of Dogs – was now crawling with previously disgruntled Danes from the last century who were carving out futures for themselves in this brave land: a small army of Olsens, Jensens, Rasmussens, Petersens, Nielsens, Madsens & Svendsens integrating themselves seamlessly and quietly, minding their Ps and Qs, honing their Vs and their Ws, and working on their English vowels until they were indistinguishable from the common stream.

Franz's own story was that of a spoiled boy. He revealed he had had a furious argument with his parents concerning his weekly allowance, & sworn to commit suicide by strapping fireworks to himself and igniting them, but then could not muster the courage. So instead he went down to Sortedams Lake, loaded his pockets with stones, and jumped.

'But as you see,' he said sheepishly, 'I did not die. The water there is no shallower than one's knees, a fact I was not aware of when I leaped. You cannot imagine how difficult it is to summon the courage to commit such an act, & then be thwarted. Most humiliating, to boot.'

Then, scrambling out of the water, he said, a hand appeared offering assistance. It was attached to an arm, which was attached to the body of a dark-cloaked balaclava'd man, who had seemingly been posting a letter. 'There is another way,' said Franz's saviour – & to cut a long & self-pitying story short, Professor Krak questioned the dripping & snivelling lad & once he had gleaned he was from a wealthy family, offered him the services of the machine. 'Being a student of philosophy, I was attracted to the idea,' whined Franz. 'But since coming here, & learning English, & reading all the philosophy that has been thought since our own era, I am keen to go back & profit from my knowledge, & make a splash with it – even though Professor Krak insisted it was impossible to alter the events of the past through intervention, for he had tried it himself to no avail & insisted it was futile for "epistemological reasons". But that door now appears to be closing in any case, with Fru Krak's marriage on the horizon. All I really want is to go home to my parents & eat *flæskesteg* for Sunday lunch,' finished Franz. 'But they believe me dead!' And he howled miserably, reaching for a tissue to blow his dejected nose.

When Franz finally departed for a place he referred to mysteriously as the Halfway Club, I resolved to confront Professor Krak as soon as I saw him again, & ask what mad & jigged-up idea he had got into his head, & was he planning to use me & Fru Schleswig as guinea-pigs? And if so, he had no right to make assumptions of any sort about what we would & would not do, unless a very tempting financial offer was involved! And then, for the first time in my life, I enacted what I later learned was a strong tradition amongst the inhabitants of that country & time in which I now found myself: I trained my eyes on the silent flickering television screen, across which passed a stream of images, by turns boring, sugary, violent, & plain incomprehensible, & fell asleep.

'To begin with,' said Professor Krak the next morning when we resumed our talk, 'I sent only animals.'

I remembered the scratching noises from the basement. 'You used rats?' I queried.

'Rats, cats, dogs. A pig, once, for they are of high intelligence. I had no luck with the smaller creatures, & I fear most were killed in transit. None returned.'

It being early morning, Fru Schleswig was still snoring in

her bed: I had pinned an explanatory note to the giant knickers draped over the chair (STAY WHERE YOU ARE, CRONE) & closed the door softly. I'd insisted to Professor Krak that if he wanted my co-operation, he take me on a tour of the Tin City (yes, I had to go there! I had seen it sparkle & glitter, I had seen it was where the magical green line pointed to, from the Observatory! Who says a girl can't have dreams?) whilst explaining his method & purpose in more detail.

'The problem was, the Time Machine does not travel: it remains where it is, while those inside it are catapulted into the void. I simply did not know how to make the creatures return to Copenhagen, for once they had been decanted into another era, how could I explain that the only way of returning was to keep to the meridian, & hope that a miniature earth tremor might be triggered, thus setting the Time-Sucker's Magnetic Memory Imperative in motion?' Professor Krak was saying as he steered me down the pavement of a street along which vehicles rampaged, spurting cacophony & acrid fumes.

'It's just everyday pollution, for there is a hole in the ozone layer,' he explained with a dismissive wave of his hand. 'But Nero fiddles while Rome burns. I have seen the devastation it will lead to a hundred years hence – but heigh ho, man will be man.'

The street was still heaving with people, many of them as fat as Fru Schleswig, with skins of all hues, like a foreign bazaar, many of them seemingly speaking aloud to themselves, with strange, ugly black jewellery clamped to their ears or dangling near their mouths like laces of liquorice. I saw tattooed sailors adorned with silver face-jewellery such as one finds in illustrations of Amazonian tribesmen, and ruffian females, too, similarly bedecked, some pushing small perambulators containing babes whose little mouths were stoppered by handy corks. Amid the bustle, no one paid the slightest heed to either me or Professor Krak, camouflaged as we were in the uniform of that freakish era: I in my unflattering men's trousers, loose shirt & the grotesquely bulbous footwear that seemed *de rigueur* among England's futurefolk, & my companion shod likewise, but clad above in a monkish hooded jerkin & flapping long-johns.

'I will admit' – here he had to raise his voice to be heard above the roar of the horseless vehicles, 'that solving the riddle of time became something of an obsession to me.' I remembered what Gudrun had said about the way Professor Krak locked himself down in the basement, where she would leave meals outside his door, & hear strange shrieks & noises emanating from his rooms. 'And then along came Pandora. My first pioneer.' A note of terrible portentousness entered his voice then, & although he was much taller than me (I fair had to skip to keep up with his lanky-legged pace) & I saw him in profile, it seemed to me he blinked away a tear.

'Who is Pandora?'

'She was an orang-utan from Borneo, originally. I purchased her from a Moroccan trader who ran a carpet shop. As soon as I saw her climbing his curtains, I knew I must have her. Herr Couscous drove a hard bargain, for he was fond of the animal & said she was more intelligent than his own wife.' Here Professor Krak broke off & seemed to wipe another tear from the corner of his eye, then got out his hip-flask – 'ah, the great human antidote!' – & slugged a mouthful down, then passed it to me, but I declined for I needed to keep my head clear to digest the progression of events. Blimey, had I not seen a stuffed animal with a dejected-looking face, in the Oblivion Room, opposite the bicycle? Yes, indeed I had!

'This is the train station,' he said as we next joined a mixed herd of scoundrels, gentlefolk, tarts & ragamuffins all queuing before a tall metal box. 'I'll take you to a place where things are more modern & a lot cleaner, in case you get the wrong idea about London. Rents are very high and we Danes have to duck and dive.'

The machine spat us two pink tickets & we waited on a platform where a sleek vehicle glided in with speed & slyness; entering, we then stood packed together in a bemusing state of wordlessness which I later discovered to be the norm on such transport. I was once again feeling queasiatious, & prayed that we would soon reach our destination, but Professor Krak was now taking up where he had left off. 'When I sent Pandora travelling, I think she went looking for her ancestors,' he said, 'or at least in search of others who resembled her, & could share her primitive urges. Be that as it may, she always returned with intriguing clues about the societies she had visited. I never knew when or if she would reappear, so as you can imagine, my life began to revolve around her arrivals & departures. She taught me courage, & I am forever grateful to her for that.' He wiped another tear away, & blew his nose. 'She had gone on twenty missions before she met her most untimely end.'

The train stopped, disgorged more passengers, then restarted its hair-raising journey into the vortex of God-Knew-Where.

'But how did she get back, pray?'

'I fitted her with a magnetic device, for by now I had calculated the physics. I concocted a special collar which picked up earth tremors: I trained her to respond to them by heading for the source, which was always the spot where the Time-Sucker & the meridian conjoined. Then she would go through the situational magnetism routine I had taught her, & the next thing she knew, she'd be back in Østerbro.' He laughed. 'My, she had the strangest taste in the souvenirs she brought home. For what takes the fancy of a female orang-utan will not closely coincide with whatever objects of interest one might select oneself, if one were free to plunder riches from the Great Beyond.'

'What did she bring?' I asked, for I will admit I was intrigued despite myself, & could feel my hostile stance beginning to erode, for it was plain there was no malice in the Professor: only the most reckless & foolhardy enthusiasm.

'There was a whole collection,' he replied. 'A human skull she brought back once,' continued Professor Krak. 'A handbag made from scaly hide, padded with fabric. A ram's horn. She tended to forage much for exotic fruit, which she devoured most happily on her return. Once, a small black box with a curious disc inside, which I did not understand the meaning of until I came to this century & discovered it to be a music CD.' (He ignored my bafflement.) 'A prayer mat. A mobile tele-phone likewise.'

'I saw what I now know to be such a speaking device in Fru Krak's home,' I confessed. 'Fru Schleswig found it.'

He smiled & nodded. 'No use to anyone there,' he said. 'Though I have a theory that there is no reason why today's telephone signals should not transport easily to the past, if positioned at the correct angle on a Time-Sucker fault-line in an area where there will *one day* stand a transmitter. Ah, I see that the next stop is ours, my dear: prepare to disembark.

Anyway, to return to poor Pandora: the nightmares she would have, after she came home! How she screamed in the night, *stakkels lille skat.* I fed her grapes & pastries & marzipan, for she had the sweetest tooth I have ever come across. O, I treated her like a princess!' he sighed happily, and it struck me then that, the Kraks being childless, this dumb creature might have filled a sentimental void in the basement world of Rosen-vængets Allé. 'But in the most cruel of ironies, the one thing I was unable to protect her from was the danger lurking in my own home, the very place I thought to be the safest in the world,' he went on, his tone of voice now heavy with dejection. 'For it was there that the dear creature met her dreadful fate.' Here he stopped to gaze out of the window, his eyes misting over with tears.

'What happened?' I asked, as the train came to a halt and we disembarked on to a clean and mysteriously empty platform, upon which stood a bench where he gestured we might sit.

'What happened was a housekeeper woman by the name of Gudrun Olsen.'

'Oh my,' I breathed. And there, on the bench, with the occasional tin train whirring in and disgorging passengers, all more neatly & pleasingly dressed than those we had seen before, Professor Krak pursued his tragic theme.

'Gudrun, as housekeeper, was under strict instructions not to enter my workshop, no matter what strange cries she heard. But for all her many qualities – & she assisted me a great deal in the construction of the machine – Gudrun has the most insatiable curiosity, & she could not leave well alone. One night Pandora was recovering from a particularly difficult mission – I knew this for she had come back bloody & scarred, as though animals had attacked her. Anyway, that night she had one of her nightmares. It was quite a screaming fit.'

Here the Professor sighed.

'And then?' I prompted.

'Well, despite being barred from my quarters, in walked Gudrun, brandishing a poker. Pandora awoke at that moment & leaped up, & so did I, shouting to Gudrun to move not a centimetre, but Pandora had by then attacked her poor face.'

I shuddered, horrified, as I pictured Gudrun's eye-socket split raggedly by a swipe of the creature's filthy claw, the wound gushing crimson blood upon her impeccably starched pinafore.

'And then –' he broke off, unable to continue.

But I imagined the rest: the screaming Gudrun, blood pouring from her cheek, bashing the monkey with her lethal poker, cracking open its little skull like a walnut, uncasing the throbbing brain, a pale translucent mauve, spotted with gore, & ending that small, brave life. And what followed: a man racked with grief for his murdered monkey, & a beautiful woman, disfigured for life, lost to a world of laundry & steam, never to marry, or fully understand what had transpired on the fateful day she entered the Professor's territory unbidden.

But bless you: let us expunge the image of that ghastly female inter-species confrontation & move on. Professor Krak & I left the bench, & rose upwards on another moving stairway, this one shining & clean, adorned with gleaming brass. Carried heavenward by this, amid a throng of other passengers, all gentlefolk it seemed, we were next propelled into an airy balconied temple of light, high-ceilinged & dotted with magnificent exotic plants, the like of which I had never seen before except in paintings of the jungle. I gasped in wonderment, half expecting an Indian tiger to pounce at us from its upper reaches, or a troupe of minstrels to burst into a glitter of harmonies. And all above us & around us, folk, folk, folk, & dwarfing them, glass, glass, glass! Never had I seen such huge sheets of it, so unsmudged, so unbroken & so unadorned by colour or leadwork! Outside, water shone flat, reflecting the highest buildings, and in them, the skies reflected back, until it seemed there were a thousand mirrors, out-staring one another. We exited through a portal & found ourselves upon an odd-shaped, curving bridge, that straddled a stretch of water, below which a row of manned vehicles sat, clawing into the water with articulated arms, & dredging out mud that they swung aloft, dripping. Above us, in the sky, buzzed a giant metal insect which Professor Krak said was a 'helicopter', bearing intrepid humans; & all around, the buildings reared up like magical steel cliffs, blank-faced & heroic.

'Seductive, is it not?' he said, as though reading my thoughts. At which a pang of loyalty to my own place & time overwhelmed me, & I retorted that Canary Wharf was all very well but I saw neither canaries nor wharves, & in any case it was nothing in comparison to Amalienborg, & all of a sudden the memory of that noble palace made me long for Copenhagen so sharply that I felt the tears prick.

'So exactly how do I get home?' I asked, as we passed a mirror in which at first I did not recognize myself, for I looked so like a prisoner, or a simpleton, or the inhabitant of an asylum, in the ugly garb of that century.

He glanced at me with what I feared was pity. 'Let us find ourselves a little coffee house,' he suggested. 'And I will explain the, er . . . *parameters*.'

*   *   *

And it was, in a nutshell, just as Franz Poppersen Muhl had described – only far, far worse. The predicament was thus: the arrival of Pastor Dahlberg in Fru Krak's life compromised the Mother Machine, as Krak called the contraption – which he referred to like a nautical vessel, as 'she'. The house was no longer a safe place to keep her, & yet because of her shape & size, & the fact that her inventor had (foolishly, he admitted with hindsight) assembled her in the basement in such a way that she could not be removed, swift action must be taken before the contraption was discovered & destroyed in the wake of the forthcoming nuptials. All this Professor Krak explained as a black savage (whom to my extreme discomfiture I found to be most attractive, so much so that I even wondered, pervertedly, what it might be like to have him in my bed) served us the frothed coffee known as *latte*, and fresh, moist croissants as good as anything you might buy at Herr Møller's bakery on Classensgade. Just like the driver of the vehicle we entered when we first arrived, the blackamoor spoke fluent English.

'Do normal people not find it disturbing to have cannibals in their midst?' I asked Professor Krak, as we watched the disconcerting waiter walk away. He merely laughed & told me to 'keep an open mind, for the world is a wider place than we Danes can easily dream of', & then returned to the subject in hand, viz how to rid the Krak homestead of its occupants, and save the Mother Machine.

'But why on earth should I help you?' I asked, as his logistical plight became apparent. 'You spied on me, did you not? Wearing a balaclava?'

He nodded in the affirmative. 'I needed to see how curious you were,' he admitted. 'And what you would do with the information you came by.'

'And then you lured me to the machine.'

'By warning you away from it!' he smiled. 'Remember? I knew you would not resist that challenge. The manner of your arrival was a little unexpected, I must admit, due to the intervention of Fru Schleswig: I had planned it otherwise. However, here you are!'

'But what right had you to bring me to this place?' I asked, peeved that he should have anticipated my behaviour so well.

'None, my dear,' he confessed, patting my hand. 'None whatsoever. You ask why you should help me. Well, I hope to show you that *there is much in this for you*, if you will be so good as to listen further. For my belief is that we can mutually assist one another,' he smiled, sipping his coffee. 'We are talking of more than merely your safe return home. You must not forget, dear Frøken Charlotte, that I have been watching you, & was acquainted well enough with your plucky character to know how to tempt you to the Oblivion Room. Now I will come straight to the point of why I did so. What I need is someone whom I can trust, to occupy that house & safeguard the machine, so I can continue to come & go as I please. That someone, in my scheme of things, is *you*. Now in return –' (& here he paused for effect) '– you may not only have the run of the entire house, but become its legal mistress.'

At this he grinned at me most winningly, & winked. Well, I'll grant him this much, I thought: he knows how my heart works all right. A young whore raised in an orphanage, mistress of a huge & imposing mansion in a grand part of town! The things I could do if I got my hands on that place! Lord, I could run my own brothel! I'd call it Hotel Charlotte. I'd employ ten, no, twenty girls, & have Doktor Thorning check their *tissekoner* for diseases once a month. I'd buy good beds, with the best linen & the softest pillows, & there would be hot & cold running water in each room, & scented soaps, & –

As though reading my thoughts, he smiled. 'And do with it as you wish, within reason. But you must stay discreet.'

'But how is this to be achieved?' I asked, so excited by my fantasy that I nearly spilled my frothy beverage. 'I can understand your need to protect the Mother Machine, as you call it, but you will never prise your wife out of that house!'

'Aha,' he said, wiping his mouth on a paper napkin as the waiter came and cleared the crockery. 'Let me explain something that might give you hope. In the seven years since I have regularly been returning to Copenhagen, I have been able to influence my wife's movements,' he said slowly. 'And with your help, I hope to influence them further. So far, indeed, as to send her packing, never to return.'

Much as I wanted to believe this, I found it most puzzling & frankly hard to credit. 'Influence a woman as obtuse as Fru Krak? How so?'

'Obtuse, yes. But she is also superstitious &, in certain ways, gullible to the extreme. Are you familiar with a publication known as the *Fine Lady*?'

I nodded. 'She is a slave to it.'

'Precisely,' smiled Herr Krak. 'A Fine Lady through & through, would you not say?'

'She certainly pays most particular heed to what her horoscope commands,' I averred.

'Well, meet its author!' he beamed, showing an array of implausibly white teeth.

'What – you? You wrote the Aquarian Lady?' I gasped. Now I was indeed impressed.

'Not just Aquarius. I did all twelve. Each week, for the last few years, anonymously, & for no pay.' My eyes widened. 'I made the mistake, I fear, of encouraging her with the Pastor, as I wished never to be shackled to her again, in case I found myself trapped back there one day, God forbid. However, when I realized he might pose a threat to the machine, I decided to try & influence her into getting a domestic servant whom I might use on the other side. I know my wife's weak spots: within a week of hatching this plan, the Aquarian Lady was persuaded to hire a cleaning girl. But it was pure luck that I should end up with one as bright and clever as you.'

I was shocked. I had known it was a trap, but had never guessed the scope of it! What evil genius!

'And when you'd written this horoscope, you came to Copenhagen & you posted it to the *Fine Lady*,' I realized aloud. 'In the letterbox down by Sortedams Lake. And all those who saw you there thought you were a ghost, not stopping to wonder why a phantom might be availing itself of the Royal Mail!'

I could not help but clap my hands then & there: Lord, you had to admire the nerve of the Professor's endeavour! I was beginning to get the feeling that we might become allies after all.

Professor Krak explained then that he could not risk revealing himself to Fru Krak, but already he felt she had sensed something (this I could confirm), & was suspicious. 'Yet if she tells the Pastor she suspects I am still alive, she can't marry him without risking bigamy. So she has been burying her head in the sand like an ostrich, & reading her horoscope. Through which I was trying to ensure she kept you on as a servant, & stayed out of the basement rooms. But who knows how the situation might change when the Pastor becomes official master of the house?'

'So you need to somehow get rid of Fru Krak and the Pastor, & make me owner of the property,' I said. 'For if they sold it, someone else might discover the machine & destroy it.'

'Precisely so.'

'And do you have a plan?'

He shook his head. 'I had thought of using the horoscope again,' he said, 'but I fear that on this issue it might not be enough to budge her – especially now that you tell me she actually descended to the basement. Now you know the Pastor better than I: perhaps there is a possibility to be exploited there? Either way, I know that if you & I put our heads together . . .'

I nodded vigorously, for having assessed what life of luxury was in store for me if I entered into his scheme, my brain was already conjuring, & indeed a quite clever, nay, *brilliant* notion was beginning to crystallize in my head, inspired by the denouement of a moving picture story I had watched the previous night on television. 'Give me a moment,' I said, & scribbled some notes upon a napkin. Once I had worked out all the logistics, I clapped my hands in delight.

'What say you to this?' I cried, outlining my cunning ruse, & laying it before him on the table, where it gleamed like a freshly minted jewel.

'My, oh my!' he cried with great enthusiasm when I had finished. 'You clever girl! What sharp wits you have about you, for I would never have thought of such a thing in a century!'

Which compliment I took most prettily, for I was enjoying

the flattery, & was loath to tell him that in fact the real credit was due to a two-dimensional dog called Scooby-Doo & his human comrades, & that all I had done was to steal & refine a plan involving property fraud that they had exposed in the course of their detective work. O, how proud was I in that moment! And how joyously impressed was Professor Krak! So much so that when we had finished our coffee, he led me to a smart dress shop, & bade me choose any outfit I wanted, for I had deserved it, & what's more, he 'sensed festivities on the horizon'. And so I emerged an hour later clad in delightful lacy russet-coloured underwear, light as a cobweb, & a green robe that matched my eyes and revealed much of my legs above the knee (how deliciously naked I felt!), & high-heeled shoes & magical stockings that clung to the thigh themselves & needed no suspenders, & I was mightily pleased with my appearance: for the outfit much flattered my figure and as we walked through the streets of the Tin City, marvelling at the sheer height and power of the buildings Professor Krak aptly referred to as 'sky-scrapers', I was right glad to note that whatever progress men had undergone in the century & a bit since I last knew them, some of their habits, such as swivelling the head the better to appreciate a young woman with a stupendously good body (if you will forgive the boast, precious reader), have stayed the same.

We then hailed a taxi. Delighted with the progress we had made in formulating a plan, Professor Krak said that I was to return to Copenhagen as soon as was feasible.

'What does *as soon as is feasible* mean, exactly?' I queried, my sudden anxiety exacerbated by the swerving & lurching of our vehicle. 'What is wrong with tomorrow, in heaven's name?' For as you can imagine I was mad-keen to establish myself as mistress of Hotel Charlotte, & had been busily furnishing it in my imagination: curlicued bed-posts, fancy chamber pots, rouched curtains, ashtrays made from exotic shells, gilded spittoons.

He shook his head. 'It's a treacherous business at both ends,' he said. 'Fru Krak is not our only opponent, I fear. We have also the custodians of the Greenwich Observatory to contend with.'

It was a second or two before the import of what he had said sunk in.

'I thought you worked with them.'

'In a manner of speaking, I do,' he said carefully. 'The fact is, there is a man whom I bribe to let me in, a buildings inspector. But sadly, he only has access at certain times, & for most specific purposes. The timing is delicate. We will be forced to wait until August, I fear.'

'The month now being?'

'June.' I gasped, but he continued hastily: 'Do not worry, I beg you. Your precious time, dear Frøken Charlotte, need not be wasted. On the contrary. Let us collect the good Fru Schleswig & direct ourselves posthaste to join my pioneers at the Halfway Club. Did I not tell you I sensed festivities on the horizon?'

Show me a girl whose heart does not skip a beat at the thought of a party – a party in her honour, no less – & I will show you a liar. As our taxi crawled along dust-belching streets, the Professor explained to us in his twitchy & excitable way (I say us, for the preposterously clad & modernized Fru Schleswig had now crammed herself into our company with much

A party in my honour!

*umph*ing & *oomph*ing) that the building in which the Halfway Club was housed served a dual purpose, the ground floor being the club itself, & the basement storing tiles, cement & brickware, part of the building enterprise of Herr & Fru Jakobsen. The Jakobsens, he said, were two pillars of the community who had 'relocated' (as though changing countries & eras were as simple as uprooting to another part of town!) after an intransigent infestation of headlice drove their wig business into ruin: the couple themselves inhabited the upper floor, where they also let rooms to 'Danes of yore' in need of accommodation.

'Why, we could be back home!' I exclaimed in delight, when our taxi drew near to what looked like a schoolhouse, for the Halfway Club was painted the same traditional ochre-yellow as the orphanage of my youth, & atop it (a patriotic tear sprang to my eye!) the glorious red and white of the Danish flag fluttered at full-mast.

'Yes, the pioneers tend to get somewhat nostalgic,' sighed the Professor. 'Like all refugees, they hanker after what they left behind. The Jakobsens especially.'

As we approached, a cheer went up, & the double doors of the schoolhouse flew open to reveal a most excited-looking throng of people in modern dress, all waving miniature Danish flags. Now you do not need me to tell you how very gratifying this was! News of my arrival – and the role Professor Krak was counting on me to play – had clearly come as a most welcome event among the community of Danish time-travellers. 'Dear Frøken Charlotte, you will be our heroine for ever!' cried an elegant lady, who shook my hand warmly & introduced herself as Fru Helle Jakobsen. At which flabbergasting pronouncement I merely smiled, &

gulped down the schnapps she discreetly handed me, & then cried bravely, getting into the spirit of the thing, 'I will do my best, good madam!', & let her then present a whole muddle of people – a burly sailor-looking type with a lascivious eye called Henrik Dogger, two boys named the Jørgensen twins, & their teenaged friend, the flame-haired Mattias Rosenvinge, one Max Kong, who carried a violin, one Rigmor Schwarb, who carried no musical instrument but whispered that if I ever needed instruction in the sexual gadgetry & manners of modern times (she winked knowingly) I must not be shy to ask, the multitudinous Poulsen family, a couple named Jespersen & their mangy mastiff, then a nervous spinster called Ida Sick who shook my hand most vigorously & said she hoped I would not be staying in London long, as it were, for she knew I had important work to do & if she were frank (here she tittered) she couldn't wait to see the back of me! Next a huge man with the big matted beard of a sailor came up, & said he was Fru Jakobsen's 'other half', Georg, at my service, & then declared that what you two good ladies (for there was no shaking off Fru Schleswig) really wanted, he would wager, was a taste of his wife's fine home-baked *wienerbrød*.

At which Professor Krak clapped his hands & raised a glass: more schnapps appeared & soon some twenty people were making a toast to me & Fru Schleswig, & chattering most excitedly. Helle Jakobsen returned with a further tray of sweetmeats & took Fru Schleswig aside in a most warm & hospitable manner, exclaiming with much enthusiasm, 'I gather, madam, that you share my passion for new-fangled cleaning devices!' & in no time was waxing lyrical about dust-suction while Fru Schleswig, her prodigious backside now moulded into an armchair, listened whilst gobbling her way through a plateful of cinnamon-dusted pastries. Franz then showed up, looking a little drunk, carrying his scrapbook under one arm & supported on the other by Rigmor Schwarb, whom I now noticed sported a tattooed snake that writhed around her elbow before disappearing into the pit of her arm. As these two launched into a heated argument about Franz's 'cowardly' wish to return home, I took in the surroundings. All about us were small tables lit with candles, & in a corner, in place of an electric kettle made from the ubiquitous coloured ivory known as plastic, there was a good solid copper vessel on a fiery hob, & on the wall a large map of Denmark with all its waters & islands – Kattegat & Skagerak, Storebælt & Lillebælt, Jylland and Fyn, Fejø & Drejø, Ærø and Møn: & how just the sight of these names & the contours of my beloved homeland brought a lump to my throat! And on the back of the door was a noticeboard to which hand-written messages were pinned ('home-pickled herring for sale', 'offer gardening & odd jobs to Danish-speakers', 'swap sewing machine for English lessons') and against the facing wall a bookshelf loaded with maps & dictionaries.

Just as Franz & Rigmor's argument was teetering on the edge of lunacy, for Franz was clearly of a most nervous disposition, & Rigmor a tough-minded girl, Professor Krak swept in, distributing salted liquorice bonbons & marzipan-balls, & his arrival – whether due to his natural authority or the treats he bore – put an instant halt to their bickering. Fru Schleswig & I should realize that we were far from being alone, the Professor assured us, in arriving abruptly in this 'most fascinating of locations'. Those clustered around him nodded in vigorous agreement. Fru Helle Jakobsen put her arm around me in a motherly fashion, & promised me I would grow to love both the future and London, however short my stay was to be, & furthermore she knew I was a brave young woman.

'Those of us who have grown nostalgic for home – & my husband & I are among them – are counting on you to assure our safe passage back to Denmark,' she said, smiling at me with a winning confidence that offered no room for argument.

'Hear hear,' muttered Franz, who then took photographs of us with his tiny silver camera, before retreating to a corner where he set to gnawing his nails.

'Eat, drink & be merry,' advised Professor Krak. 'For tomorrow morning, my dear Charlotte, begins your education.'

'Education?' I queried, but he merely winked & handed me another glass of schnapps, so I ate & drank as instructed, & had a most agreeable time of it, what with the violin-jigs & the homely food, & the mix of most curious company (for had not all these people been driven, at one time, to seek oblivion?): & if I harboured anxieties about how I might perform my role as the saviour of this odd bunch of folk, I swallowed them down with the schnapps as I danced & laughed, & watched Fru Schleswig get most roaring drunk, & when Professor Krak came & asked how I was doing, & squeezed my hand, I returned the squeeze, for I was suddenly feeling most generous towards the man who had just handed me a new dream on a plate, with trimmings, & when I thought of the whorehouse that would bear my name (Charlotte, the orphan from Jutland, turned lady of business!), I smiled & felt a loud bell of happiness ring through my blood.

*   *   *

It was with a shocker of a hangover that, the next afternoon, the Professor escorted myself & the old hag & I, escorted by the Professor, arrived at the Halfway Club for our New-comers' Orientation Class. It was run by Henrik Dogger, a red-faced former helmsman whom I had met briefly at the welcome party: as he greeted us, the assessing look in his eye made me wonder if I might once have serviced him in Copenhagen, but to my relief he indicated no recognition, at which I was glad, for there was coming over me a feeling that I might advantageously reinvent myself somewhat to better suit this time & place, as my fellow time-travellers had seemingly done before me. At this notion, I felt a small worm of possibility shift inside me. For all anybody knew, I too was a Bischen-Baschen! While the implications of such a trans-formation ran through my head, Herr Dogger was instructing us to be seated, lighting his pipe & announcing that he had personally made several expeditions in the Time Machine. Being of a technical disposition, he had often been sent on missions by Professor Krak (who nodded in the affirmative), & described himself as 'Fred's right-hand man, technically speaking', to which the Professor did not demur but merely smiled & cracked his knuckles.

Dogger claimed he had visited twelfth-century Paris ('sew-age problems you won't believe') & he-knew-not-what-cen-tury island of Marroquinta in the South Atlantic, now sunk beneath the surface of the waves but once a tiny splotch of land on the Meridian Line three hundred miles south of Ghana. Here, he said excitedly, poking energetically at his pipe, the natives are presided over by the Sultan, whose myriad wives hide their faces & show their breasts, while the island's menfolk wear cosmetics & glorious woven silks bright as flamingos & hold beauty contests, & the sand whips your face & the camels make noises 'like gurgling drains or the destruction of Pompeii'.

'Well, I shall leave you in Herr Dogger's capable hands,' said Professor Krak when he saw me listening open-mouthed to this nonsense. And handing me the key to the apartment, he instructed Franz – who was working moodily on his scrapbook – to escort us home when we were done. 'I need to make a foray into the criminal underworld to get you some paperwork forged, lest you should fall foul of the British authorities at any point,' he said airily, taking a small gulp of schnapps from his hip-flask. 'Herr Dogger will teach you about the century you have missed, and about Britain and its inhabitants, will you not, Henrik? And try to combine it with a crash course in English, while you're at it!'

'Consider it done, Professor,' said Dogger, giving a nautical-looking salute, which I thought most creepy, & before we could object, Professor Krak had taken his leave & Dogger had pulled out chairs and a blackboard, and given Fru Schleswig and myself each a piece of paper on which was written in elegant cursive script:

Club Rules
1. *All Danes who have travelled through time shall hereby be deemed club members, & shall agree to abide by its rules.*
2. *Members must wear modern dress at all times, save for traditional celebrations such as Jul, Nytår and Sankt Hans Aften, held at the club.*
3. *Community obligations: All members must keep fellow-members of the Halfway Club cognizant of their whereabouts at all times. Security being paramount, they must also note the names,*

addresses and telephone numbers of all modern-age friends and acquaintances in the Club Book of Local Knowledge. Failure to do so will be regarded as a serious offence.

4. *Discretion: Members must not reveal the true circumstances of their arrival in the modern age to any non-member, including modern spouses & offspring, if applicable. This is crucial to the security of our community: breaking this rule shall be considered a punishable offence, entailing exclusion from the club & its services. Members must especially beware of Danes from modern Denmark. Should one be encountered by chance, who turns inquisitive, suggest that you represent the Danish tax authorities.*

Upon the blackboard Dogger then affixed a map of the world, dotted with small red pins: these, he explained, marked where 'Krak pioneers' had settled. 'Thanks to electronic messaging systems such as text and e-mail, we have news of those in this era, but of the other time-travellers there is no trace, if they have chosen, as they most often do, to settle where they are, & integrate.'

Fru Schleswig shifted in her chair & reached for one of last night's pastries.

'How long wil this tayke?' she muttered through a mouthful. 'I thort I woz dun wiv my skooling long ago. Did notte lyke it then & duz notte lyke it no more now.'

'There have been two world wars, & many smaller ones,' pursued Dogger, blithely ignoring the crumb-spitting creature. 'We were lucky to have missed them. The era you have come to is called the Information Age. You will have access to all the knowledge in the world, but never, I'll wager, will you have met folk with less wisdom, curiosity or insight.' Then he whipped the map away & proceeded to illustrate his themes on the blackboard beneath, writing 'useful English vocabulary' on the margins as he did so. And so my head was crammed with twelve-carat gobbledegook, while Fru Schleswig, armed as she was with seemingly endless supplies of *wienerbrød*, was not even pretending to pay attention, & once she had cleared the buffet, settled deep in her chair & began to snore. Whereupon, in a most haphazard & scattergun fashion, Dogger – who turned out to be a most fanatical pedagogue, much in love with the sound of his own voice but also with a lecherous eye that roamed breastward with alarming frequency – waxed garrulous on whatever diverse subjects caught his fancy, all of which announced themselves to be of a scientific & meteorological nature, & of deep unlikeliness: freeze-dried coffee granules, a man sent to the moon in a rocket at great expense, who returned with only a few dirty pebbles, flooding & drought in a place called 'the Third World' ('O Lord,' I gasped, 'there are now three? Spare me, sir, I pray!), the phenomenon of living offal being transplanted from pigs into humans who had killed their liver by excess drinking, 'computer dating', a cold soup called gazpacho ('so revolting that you will instantly be sick'), & finally (he drew back a frieze, behind which a television-like machine sat, its window flashing) Google, the means by which any supplementary questions I had could be settled. This, he said, was a 'computer', an information-containing device which could answer any enquiry one should care to ask within a matter of seconds, at the click of a button, just like a crystal ball. With a flourish he sat before it & ran his hands across the keys, much like a player of a miniature piano, & brightly coloured rectangles covered in pretty script & symbols blossomed on its blackboard.

'Go on, Frøken Charlotte, then, ask away!'

'Does God exist?' I asked, intrigued.

'Try another,' he said, clearly rattled. 'Less ambitious, if you can manage it.'

'How do I get home?'

'You need to be more specific. It isn't geared –'

'Will I, Charlotte Dagmar Marie of Østerbro, one day run my very own broth—'

But here I halted my tongue, for I did not want to give too much away, & instead asked him how one might measure the breeding rate of flies, to which he instantly found several answers, some of them illustrated by screenfuls of writhing maggots.

And so two long hours passed, during which, impressed though I was by the memory capacities of the computer, the more Dogger propounded, the more I realized that never, in the whole of my twenty-five years, had I heard such a quantity of rubbish spouted at me, even by boring clients who had paid for the privilege. However, when the lesson ended & I voiced my scorn, the old helmsman merely laughed, & insisted there was 'photographic & documentary evidence' to back up his preposterous claims, & in any case I would soon enough see for myself that my scepticism was merely 'old-world prejudice', the lowest common denominator of new-comers. Suffice it to say that by the time Franz finally escorted us home on the railway (in preparation for which subterranean journey Fru Schleswig insisted on downing three further glasses of schnapps), I had developed an intense hostility to my new teacher, who had run his eye up & down my body too often for my liking, & added insult to injury by addling my brain with so much toxic gibberish that when I fell asleep that night, it was to dream of flying pigs.

O Chance, how like a game of bagatelle! Who could have foreseen what was to come & skew my fortunes next? For be warned, my dearest one: my tale, which has so far, I fervently hope, amused you, or at least kept the wolf of boredom from your door, is shortly to change shape in a most abrupt manner: indeed, it is about to swerve almost off the page due to a most unexpected event. So bear with me, & 'fasten your seatbelt' as they say in modern times, while we approach this shocking bend.

I will not bother you, darling reader, with more about my acquaintanceship with the modern world, for you know its nature better than I, & it is no source of wonderment to you. All I need say therefore is that over the next fortnight I became more accustomed to the future present into which Fate had thrust me, & was forced to acknowledge that some, if not all, of the *pølsesnak* Dogger spouted with such confident pomposity bore some correspondence to reality, & that instead of reeling with shock at every novelty I encountered, my time would be better spent judging whether or not the conundrum in question, whether it be the dizzying concept of 'post-post-feminism' or a walrus that shat underwater fire-works (for by then nothing would have surprised me), was worth paying heed to, given that my stay here would be short.

Meanwhile, although with the exception of a few phrases such as 'yes please', 'no thank you' & 'do you want me to call the police?' I still spoke none of the local language, my lack of English would not be a problem, Professor Krak assured me, for there were plenty of foreigners in London. All I need do, therefore, was learn two phrases: 'Sorry I no speak English' & 'I from Croatia'. ('Don't say Denmark,' he warned, 'for all today's young Danes are perfectly fluent in English, nay bilingual, & you will be instantly misprized.') Which I duly did, & found it was indeed all I needed, until an unexpected revolution of the psyche occurred, & all the words of all the languages of the world could not express –

But (time-traveller that I am) I once again leap ahead.

So to get back to the present, if I may speak of the future thus: together, Professor Krak & I spent many an hour laying meticulous plans for the journey back to Copenhagen – a voyage he insisted we undertake with the excruciating Fru Schleswig at our side, for we would need her assistance 'in an emergency'.

'But she herself is an emergency! A veritable human calamity!' I protested, for as you can well imagine, dear one, I was more than keen to leave the old swine behind me for ever, & dumping her in another era entirely, where she need never trouble me more, seemed like an excellent notion. 'She will once again do something typically galumphing & foolish, & wreck –'

'A risk we must take,' the Professor interrupted, 'for my wife will want to know her whereabouts if our plan is to work. And remember, your mother has the strength of an ox, which can come in handy if one finds oneself in a tight spot. Franz will also accompany us, as he wishes to return to his parents. He will remain in Copenhagen as Liaison Officer, & will be available for further reinforcement, should you need it. I, too, will be on hand, of course, masterminding proceedings – though, unlike you, I shall need to keep my profile very low. Fru Jakobsen is knitting me a new balaclava as we speak.'

And so, once I had corrected him for the umpteenth time on the erroneousness of the genealogical link between me and Fru S which he so annoyingly and persistently harked on about, we continued to choreograph the possibilities, drawing what Professor Krak called 'flow-charts' to decide in advance what path to take should this-or-that happen instead of such-and-such, & if so . . . ad infinitum. But O, how I laugh now, when I look back at all that careful plotting we did of all the 'variables', for was it not what the English call 'Sod's Law' indeed that the one very thing we could never have foreseen was the very thing that would transpire, & that before we even set off?

In the afternoons, Professor Krak would don a tie & disappear on what he called 'business' (I later discovered he ran quite a brisk trade in the Danish antiques smuggled across time) & I would listen to the increasingly lecherous Dogger spout more absurdities about modern life, which I would then compare to the evidence before me, & add much salt before assimilating. It was on one of these afternoons, while Dogger & I were taking a half-hour break from the irritating intensity of one another's company, that I took a stroll down to the local gardens & met with what I think of as my great accident. The gardens, a short distance from the Halfway Club, contained a pond, dotted with mauve and white lily-flowers, & it was to this small oasis of calm that I was wont to direct my steps, while puzzling over whatever new phenomenon of the modern age Herr Dogger had presented me with, whilst he stared at my breasts or fiddled with his pipe, or both. More often than not, however, I would find myself making plans for Hotel Charlotte

– where the advantages of the future could, I soon realized, prove lucrative in my own era. As I approached the pond, I pondered the new possibilities that had opened up after I took Rigmor Schwarb into my confidence. Catching my drift at once (for it quickly emerged that she too had been a harlot back home), she had enthusiastically shown me an object called the 'ribbed & flavoured condom', & indicated how I might purchase 'sex gadgets' in bulk on the 'World Wide Web', not to mention erotic magazines & other paraphernalia of the trade. I became much excited at the prospect of using such equipment at Hotel Charlotte, but to buy them, we agreed, I would need funds, & for funds, I would need clients. How much could a girl charge in London? Rigmor Schwarb said she did not know, really, but could investigate. 'At least fifty British pounds a go,' she guessed. 'If you include aromatherapy.' That sounded a fortune to me, but I immediately thought of doubling it – easily enough done, if one avoided the small fry & headed straight for the rich pickings in the higher echelons, for time was of the essence. But how to identify a gentleman, when modern garb was so hard to decipher? Or should I simply return to Canary Wharf, where a suit might (I hazarded) be construed as a sign of money?

It was on this subject, as I walked in the park, that I was applying my concentration when a smatter of rain set up, the kind of shower that is the hallmark of England, just as it is of my own land. Having borrowed a most intriguingly designed telescopic umbrella from Fru Helle Jakobsen in anticipation of such an event, I was struggling with the mechanism by which one opened it when I saw them before me by the pond: a man & a boy feeding the ducks & swans with chunks of bread from a bag. Unusual that it should have been the child I noticed first, rather than its father, for I could not abide children, or rather did not know any, & classified them as belonging to a separate species which it was best to avoid, but it was surely the oddity of the lad's brightly coloured outfit that first drew my attention: a screaming red & blue suit with a flowing cape, & a mask that covered his whole head, & featured staring insect-like eyes. The child seemed about nine years of age, but I later learned it was younger, for they make them two sizes larger in the future: girls are bleeding by ten in that world, yet they are still just babes, despite all the grown-up knowledge they have, & all the speedy texting they do. As I walked past, the child continued flinging bread-crusts while the man – his father – looked on. He had the air of a gentleman, with his dark hair & a handsome face that rested easy on the eye, but as I pondered the value & significance of his somewhat neutral trousers & jacket it slowly struck me that perhaps – *perhaps* – it was odd that he be here at all. What man looks after his own child in the middle of the day, when surely most breadwinners are out at work? *Might he be a Man of Leisure?* The idea made me feel most perky, for it is a truth universally acknowledged that any man in possession of a good fortune must be in want of a mistress.

What instinct told me to experiment with him, as I observed him lovingly supervising his little son? His pirate-dark features, so different from the fuzzy paleness of my native folk? My suspicion that he was an extremely rich man, & that I might have some fun along the way?

Yes, beloved one. Put your hand to my brow at this point, & feel the click of my mental abacus. But the path of aspiration never runs smooth. And nor did it with me & my new client. For first of all, in order that our financial relationship might be initiated, my sudden enthusiasm must be reciprocated, & for that to happen (& how could it not, once he had seen me?) I realized that I must attract his attention, pronto, or lose him for ever. But by what means to go about it? He & his oddly clad child seemed in another world, all of their own, that was of just the right dimension to contain but the two of them, & I saw no chink by which I might enter & be part of it. I circled the large pond thrice, in the expectation that my new-found object of desire – whose close-cropped dark hair, & determined & manly jaw, I used the circumnavigation to scrutinize, linger over & appreciate – would glance at me, for I was clad in my green short-skirted finery & high heels, but glance he did not, being busy with the duck-feeding of fatherhood, & all my sorry flip-flap seemed for naught, & I was ready to explode with the frustration of it, until I hatched the ruse of accidentally-on-purpose chucking my opened umbrella into the drink with a small & feminine cry of OOH!

At which sound the child set about laughing & pointing, not at my upside-down umbrella floating there amid the pecking swans like a giant tea-saucer, but at me. (Later I learned I had seemingly hurled my umbrella into the water 'like a cavewoman with a parachute', but I knew none of this as I watched the child speak excitedly to its father, who then looked across at me in a puzzled fashion, & smiled questioningly.)

'Ooh,' I said again, & indicated the pond, where my umbrella floated sadly. 'Oh *pokkers også!*' & then, for lack of any other means of expressing myself, I explained to him in my own tongue that I had accidentally dropped my dear departed grandmother's favourite umbrella, a family heirloom & object of great sentimental value, & might he help me to retrieve it?

The man's brown eyes sparkled with amusement – though what he found so hilarious about my plight I could not fathom – & the more animatedly I spoke, the more he grinned at me (& he must be rich indeed to afford such beautiful teeth!) as though it were all a huge & preposterous joke that I had suffered such a mishap & might need to call on his kindness for assistance. And all the while his child jumped up & down, repeating something over & over again the way children do, making the man laugh even more. Then he shook his head, & addressed me kindly in English & gestured towards the water, where my 'family heirloom' had now tipped to one side, its hemispheric hull slowly pooling with pond-water & chick-weed. O calamity!

'Quick,' I urged in Danish, 'before it sinks!'

And so not understanding my words, but sensing the desperation they conveyed, my Man of Leisure proved himself most resourceful by locating a small branch, which he then stripped to make a stick with which to hook the telescopic umbrella from the watery grave that would other-wise be its destiny.

Meanwhile, as luck would have it, four sizeable swans had decided Fru Jakobsen's umbrella was their rightful property, & amid much hissing, they made to intercept & colonize the ever-sinking apparatus. Seeing this, my new-found saviour stepped boldly & agilely on to a rock that stood in the water, in order to reach closer, but the aggressive birds merely hissed more, causing the child to cry out in terror. Hesitantly, I patted the young thing on its masked head: I have seen others so doing with children, which apparently much resemble dogs in this way. The gesture seemed to calm the child, & together we watched its father as, with a triumphant flourish, he caught

O calamity!

the handle of the umbrella with his stick, & raised it high in the air, to the great anger of the swans, which flapped their wings & stretched their snaky hissing necks just as he lost his footing on the stone, causing the umbrella to tip sideways & release a torrent of water on to the birds, spattering them with muddy chickweed. Knowing the swan to be a proud creature, easily humiliated, I gestured to the boy to throw more bread to distract them from their shame, which he duly did while I hurried to join Moneybags on his stone, where I assumed he would look deep into my eyes, recognize his future mistress when he saw her, & kiss me passionately. But I had misjudged this element of the proceedings, for my alighting on the stone caused him to sway, at which the umbrella tipped further, & to stop us both falling I clung to him. The result of this, which you may well have predicted, you clever one, though I did not, was to send us both crashing headlong into the freezing deep, whence we emerged a moment later gulping filthy brine.

Did he finally fall for me headlong, reader, as we faced death by drowning? You would have expected so, but the fact was that he was not as speedy as I had hoped in that department & indeed at the time seemed merely disconcerted & more eager to get us both out of the water (what a mercy one of us could swim!) & reassure his son that all was well, & that they would soon be home & dry, than to pronounce undying financial devotion to his new-found object of desire. Or so at least did I glean from the conversation between the two of them, which appeared not to include me. He eventually glanced at me nonetheless and I shrugged my shivering helplessness. 'Sorry: I no speak English,' I said dejectedly, for by now I was beginning to feel foolish about my misjudgement of his intentions. 'I from Croatia.' At which he hesitated for a moment, then pointed to himself and said, 'Fergus McCrombie,' and then at the boy & said, 'Josie McCrombie' (as if the lad should figure in my equation!), and I pointed to my prettily heaving cleavage & said, 'Frøken Charlotte Dagmar Marie of Østerbro,' & thus were the introductions made, after which both father & son nodded happily, which cheered me a little, & then my spirits rose once more, for next Herr McCrombie gestured me to follow him to a place where (I surmised) we could dry off, pass the child over to a servant, & get down to business. And I would not content myself with a single encounter; O no. Here was a goose who would lay me a golden egg, I was sure of it. And another & another! No one-off client he, but a single provider!

Not looking my dazzling best, I felt a little wary of a chance encounter with his wife, lest my bedraggled state should lead the woman grandiosely to consider herself more worthy of his financial favours than I, but when we arrived at his house (disappointingly smaller than Fru Krak's but of the same era), & he had shown me to his bedroom where I might change into the clothes that he offered (which were clearly his – how quaint! Did he like mannish women, I wondered?), I spotted no signs of another woman's presence: no lace-frilled undergarments in the chest of drawers (and yes, reader, you can be most sure I made a thorough inspection, just as you would have done in my circumstances), nor hand-picked roses in vases, nor smell of apple and cinnamon a-bubble wafting from the hearth, nor intimate feminine objects in the bathroom, & I was right pleased about that, but did not then have the language to ask him where the temporary usurper of my rightful economic status might be & when we might expect her to return.

Instead, everywhere, I saw signs of Herr McCrombie's life, quite chaotically displayed: paintings and coloured daguerreotypes of a most accurate nature adorned the walls, & all about stood glass cases containing artefacts of great fascination: animal skulls & bones, & small sculptures & pots fashioned from clay & bronze & many plaster of Paris moulds of objects whose shapes I could not determine: it seemed my Man of Leisure enjoyed collecting things, or was perhaps an amateur explorer. Seeing the amazement & curiosity on my face, he waved at it all & said something & laughed, & I shook my head for the thousandth time & repeated that I was sorry, I no speak English, I from Croatia, & he repeated a many-syllabled word several times, that began with A, but I knew it not, and did not have a dictionary with me.

And then instead of discussing the practicalities of getting shot of his child (which, having shed its costume & mask, appeared to have changed sex & become a pretty girl, of the short-haired & tomboyish variety), & perhaps settling my fee in advance, he gestured to ask whether I was hungry. Puzzled, for I had not yet learned the sexual etiquette of that era, I nodded yes, & soon – to my amazement – he was motioning at me to peel & chop, whilst he cleared the table & took out a recipe book with many an illustration of the succulent fare one might manufacture from the ingredients we had to hand, viz one chicken. My lesson with Dogger quite forgotten, we then set about cooking in a most *hyggelig*-domestic manner while Josie prattled in their language & made elaborate & most impressive drawings of a fantastical semi-human figure that much resembled her earlier costumed self, called 'Spider-man'. As preludes to erotic encounters go, the evening was veering a long way from the normal, but the meal was nevertheless accompanied by much laughter, for Josie was a girl who liked to pull faces, & as it happens I am also rather good at pulling faces, not to mention walking on my hands, & this I did to amuse the child, whose English was easier to follow than her father's, for she cried, 'Again!', a word I knew, & 'Look at me!', a phrase I could also decipher, & then she demonstrated her skill at somersaulting on the bed & I joined in, despite a small worry that it might make me look unfeminine & thus diminish my air of womanly mystery, a bad start for an ambitious mistress. Later, while Herr McCrombie was bathing Josie, I explored the house more, with a view to doing a little light pilfering, but I got no further than the child's bedroom, for there I was waylaid by the sight of many shelves of books, one of which caused me to cry out in a bright shock of delight, for the name on its spine was none other than Hans Christian Andersen, so when the bath was done, seeing that our own bed-time must wait until after the child's, I waved the book & pointed, urging Herr McCrombie to read Josie *The Ugly Duckling*, & the three of us settled together on the sofa, Herr McCrombie next to me, & Josie straddled easily on my lap, as though this were the most natural place in the world for her, & if she were a cat, she would purr, & soon I was stroking her dark head & feeling (most odd, for I hated children!) that if I were a cat, I would purr too. And as Herr McCrombie read about the duckling who looked at himself in the water & saw himself to be ugly, & grew apart from his siblings who scorned him, but then found himself to belong to another breed, far more beautiful, & hatched from a swan's egg, I strained to catch words I might identify, & then & there made a silent vow to learn this foreign patter faster than you can say *rødgrød med fløde*, for speaking it would surely be the key to my new patron's bank account.

Though later that evening, when Josie was sleeping, I found a much swifter method, which began with me dropping a plate to the floor and smashing it, & both of us stooping to pick up the pieces, & banging our heads together, & laughing, & then hugging, & thence making our way to the bedroom, the better to explore & enjoy one another's anatomy. And most happy & joyful it was, for we were like two greedy children at a bottomless jar of sweets, & in the heat of the moment I quite forgot that it was a means to an end, & I will confess that I enjoyed the act, as performed by our two most well-fitting bodies, in a most unprofessional manner. And when we had done & were quite ravished & exhausted, he kissed me & murmured sweet things in his language, & I lay there in a great state of contentment until I suddenly returned to my fiscal senses & explained in my own tongue what my terms, fees & conditions were, & that I would keep a tally in a notebook so he could pay the final bill when we were finished, but I would be happy to take on the role of his exclusive mistress for as long as I stayed in London.

Tick, tock. The days passed, & I spent much time in Herr McCrombie's company. I would not normally take the liberty of calling a client by his first name, for I have always considered it an intimacy too far, but after our first night together my new provider became most insistent upon the matter, & so I finally succumbed to the exigencies of his era & culture, & began to address him as 'Fergus'.

'So what's Croatia like?' he asked me one morn, as I fingered a beautiful Roman horse. 'You've hardly told me anything. I know the Balkans a little bit. What city do you come from? Were you there during the war? Did you follow the trial of Miloševic?'

And so, not knowing anything of Croatia (for I had never heard of it), let alone its wars, while I dressed to return to Professor Krak's apartment, where I was still occasionally lodging for fear of arousing suspicions, I summoned the courage to tell him in my halting but increasingly serviceable English that I was not from that country at all, but from Denmark, & that there were reasons for my small deception which I could not go into now, but I would recount my full story as soon as my teacher, Herr Dogger, had supplied me with the necessary words.

At which he looked at me quizzically. 'You are quite a mystery, Lottie,' he said, Lottie being his pet name for me. 'But I will solve you. Remember, I'm an archaeologist: I'm good at removing layers.' Upon which he grabbed me & set about undressing me again, & I never left the house after all.

'Where your wife?' I asked him when we woke the next morning, for I had by now assumed she was away visiting sick relatives or somesuch, which is one of the things wives seem to do, but would be coming back soon to spoil our fun, & the prospect of this interruption had been working on my psyche in a most discomfiting manner. But he seemed most puzzled, & I fancied I even detected shock on his face.

'Lottie, if I had a wife, do you really think you'd be here?' he asked. A question I was at a loss to answer, for the fact was, I did indeed think I might be here if he had a wife, for he was a man like any other, & indeed more so, in his enthusiasm for my body. (And here I will confess, dear one, I was much enamoured of his too, & had been from the very first moment

I was in his arms.) In my sudden embarrassment (I, Charlotte Dagmar Marie of Østerbro, normally immune to such feelings!) I merely laughed, but in the silence that followed I realized that now, if any, was the time to set out the terms and conditions of my mistresshood, & show him the little book in which I had been noting down our transactions. But to my own bafflement, I said nothing.

'Actually I don't have a wife,' he said. 'So lucky you.'

'But Josie's mother?' I asked, for suddenly I was curious. 'Where is she?' But at this he looked grave.

'Dead,' he said, & I quickly struggled to reassemble my face into a shape that represented sorrow, though secretly I was most pleased, for Rigmor had told me about such things as divorce settlements & alimony, & I knew them to be a drain on a man's resources. Fergus smiled at my perplexed look. 'I was digging in Peru, & I found Josie one morning sleeping in a hole, wrapped in a blanket. She was cold & hungry & all alone. I made enquiries. It seemed the father abandoned her after the mother died. So I adopted her & brought her home. Her name's Josefina, but I shortened it and lengthened the rest, so she's now Josie Prudence Rosenberg McCrombie. The Prudence is after my grandmother, who was anything but prudent. She died in a hot-air balloon accident when she was eighty. And Rosenberg after Professor Rosenberg, who taught me archaeology. Now she's my daughter.'

What a story! I thought, unable to fathom it entirely, but somehow it caused something animal to stir in me & I kissed him again, & was just beginning to feel another urge to explore his anatomy when the alarm-clock sounded & Josie Prudence Rosenberg McCrombie came in and tumbled on to the eiderdown, so we played an English game called Crazy Frog Pillow Wars instead.

But after that conversation something had shifted within me & I felt unaccountably perturbed, almost as though I had a brain fever coming on, for there welled in my breast a confusion whose origins I could not place, but which seemed to underline the notion that the thing I most desired – Herr Fergus McCrombie's money – was somehow incompatible with the means of getting it.

'You must tell him the truth forthwith,' said Rigmor Schwarb firmly when I explained the situation. 'For I fear he has misunderstood the nature of your relationship. They do things differently here, Charlotte. Women of the future commonly lie with men out of neither duty nor financial gain, but merely for the pleasure of the act of love, & society does not frown on them for it as it does in our era.' We were using the computer at the Halfway Club: she had logged on to the 'Crotchware Inc' website &, having taught me to manipulate the 'mouse', got me busy ticking boxes placing orders for Hotel Charlotte. 'If Fergus is unaware of the need to reward you for services rendered, how are you going to pay for all these wares?'

I smiled, & waved Fergus's credit card at her, which I had lifted from his wallet earlier. 'I'll tell him later, when my English is improved,' I said.

'But what about all this merchandise you're ordering in his name?' she cried angrily, gesturing at the screen. 'How are you going to explain that? Whatever story you dream up, he's going to have trouble believing you – gullible though he sounds.'

'He is not gullible!' I snapped. 'He is simply a –'

'A what?' she asked, her tone changing to curiosity.

'A good man,' I said, suddenly in a rush to talk about him. 'He is a good man. He thinks I'm good too. He has a daughter called Josie. He cooks meals that taste like a chef has made them. He's an archaeologist & has been all around the world. And he calls me "darling" & "*hen*". Hen is Scottish for *skat*.' At which she gave me a long look, & slowly nodded, but said nothing.

Hen, I thought as I wandered back through the park where I had first met Fergus. The lilies were in full bloom now, and I wanted him to see them with me, but he was at a 'conference' where they were discussing the contents of an Egyptian mummy's stomach. *Hen* is a beautiful word. I had been called many affectionate names by clients before, such as *Lotte-pige* & *drømmekvinde* & *tuttenutte*, but *hen* awoke something new in me & unidentifiable, a nameless feeling that was neither longing nor solace nor pleasure nor lust nor hope nor joy, but more a mixture of all, mingled with something that one perhaps might call comfort or content-ment, & the word kept ringing in my head like a soft & lovely bell: hen, hen, hen.

And when he returned home with Josie I had fabricated a meal for all of us, & it did not taste too inferior at all, despite my lack of skills, & that night after we had rolled around together on the bed & had much fun, we slept locked in one another's arms, & in the morning he turned to me drowsily & said, 'Lottie, what would you say if I told you I love you?'

At these words I snapped awake, instantly in a state of extreme anxiety, for this was not in the scheme of things at all!

I grabbed the bedclothes & covered my body, all at once shy as a virgin.

'What?'

'What would you say if –'

'I say no! You can't!'

But he was smiling.

'I can and I will, because you're the most lovable Croatian–Dane I've ever met. A wee bit eccentric maybe, but it suits you. And what you lack in basic knowledge – because my theory is you are a woman who actually *does* come from Venus – you make up for in basic sexiness. Plus you have the most gorgeous breasts I've ever set eyes on, and I've seen a few in my time.'

Upon which he reached for me and gave me a long kiss.

'But you can't love me!' I cried, tearing myself away with some reluctance, for his kisses were like honey. 'And I can't fall in love with you!'

He smiled & shook his head in amusement. 'But you already have, hen.'

'Not true!'

'Why else do you reach for me in your sleep and say *Fergus*, in that funny accent of yours? We're made for each other. Why fight it?'

'Because it is not part of the plan!'

'What plan?'

'My plan!'

'Oh, my wee Venutian has a plan! That's news to me!'

'Yes! I have a plan.'

'Well,' he said, pulling me down to the bed. 'If this plan of yours doesn't involve me and Josie, and making lots of babies, you'd better change it.'

*   *   *

Later that morning I emerged from my shower to see a delivery van parked in the road outside the house. Gripped by a sudden unease, I hastened down to the parlour to find Fergus seated on the sofa with a large cardboard box, freshly opened to reveal fifty multi-packs of ribbed & flavoured condoms.

He looked up in puzzlement. 'Darling,' he said gently. 'I had no idea you were so nervous about falling pregnant. Or,' he said, scrutinizing a wrapper, 'that you were quite so fond of avocado. Is there something you'd perhaps like to explain?'

Yes: the moment of truth was upon us, it seemed. But, dear reader (and think less of me if you will!), I could not do it, even when he investigated the box further & encountered basques of every size & shape, fluffy handcuffs, plastic male members & the like (at which I feigned ignorance & perplexity): no, I could not, would not! Can you blame me, precious one (I do not deserve your sympathy, but I beg it nonetheless!), if found myself incapable of telling the man to whom I was swiftly & despite myself becoming increasingly attached, that I was not after all the creature of his dreams, but a time-travelling harlot who had cheated him into the unwitting purchase of a panoply of erotic gadgetry for the titillation of Hotel Charlotte's nineteenth-century clientèle?

So I informed him merely that I had used his credit card thinking it was my own, for it was almost *exactly* the same shade of blue, & then my friend Rigmor must have clicked the wrong box on the 'World Wide Web', for in fact it was not sex toys from Crotchware Inc that I required, as she mistakenly understood, but a *Compendium of Common English Idioms* from Amazon Dot Com, & furthermore I told him – now much aware that something was required of me by way of elaboration – that I was

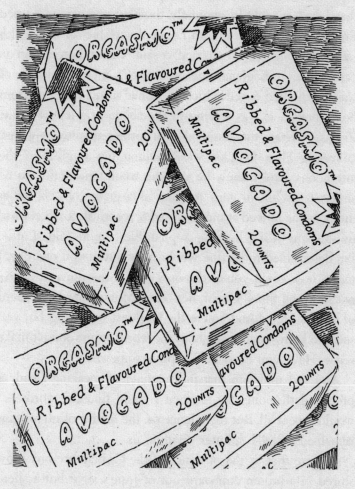

'I had no idea you were so nervous about falling pregnant!'

not from Venus, as he constantly teased, but from Copenhagen, & had worked in the entertainment industry & sometimes helped out in a flower shop owned by my friend Else, that I had an elderly, mentally disabled companion named Fru Schleswig who came to England with me for her health (at this he looked most puzzled, & said, 'Christ, Lottie, who on earth comes to England for their health?'), & I explained that I was unschooled & self-educated, & had never travelled from home before, & was staying in the abode of a fellow Dane, Professor Krak, the husband of a former employer, whose colleague Herr Dogger was teaching me English in the afternoons. And I knew he saw the whole concoction to be shaky, & as full of gaps & holes as a giant cobweb, for at moments he looked at me most sad & sceptical, & when I had finished my sorry, limping implausible tale, he said, 'Lottie, I'm determined to get the whole story out of you one day. I mean, how come you're the only girl in the universe who's not seen any films? Christ, hen, even Mongolians have heard of Johnny Depp! And you're the brightest wee thing, but you seem to know bugger all about the world. It just doesn't make sense. Have you been held captive somewhere?'

And so I told him that in a manner of speaking I had, & promised that one day – when I could find the words – I would reveal all. But my silence on the matter of my origins remained a chilly splinter dividing us.

Despite that, & the presence of the Crotchware box (now stored in a broom cupboard out of Josie's sight but a silent reproach to me nonetheless), we were constantly together in the days that followed. And just as I'll wager you too would have done in the same circumstances, precious, I neglected more & more to visit Professor Krak's apartment & even missed a few of my lessons with Herr Dogger, to the glee of Fru Schleswig, who had boycotted them from the second day, & had called me a 'silly swotte' for taking an interest, & who now felt vindicated. I saw little of Professor Krak on these occasions, & so immersed did he seem in his plans for our return that he was too distracted to enter into conversation. Often, though, I would glimpse him at the Halfway Club in deep conference with Franz who, since learning that he would accompany us on the journey, had become most animated & light-hearted, & exceedingly friendly towards me. And if from time to time I caught Herr Dogger glancing at me oddly, I did not pay heed to it, for he was a ruttish man & I am used to such looks. And if Fru Schleswig sometimes muttered to me, 'Woch out, gurl,' I paid no heed to that neither, for the crone has always tried to kill my fun, & if Fru Jakobsen on one occasion murmured to me, 'We are counting on you,' with some urgency, & thrust a copy of the Club Rules into my hand, I saw not the significance of it.

No: none of these small signs penetrated my consciousness, for what preoccupied me now was my discovery of Love. You may have spotted that I was heading in that direction, dear observant reader, but I had not, & the realization left me most perplexed, for in some respects I am quite blind to the will of my own heart! I investigated my symptoms like a scientist might dissect & scrutinize a squirming specimen, & then drew back, appalled & simultaneous in awe, at the conclusion I reached: Love makes your heart & soul so naked! What if it should hurt me? All my life I had avoided it most effectively, but now –

Could I trust my Englishman who, it now transpired, was

apparently not an Englishman at all, but a native of the Firth of Forth?

What knew I of the Firth of Forth? My head warned me off, but my heart shouted yes. And which organ did I heed? You can guess the answer, for you know me so well, sweetest. And you would have done the same, if I know you at all.

In the meantime I discovered more about Herr Fergus McCrombie. I saw photographs of his archaeological voyages around the world both before & after the arrival of Josie, heard stories about his wise professor, listened to the gory details of his two disastrous love affairs with 'entirely unhinged' women, & his happier 'wham-bam' ones, with 'unsuitables' (how quickly I was learning his language!) – while he in turn discovered the minimum about me. I knew, dear one, that I must tell him the truth. But how to do it? If you are thinking that my reason for stalling was a keenness to abide by the absurd Club Rules, then think again, for it was not so much the Halfway Club's petty bureaucracy that hindered me, as my own inability to imagine how I might begin to convince him of a story – ie, that I was not only from another place but another time – that sounded so patently preposterous.

Tick, tock.

The days passed: three perfect weeks. O, to have found such happiness, & lost it, out of my own foolishness! But in that time, this much I learned about Love: that it involves much laughter. Lord, how we laughed, & were filled with such joy as I have never known, & what better thing is there than that, for my modern Scottishman was also brimful of fun & play & teasing, & there were moments when we were children together & roared at foolish jokes, & kissed & kissed again & rolled on the bed tickling one another like innocent babes. What sweeter thing is there than to be in the arms of the one you adore all night long, & reach out & stroke his chest or his arm or his shoulder or his dear dreaming head. That sweet sleeping face, that quiet soft breathing. And when he wakes you tell him, in your now halting English, your dreams & he tells you his, & you laugh & kiss & kiss again, & the world is a good place despite all the bad in it, & you know that human beings are not monsters, for as long as Love dwells in men's hearts all shall be well & all manner of things shall be well.

But within all this joy there were little cold moments, too, for I had been forgetting my past life, & doing so at my peril, & he had desisted from questioning me further, at his: & we both knew that soon I must speak, for it was in his eyes: he could never be fully mine until I did.

'You must tell me the truth, Lottie,' he said. 'I'm sorry, hen. But if you don't, it's just not going to work.'

'Just give me more time.'

He looked at his watch.

Love turns a girl foolish: I had not been on my guard, not seen the signs. For the first I knew of my forthcoming disgrace was the day I arrived for my lesson at the Halfway Club to find the hall chock-a-block with people, all seemingly in a heated debate. I could see at once that something was very much amiss, & that it concerned me, for a group of fifty or so folk – among them the Jakobsens, Franz, Rigmor Schwarb, the Poulsen family, Professor Krak, an elderly couple called Brogaard, Herr Dogger & Fru Schleswig – immediately stopped talking and looked at me with stony faces. They had clearly been holding some kind of conference – to which I had not been invited.

'Talk of the Devil,' murmured Herr Dogger.

'Come and sit,' said Professor Krak, rising and indicating that I should take the chair from which he had been addressing them, face to the throng. I felt most uneasy. What had I done to be so excluded? Did they no longer believe me to be their heroine? As I sat, Herr Dogger, seated in the front row, leered at me waggling a small pair of binoculars. I gulped: a horrible suspicion was beginning to hatch in my breast.

'What's going on?' I asked as lightly as I could. Fifty pairs of eyes stared in my direction.

'We thought that perhaps that was something you could tell us,' said Professor Krak with a gentleness that much discomposed me.

'What mean you by that, good sir?'

'You are aware of the Club Rules?' said Professor Krak. 'Concerning mixing with people from the modern age?'

'I have broken no rules,' I retorted sharply. 'I have divulged nothing about my status as a time-traveller, or anyone else's.'

Was it my imagination, or did I sense a slight decrease in the tension, as I said this? But the interrogation continued nonetheless.

'We understand from Herr Dogger, our Head of Security, that you have entered into a relationship with a contemporaneous man,' began Professor Krak. I gasped. So Herr Dogger had indeed been spying on me! I shot him a furious glance, & he winked at me affirmatively.

'How dare you!' I cried, quite winded by the audacity of it.

'Club policy,' he said smugly.

'Anyway, dear Charlotte,' Professor Krak went on in a tone

that I did not much trust. 'I am sure we are all very happy for you. You are not the first to have met Love in this new era. But there are serious implications for the community, as you must be aware. If you should change your mind about returning to Copenhagen & securing the Time Machine, & thus assuring our liberty of passage . . .'

There was a silence as they all looked at me. During which long, uncomfortable moment I forced myself to consider my situation, which resulted in the following heart-piercing question: how could I possibly run the risk of going back, if it meant saying farewell to the man I loved, & young Spiderman? Clearly the club members had been more perspicacious than I on this matter, & had anticipated my rush of conflicting feelings.

'I shall not go back,' I said eventually. 'I cannot. I regret having to disappoint you, but I must remind you that I did not come here by choice in the first place, & my role in the Professor's scheme was not of my own devising. The truth is, I no longer wish to go back to Copenhagen, & I cannot take the risk of going there, if I might be unable to return. I cannot gainsay Love. My life is now here.'

There was a huge collective wail.

'But you are our last hope!' cried Helle Jakobsen, standing up & then seeming to collapse into the lap of her husband. Franz blew his nose at length. The Jørgensen twins took to their feet as a single being & shook their fists at me. Mattias Rosenvinge booed. Rigmor Schwarb looked grim, & scratched her tattoo.

'But you owe it to us!' piped up a small female voice from the back row: Ida Sick.

'I owe you nothing!' I expostulated. And stormed out.

*   *   *

On my return, Fergus saw my distress & was most solici-
tous, but I would not tell him what had transpired, save that
I had had an argument with some fellow Danes, & so the
chilly splinter – already well embedded – dug itself deeper,
& there was a terrible silence between us until finally he
sighed deeply & said, 'Lottie, I've been doing some thinking.
I love you, & I want to be with you, hen. I want to marry
you. But –'

'Marry?'

'Yes. Does that idea appeal to you, sweetheart? Do they
do marriage on Venus?' (O, reader! Hold my hand! Do you
feel it tremble?) 'But if you won't tell me about yourself—
Well, how can I give myself to a woman who won't do the
same for me? We have to at least start from a basis of
equality, hen.'

O, beloved! Do you think he would still want to marry me,
if he knew the truth? All at once I felt the squeeze of two
insistent incompatibilities: together, they were crushing my
heart.

'I'm going to fetch Josie,' he said. 'So you have till I get
back.'

Tick, tock.

I have learned that in English, time is a commodity that can
be made, stolen, bought, wasted, trodden, marked, put off, &
raced against. That things can happen from time to time, all in
good time, time & time again. That from time immemorial,
'Old Father' Time has been considered precious, & *of the
essence*, that there is a time to live & a time to die, a time to
love & a time to hate, & a time to read 'Useful Temporal
Expressions' in Herr Dogger's recommended tome, *Infinite
English Grammar* by Professor H.W. Biggs-Gusset, all the

while scarcely able to hold back your tears, for you are about to take another dangerous leap into an unknown fate.

'I was born in Jutland in 1872,' I blurted as soon as the door opened, '& raised in an orphanage. In 1888 I ran away to Copenhagen but Fru Schleswig followed me.'

Fergus, still removing his jacket, looked bemused, & Josie intrigued.

'You wanted to hear my story?' I continued. 'So now you listen.'

'A story?' asked Josie. 'Can I hear it too, Lottie?'

'This one is not for children, *min lille skat*,' I said. 'It is full of boring grown-up *pølsesnak*.'

'Chock-a-block with tedious twaddle, pet,' affirmed Fergus, & ushered his daughter to the living room, where he fed a video of her beloved Spiderman into the machine & I brought her a plate of lemon biscuits I had cooked that morning, for Love had turned me into a creature quite unexpectedly fired up with domesticity. When Fergus came back he sat opposite me at the kitchen table and said, 'OK. Let's take this slowly. Did you say *eighteen* something?'

'Eighteen hundred and seventy-two,' I said. 'July 4th. In Copenhagen I did a dancing show with Else, we were the Østerbro Coquettes. But then she had an accident, & fell on the skin of a pig & her father died & she started a flower shop & I was selling my body & then one day I was in the bakery on Classensgade . . .'

And as I recounted it all to him, in a somewhat gabbling & haphazard manner with much looping to & fro, I saw many emotions cross his visage, from sympathy (my orphanage years) to concern (the whoring) to amusement (Fru Krak) to deep puzzlement (the Time Machine), to alarm

(Fru Krak's gun), to disbelief (the Greenwich Observatory), followed by – yes! For was he not an adventurer at heart? Had I not spotted it in him? And was he not in love with history? – excitement! Joy! Nay, hilarity! For now that I had reached the part about arriving in London & getting acquainted with English life, & needing condoms for my brothel in Copenhagen, & seducing him as a whore but falling in love with him as a woman, he began laughing: laughing & laughing, with tears in his eyes!

'My God, I enjoyed that, sweetheart,' he said when I was quite done with my tale. He shook his head, still amused. 'You're quite a storyteller. The bit about the Professor writing his wife's horoscope: I love it.' But then he took my hand & his face became serious. 'But look, Lottie. When exactly do I get the real version of why you borrowed my credit card to order five thousand avocado-flavoured condoms and a load of fluffy handcuffs? Because, joking apart, I do think you owe me an explanation. A proper one.'

O, how my heart plummeted! Reader, he had believed not a word! O woe was me! Now although I had perhaps expected my love to question parts of my story, I was nonetheless quite flabbergasted that *none* of it had convinced him – not even those elements it most pained me to confess: viz, my designs upon his wallet. O, beloved, can you imagine how I felt at that moment, when it seemed there was naught that I could do save provide more detail, which would bury me further in what my lover perceived to be an elaborate & fantastical web of lies? I was at a loss. Looking out of the window I saw an old lady by a pedestrian crossing, waiting for 'the green man'. As the figure lit up, he became a wobbling blur & a lump came to my throat.

'Lottie,' Fergus said. He looked worried, & handed me a tissue. 'I'd love to believe you. But— Well, it's so incredible. And really *thoroughly imagined*. I bet you could even tell me the colour of Fru Krak's kitchen floor!'

'It's wood, whitewashed,' I said without hesitation. 'Fru Schleswig, she uses bleach.'

He nodded thoughtfully. 'Impressive. You should put this talent to use,' he said, & he seemed to mean it.

'But it is all the truth!' I cried, standing up so suddenly that my chair crashed to the ground. The noise of *Spiderman* came through from the next room: an insistent musical beat beneath the quick to-&-fro of voices. Fergus, still seated at the table, began playing with a metal corkscrew shaped like a fish.

'Darling,' he said, sighing. 'It's no good. This isn't working.' So this is how it is done, I thought. This is the pain that Love brings. 'How can we live together if you're hiding from me behind a story that sounds like something straight out of *Doctor Who*?' And then I saw that he had tears in his eyes, too, but a new kind I had not seen before.

'Doctor what?'

'It's a television series.'

'*Television?*' I cried, all at once most offended & distraught. We were a pair of sweethearts having their first row. But I knew not the rules of how sweethearts disagree. All I knew was that the emotions involved were unbearable. 'But I am real. I am not television! What happened is the truth! How can I prove it to you?' I exclaimed, boiling with annoyance – at myself as much as him, for had I not spent much of my life thus far practising deceit on men? Most agonizingly ironic, then, that on the one occasion I should choose to tell the truth,

I would be disbelieved! How frustrating was my lover's obstinacy! I stamped my foot so hard upon the tiled floor that it hurt: he merely carried on playing with the fish corkscrew.

'OK,' he began wearily. 'If I've understood you right, this recent argument you had with the other Danish people was about –'

But I interrupted. 'They're expecting me to go back & save the Mother Machine with Fru Schleswig & Professor Krak. But I told them I will not do it. Because I am in love with you!' I snapped.

'So go back and tell them yes,' he said, pulling the extendable fish to its maximum length & then letting it contract back. And his soft brown eyes looked at me steadily.

'*What?* I shouted. 'Are you mad?'

'No, I'm quite sane, Lottie. Tell them you've changed your mind. Tell them that you'll go.' O, insupportable! No sooner had my own heart been awakened, than it was made to bleed!

'You want me to leave you? Go back, be gone for ever, set up Hotel Charlotte in Østerbro & never see you again? And get stuck there just to show to you I am not *television?*' I was ready to tear out my hair by the roots.

'I never said that, hen.' Lord, his calmness drove me to distraction.

'Yes! More or less you did!'

'Lottie,' he said, getting to his feet & grabbing me by the shoulders, which forced me to stand still. He looked into my eyes as if searching for something: the way a doctor might look to see if there was any hope in the brain of a madman. 'Listen, hen. Wherever it is you have to go, and whatever you have to do there, I want you to take me with you.'

'What?'

'You want me to believe you. But unless I see it for myself, how can I?'

'But it's dangerous!'

He shrugged, for this reply clearly bolstered his scepticism. 'That definitely sounds like another reason to say no.'

'No! It's not that! Anyway, what about Josie?'

'Josie always comes with me on my archaeological trips abroad. Why should a journey to the past be any different?'

He was still challenging me.

'You have to trust me!' I cried. 'I tell you, it is dangerous!' How pig-headed he was!

'Lottie: seeing is believing. So show me it's true and I'm yours for ever.'

Much hoo-ha ensued.

I will spare you the stormy details of my meeting with Professor Krak, who muttered 'blackmail' when I gave him the ultimatum, but brightened when he learned that Fergus was an archaeologist; of my address to the Halfway Club, which met with a mixed reaction of frantic pleas & outrage; of the wrath of Herr Dogger, who shouted that a certain worthless, brazen hussy had caused the club rule of confidentiality to be broken 'for the first time in history'; of the emphatically expressed support of Fru Jakobsen & Franz, who argued that the necessity of a connection with home should over-ride the aforementioned rule; & finally of my own intervention. I spoke to the assembled throng at the Halfway

Club with much passion & eloquence, declaring that whilst understanding the vital nature of our mission, supporting it wholeheartedly, & respecting the need for secrecy concerning the machine, the love of my life could under no circumstances permit the woman he loved to travel unprotected &, if she wished to go, insisted upon accompanying her. At which declaration I, being the she in question, was moved to tears, as were all of the shes in the hall (with the exception of Fru S, who merely snorted that I was 'nuthing but a spoyled bratte'), & in the end by a show of hands it was democratically agreed by all but Herr Dogger, who opposed it, & Fru S, who was by now snoring vibrantly, that desperate times required desperate measures.

'OK, they agree. But if we do this, we must do what Professor Krak & I have already planned,' I told Fergus when I returned, triumphant, from the meeting. 'You & Josie must help. You must know we may be stuck there.' I was beginning to become anxious. How could I acquaint him with the dangers of our journey, if he so thoroughly questioned its likelihood?

'Whatever you say,' he grinned. To him the undertaking was still a source of benign amusement & curiosity – but as the days passed, my seriousness about equipping him & Josie for the 'surprise trip to Denmark' began to dent his confidence. 'Er, how long do you expect us to be gone?' he asked, as I measured him up for clothing.

'I am no philosopher,' I said, kissing his left cheekbone, of which I was particularly fond. 'But it all depends on how you measure time.'

* * *

Just over six weeks had passed since Fru Schleswig & I began our adventures: Professor Krak had calculated that we should therefore land in Copenhagen sometime in late December 1897, nigh on Christmas. 'A good time,' he assured us, 'for it is a preoccupied season, involving much drunkenness & high spirits, & we can take cover behind the revelry.' So thus it is that after further intensive discussions concerning the logistics of the mission, Fergus, Josie & myself, with Franz, Fru Schleswig & Professor Krak, all clad in appropriate 1890s dress (ah, how at home do I feel in my familiar bodice & dress, freshly dry-cleaned! And how splendid does my love look in Herr Jakobsen's waistcoat, jacket, breeches & frock coat, & how adorable Josie, in the woollen sailor's outfit Fru Jakobsen has knitted for her!), now pile into a hired minibus along with several large suitcases of equipment, medical drugs & other modern paraphernalia including the vacuum cleaner from which Fru Schleswig has most obstinately refused to be parted, & travel to the Greenwich Observatory where, tiptoeing in, we crowd together next to the telescope, beneath the green laser Meridian Line in the upstairs hall. In which anxious tableau try to picture us, O precious one, as we stand quaking on the brink of our adventure – a small throng sizzling with nerves & uttering jumbled, hapless prayers to whatever idea of God our imaginations can summon, while Professor Krak prepares to trigger, with a long, curved magnetic wand, the tiny earth-shudder that will (*hopefully*) awaken the Time-Sucker & catapult us back to whence we came.

Whoosh! Ping!

We gasp as –

Yes!

No!

Yes!

A loud crack, a puff of noxious smoke –

HELP!

The time is exactly 11pm on Wednesday July 30th.

But not for long.

Part the Third: Back from Beyond

T his journey was quite different from the last. Not least because I, for one, was wide awake for the whole excruciating process, which involved a hideous whirling that seemed to last both seconds & years (as indeed it did), & featuring many coloured flashing lights and screaming, hissy noises, much like a fairground jamboree randomly & cata-strophically melting: but then, just as I was beginning to believe that this was Hell, & I should never be out of it, & that nor would I forgive myself for assigning my poor Fergus & Josie to the same Fate, the monstrous experience came to an abrupt halt, & we landed with a shoddy & uncompromising thud in a place of pitch darkness & searing cold where, dizzily recovering our bearings, we discovered ourselves crushed together in a higgledy-piggledy amalgam of heads, torsos & limbs within the velvet interior of the Time Machine in the Krak basement. Or there, at least, we surmised we were, for a moment passed before Herr Krak located his powerful mod-ern torch. Disentangling ourselves from one another & struggling out (this time, I was pleased to note, we had not travelled the maritime route, & were quite dry), we looked around to find the basement room exactly as we had left it, but thankfully minus Fru Krak & her blunderbuss.

Pandora the orang-utan looked down upon us mournfully from her high glass-walled perch. Josie – who seemed not to have been aware of the journey, unlike the adults in our party, all of whom were feeling nauseous – was already jumping up & down with excited glee, & clambering all over the machine ('Touch nothing!' warned Professor Krak. 'She is the most delicate of beasts!'), while Fergus simply stood staring open-mouthed in amazement, that all I had recounted was indeed true and not the ravings of a fantasticator, lunatic or sect member.

I turned to him triumphantly. 'You see?'

He blinked several times, acknowledging the fact that we were no longer in Greenwich. I saw him taking in the dresser, the pictures on the walls, the ornamental table. Professor Krak smiled at his consternation and said in English: 'It's all very much vintage *klunkestil,* as we call it in Denmark – late Victorian, to you. Except the exercise bicycle, which is an import.'

Fergus fell before me on his knees, & when he finally spoke, it was with the slowness & deliberation of an oracle.

'If you can ever forgive me, Lottie,' he said – still looking around him like a sleepwalker, or Lazarus returned from the dead – 'then please marry me.'

'All in good time,' interrupted Professor Krak, before I could reply. 'But first things first, if you do not mind. We are on a mission here, Mr McCrombie, & shall be requiring your assistance.'

'I didn't believe her, Professor,' said Fergus, rising to his feet, but looking so dazed I feared he might swoon. 'I was beginning to think it was, well, something mental. Delusions, you know, from her imagination being too big for her wee head. I figured we'd just have to tread water till the right pharmaceutical solution came along.'

'Well, frankly she should never have told you,' the Professor replied, looking at me reproachfully and rubbing his hands against the sudden cold. Chilly vapours puffed from his mouth as he spoke. 'It is quite against regulations. But now you are with us, I am sure you can be of help. Perhaps you could begin by asking young Josie to get off the exercise bicycle? All the equipment here is most delicate & irreplaceable.'

'Hoam, & not a minnit too soone,' harrumphed Fru Schleswig, detaching herself from the vacuum cleaner & directing a punishing glance at Professor Krak, before reaching for the crate of food Fru Jakobsen had prepared for us. 'I am not doin nuthing lyke thatte aggen as long as I lyvve. So putte that in yor pype and smoke it. Now wer is the bred? I cud eet a hors.'

And so could we all, for our time-journeying had engendered a fearsome hunger, so it was with gusto that we attacked the home-made *rugbrød*, & the cheese & sausage Fru Jakobsen had packed for us, devouring it picnic-style along with hot, sweetened tea from a clever hotty-botty flask known as a Thermos. Upon which, with all but Fru Schleswig's mighty appetite then assuaged ('How cud anywun think this is enuffe to keep boddie & sole together?' she grumbled), we set about our appointed tasks, according to the extensive flow-chart which we had now pinned to the wall, which Professor Krak had begged us to consider as our Bible. He also had instilled in us the need to co-operate 'like a highly motivated populace, under the leadership of, say, Stalin in his heyday', & this we did insofar as our understanding of this allowed, I at least never having heard of that good gentleman. First Fergus, Josie, Fru Schleswig & I unrolled the inflatable mattresses we had brought with us, & set up a temporary home in the two spare rooms of the basement not occupied by the machine, to which we now laid claim as safe territory. As we had anticipated, Fru Krak had barred entry to the upper rooms by a heavy metal grille at the top of the staircase, but our access to the outdoors remained unjeopardized, for it could be effected by all but the monstrously bloated Fru Schleswig via a narrow ventilation tunnel which finalized in the garden, & it was through this that Professor Krak & Franz planned to venture when dusk fell, Franz for the long-anticipated re-union with his parents, the wealthy & distinguished Herr & Fru Poppersen Muhl, & Professor Krak to sell modern medicines on the black market, & thereby procure us enough money to last for the duration of our stay.

There is a fever for things mechanical which comes over certain men when in the presence of anything bolted, wired, wheeled or pistonned – a fever to which my beloved Fergus unexpectedly turned out to be no more immune than a member of my own sex is to the allure of a diamond necklace or an elegant high-heeled shoe. So animated had I been by the charm of Fergus's mind, thus far, & how busily besotted with his physique, that the practical aspect of his character had never surfaced, hitherto, in my presence. But now it had found its element. With Josie at his side (the child fair bubbling with energy like an overheated cooking pot), my husband-to-be excitedly investigated the incomprehensible innards of the Time Machine, quizzing our host about its capacities all the while. This curious attention flattered Professor Krak.

'I will show you the plans if you wish,' he beamed. 'I keep a copy in there, as well as in London,' he said, pointing to a large bureau in the corner, sporting many drawers. 'But be warned; the machine can never be reproduced by anyone other than me: I have seen to that.'

'How so?' I queried, yawning, for the phenomenon of men being masculine together always renders me somewhat bored & I will confess I felt a little disappointed that my dearest seemed more fascinated by the engineering of our vehicle than with the aesthetics of my attire, which the dry-cleaning process had rendered most glorious, to match the woman wearing it, if I may say so myself, for now that my nausea had subsided, a pretty flush had blossomed on my cheeks.

'I have incorporated in it a uniqueness,' replied Professor Krak. 'In the form of a liquid component whose four in-gredients are known only to myself, which cannot be stored, & which remains fresh for only twenty-four hours. Without its presence in the spherical receptacle I call the Catalysing Orb, the contraption's acceleration device remains inactive & dormant. For the purposes of security, the recipe for this delicate activating element remains a secret held only by me. We cannot have everyone criss-crossing time, now can we? And I am pleased to see from all my forays into the future, that I appear to be the only man in history who has ever engineered such a device. And that is how I wish to keep it. In the hands of the uninitiated, a Time Machine could be all too easily abused.'

'That sounds fair enough,' said Fergus, but a worried look

came to his face & he presently voiced his concern. 'But Professor (can I call you Fred?), you must have some sort of back-up plan for us? I mean, in case we should find ourselves . . .'

But Professor Krak was now delving into a trunk, from which he pulled a long knotted rope. 'Now help me attach this to the vent,' he said breezily, 'the better to facilitate our exit.'

No more was said, & the moment was gone faster than a wink.

After Professor Krak and Franz had left on their missions to the unsafe territory of the outer world, Fergus & I lay nestled in one another's arms, listening to the distant footsteps of Fru Krak in the house above us, the sleeping Josie beside us on the mattress, adorably sucking her thumb, & in the next room, Fru Schleswig snoring reverberatively in a way that, instead of provoking the usual annoyance in me, bore for once the comfort of the familiar. I sighed in happiness. All seemed right with the world. Would that it might stay that way. (Though guess what, dear reader: fat chance!)

The next morning, as planned, we ventured out, carefully timing our exit to coincide with Fru Krak's visit from young Franz, who rang the doorbell at precisely 10am, as agreed, posing as a salesman of ladies' restorative products, peddling a powerful sleeping potion sold in the English retail outlet Superdrug under the trade-name of Nytol. With the Krakster thus engaged buying this miracle cure, along with the yellow 'kick-starting' pills that came with it, three of which must be swallowed most religiously with a swig of cod-liver oil on the twenty-third day of every month, we were able to slip out through the ventilation shaft by means of the knotted rope, &

turn swiftly off Rosenvængets Allé into Faksegade, whence to the broader sweep of Odensegade, where Fergus and Josie became so instantly and amazedly agog with the sight of people all dressed like ourselves, in hats & veils & muffs, & with other such archaic oddities, that I had to remind them to keep their mouths closed. But what an unexpected joy it was, through them, to see my beloved city through new-opened eyes, and marvel at the way those things I had previously ignored or taken for granted had transformed themselves into quaint & charming quirks! The frosted cobblestones that glinted in the morning sun; the cries of the street-hawkers & newspaper-sellers on Østerbrogade; the clatter of the horse-drawn trams & the sight of a fat, red-nosed man wobbling high on a pennyfarthing, balancing umpteen Christmas packages; while across the wide boulevard, the long-necked swans pecked at the icy surface of Sortedams Lake, and all around, the merry Christmas lights strung between the gas-lamps, and the little *Jul* candles that flickered in every window, high and low!

And what joy too, to see my Fergus's countenance, so full of relief that I was not a madwoman after all, & so enthralled with all he beheld about him, for was not this an adventure to end all adventures?

And I – O, home I was again! And how joyful was this reunion, for I swear there is no country better to be in at Christmas-time than Denmark, & no people more in love with that festive season than we sentimental Danes, & thus we walked along, past the little match-selling girl sitting propped against the wall with her red, red cheeks and a sweet smile on her lips (so happy she looked, as though she had just seen her long-lost grandmother! I threw her a coin but she did not move, so entranced was she with her heavenly vision), & peeked into people's homes & spied decorated fir trees from whose branches hung the dearest little baskets cut from paper, stuffed with sweetmeats, & elsewhere gilded apples and walnuts, and red candles shimmering with orange flames. It was magnificent, quite incomparably magnificent! At every window we passed, we stopped for Josie to press her nose against the pane, entranced by what she saw, for how intoxicating it was for a child, suddenly to find herself in the land of Juletide! How blessed we felt as we witnessed her happy smiles and heard her shrieks of joy, & we all three linked hands as we walked, while I set to musing about all the little presents we might muster or forage for her, such as liquorice pipes & cinnamon lollipops & maybe even a toy elephant with moving joints, so that she could enjoy the occasion as children should, & I pictured us all returning next year, I pushing a baby in a perambulator up Holsteinsgade, & the year after that with that same baby plus another child, up Rosenvængets Hovedvej. Then in future years more, I pregnant at all times, & we would walk along Østergade, for I was now busy cooking up a grandiose & many-offsprung dream. I squeezed Fergus's hand, & he squeezed mine back, & I knew he was cooking up the same thing, for if he was my steadfast tin soldier, then I was his little ballerina, just like in the story: in any case as you can see, dear one, we were made for each other, & if this brings a romantic tear to your eye then I will not apologize, for there are worse things that can befall a reader.

Then imagine the sheer delight of walking into Else's flower shop on Slagelsegade with Fergus on my arm (and have I forgotten to tell you what a fine figure of a gentleman he looked in his aristocratic get-up?), & Josie, swaddled in her blue woollen winterwear, at my side! The bell rang as we entered: Else was nowhere to be seen, but Josie gasped with delight, for the shop was chock-a-block with marvellous glittering nonsense: Else has a magic talent for concocting much from little, & she had swathed every surface with a flutter of artificial snowflakes, upon whose soft whiteness squatted glorious crimson flower-bouquets, and *nisse*-dwarves, silver-dusted candles, and a splendid nativity scene with pine-cones that sparkled silver, bronze & gold, fat pink cherubs, marzipan pigs as small as your thumb, & minuscule sheep with real pink & green-dyed fleece: Josie's eyes saucered at the sight of all the shining trinkets, riches, baubles and wonders my clever friend had conjured in the confines of such a small space, at the perfumed hyacinths, the dark fir-fronds, the blood-red berries & the snowdrops, & the chocolate angels and red hearts dangling from the small Christmas tree in the window, whose candles flickered with every little gust of breath, & seemed to whisper to us, 'Hooray, & *Glædelig Jul!*'

And then from the back store room came the sound of a nose being blown, & with a muffled cry of, 'Welcome, & do look around!' in burst Else, dressed in festive scarlet & bottle-green, with jingle-bells in her hair – a happy sight indeed at first glance, until you beheld her face, whose red nose and eyes belied the cheeriness of her apparel, for it was plain to see that she had just been weeping. And then immediately I understood why, for my beloved friend was bearing a huge wreath of red roses in the shape of a heart, that bore the legend:

GOODBYE, DEAREST CHARLOTTE.

MUCH-LOVED FRIEND

GONE BUT NOT FORGOTTEN.

And my heart lurched bootwards, at the thought of all the misery that my beloved, faithful Else must have endured these past six weeks, not knowing what had become of me but clearly believing the worst.

Not recognising me beneath my veil, she immediately took me & my companions for customers &, mustering a cheerful tone, let fly a scatter of bright seasonal remarks about how freezing the weather had become, & what madness was all this last-minute gift-buying, & she supposed that sir & madam & the young master had come for a *Jul* bouquet & luckily for us, over there on that shelf to the left of the pompoms . . .' But then, sensing something out-of-kilter, she stopped mid-flow & looked us over, puzzled.

'Excuse me, madam, but I know that dress,' she faltered, taking me in thoroughly now, from neck to hemline. There was a tiny indignance in her voice. 'I've seen it worn by someone else, though it was dirtier then. It . . . fitted her figure exactly the same.'

'Yes, Else,' I said, my voice quiet & most gentlesome. 'You are not mistaken,' & then I raised my veil & smiled wide, wide, wide. At which she shrieked & stepped back, for as she told me afterwards, she was convinced she had seen a very pretty ghost. 'Else,' I laughed, too happy for words, 'do you not recognize your fellow Østerbro Coquette? For it is I! Dry your tears, for I have returned!' At which I removed my glove & touched her hand with mine, & when she felt its warmth she knew that I was made of real flesh, & then she was mine again.

O, the happiness of us both! O what lotion, salve, pomade & ointment was then applied to our hearts' wounds in that loving moment! My dear friend whooped out in joy, & hurling my premature wreath to the floor, leaped over the counter in the most unladylike fashion, revealing her bottle-green lace bloomers, & threw herself into my arms. How we hugged & kissed! 'We all thought you was dead!' she cried tearfully, & embraced me more, while Fergus & Josie looked on in happy bewilderment, until I stopped & introduced them to her, explaining hurriedly that I had accidentally time-travelled to London where I had found myself a beau, who came from the future. Who now smilingly shook her hand and uttered the only Danish he knew, to wit, '*Du er verdens dejligste kvinde og du har mirakuløse bryster*,' and bade Josie do the same, to the uproarious amusement of us both, for they had unwittingly sweet-talked her bazookas. Then Else commanded that I must explain this nonsense about London to her before she *expostulated* with curiosity – all this in Danish, you can be sure, so that Fergus missed her quick-fired questions about his abilities as a lover, my enthusiastic & fulsome answers to which would have made him redden with manly pride.

'Now tell me, have you seen Fru Krak of late?' I asked her, when I had finished outlining the tale of my sudden disappearance, & that of Fru Schleswig. 'For I would much like to discover how the shooting incident affected her nerves, which I know to be most frayed & jumpy at the best of times.'

Else nodded as she listened, then broke into a grin. 'That explains why she's been looking so shocking awful of late,' she said. 'I've spotted her in the bakery several times, pale as a ghost, buying cakes. Judging from how fat she's got, seems like she's stuffing her face with them for solace. I spoke to her once, after you disappeared. She couldn't wait to get away, but I says, excuse me, madam, but I must enquire what happened to your cleaning girl. Coz I was desperate, & couldn't find you nowhere, nor Fru Schleswig neither. I reckoned something fishy had happened down in that basement of hers.'

'As indeed it had! So what did she say?'

'First she looked alarmed, but then she got angry.' At which Else pulled herself up tall & haughty & pouted out her mouth grump-wise, & was at once a parody of Fru Krak. '*I know of no such little cleaning whore!*' spat Else, mimicking the Krakster's fancy-pants accent perfectly. '*Nor nothing of her repellent mother either, & if anyone should insinuate otherwise & thus disrespect me, I shall speak instantly to my lawyer, who will do all in his power to take away any rights that anyone might presume to have in relation to me, & claim damages into the bargain.* And then she simply turned on her heel and buggered off. Leaving me in no doubt that she knew something she wasn't letting on about, & the few times I spotted her after that, she'd cross the street to avoid me. I went to Sergeant Svendsen but he said that "without a body, or proof of foul play" there was nothing he could do.'

Quickly I relayed this in English to Fergus (thus most impressing Else) & explained to him that Else's account of Fru Krak's state of mind cheered me greatly. The fact was, the information it contained gave further fuel to the plan of destabilization & sabotage that (inspired by the discoveries of a certain detective team headed by a cartoon dog) I had already jingled up back in the Tin City & refined with her estranged husband. All of which I then relayed to Else in hurried and somewhat squozzakin fashion whilst Fergus & Josie went out to make a circuit of Sortedams Lake, & buy roast chestnuts from the nine-fingered man with the charcoal-burner, who does a roaring trade at this time of year then spends the next twelvemonth drinking the proceeds.

'So can you help us?' I finished, when I had told her the full story of my departure for England, & summarized the cunning plot in which she was to play such an important role. At which she smiled her biggest smile, threw back her head & laughed, making all the bells in her hair tinkle.

'*For helvede*, Charlotte, you know me: I'd be downright honoured!' she cried. 'I can't wait to see the look on that woman's face! What a Christmas present that'll be!'

Three days later, on December 23rd, all was set. Fergus, Josie & Professor Krak left for the home of Franz, whose indulgent parents, Herr & Fru Poppersen Muhl, were so grateful to see their Little Prince alive that they were willing to go to hallucinatory lengths to keep him sweet – including bribing the Grand Master of Tivoli Gardens to open a segment of the amusement park in his honour. Professor Krak, as already agreed with Franz, would be introduced to the Poppersen Muhls as Franz's 'saviour, mentor and guardian angel, who was fortunate enough to be able to persuade the lad to return to his loved ones' – for as the Professor put it, 'In a situation like ours, we need all the friends in high places we can get.' Fergus, meanwhile, was to be presented as Franz's English teacher, a man who had grown so fond of his young & brilliant pupil in London that he wished to visit him in Denmark with his daughter, & combine the trip with a little tourism. Then, whilst the happily reunited Poppersen Muhl family took 'the

English visitors' on a clandestine tour of Tivoli Gardens (a delight I was right sorry to miss, for I am as nuts about toffee apples & whirligigs as the next girl), Professor Krak, furnished with a lengthy shopping list & a thick wad of easily come-by cash, & clad in his balaclava, joined the heady queues at the butcher's, the baker's & the grocer's to secure the ingredients for our Christmas feast. Fru Schleswig's job, meanwhile, was to remain *in situ* & guard the machine – a task which engendered much grumbling on her part, until I lost my temper with her, & shouted that she was too fat to leave, & if she ever wanted to, she'd best do as we said or shed half a ton of lard forthwith.

And me? I was to be found crouching behind the juniper bush by Fru Krak's front door, awaiting the imminent arrival of yet another visitor. I shivered in the chill until the church clock tolled eleven, at which cue up Rosenvængets Allé waddled a tiny, bulbous, hunchbacked old dame dressed in rags who mounted the steps in far more nimble fashion than her decrepit-looking body suggested it could, & rang the Krak doorbell.

'Good luck!' I just had time to whisper from my hiding-place before the thick front door – still unoiled – creaked open and the now decidedly hefty Fru Krak, her entire visage smeared with pungent cosmetic cream, came face to face with an ancient, bent, spectacled & heavily veiled fortune-teller who had padded herself so effectively with cushions that should Fru Krak lash out & push her down the steps (not unthinkable, given my former mistress's propensity for violence), she would come to no harm, for she would roll like a *bolle*-bun.

'Who are you, & what do you want?' snapped Fru Krak, already preparing to slam the door in her visitor's face.

But the fortune-teller played a cool game. 'The question is, O my Fine Lady – now let me guess, you are an Aquarian if ever I saw one, or my name is not Tante Clairvoyante! – the question is, what do YOU want? For I see that you have problems of a domestic nature on the horizon, madam. Which need your urgent attention, if you are to have the wedding that I also see written – though in a much more shaky form, I fear to tell you – in the book of your future.'

This was enough to scare Fru Krak, & although I thought for a moment that she would simply retreat into the ostrich position, it seemed that Else had addressed directly her deepest fears, & got her hooked.

'Domestic problems?' faltered Fru Krak. 'Can you elaborate?'

'Concerning a dark place what is part of your home. Now let me see,' said Tante Clairvoyante, squinting up into the squally-looking sky as though the answer lay amidst the gathering clouds, 'could it be a cellar, or a basement?' At this, Fru Krak gasped and clutched the door: I saw her knuckles turn a gooky white. 'Something tells me you have a terrible secret hidden there,' whispered Tante Clairvoyante with deep concern. 'And that you won't be free of it till you take action,' she continued, rootling in her huge tapestry bag for a crystal ball, which she dusted off with her glove and pretended to squiz into with increasing alarm.

'I see nothing,' said Fru Krak, leaning over to look. But I could picture her *crème*-slathered face retreating to an even paler shade.

'Come closer, then, madam,' replied the fortune-teller. 'And tell me what you spy through the mystic fog.'

Fru Krak bent forward, peered deeply in, & jumped back with just the kind of sharp & squeaky cry I imagine a hyena making when a half-chewed carcass unexpectedly fights back. For there, deep within the ball, & so vividly & horribly disganglified by its contours as to seem like a three-dimensional *tableau vivant*, was a digitally taken & creepily distorted photograph of the Little Cleaning Girl Charlotte, dressed in black, lying in a coffin, stone dead.

'Cross my palm with silver, & I'll give you some advice,' whispered Else in her most menacing croak. Fru Krak's flabby jawline slumped further into the wattles of her pallid neck. 'If someone you've wronged comes looking for vengeance,' Else warned as she stepped over the threshold, for Fru Krak had by now reluctantly gestured her to enter, 'you'll have to appease her, coz otherwise you'll be disgraced for ever. Shunned by the fine society of Copenhagen, you'll be. Posh ladies'll turn their backs on you at the haberdasher's. And forget about being invited to any more of them balls.'

And the door closed behind them.

Half an hour later Else emerged a richer woman, and we embraced. The scene was set.

Later that day the Pastor came to call, wearing a frock coat & bearing a heavy Bible: Fru Krak led him into the parlour where they sat for an hour. From the basement below, we listened as best we could with the aid of a surveillance device called a baby alarm obtained by the Professor in London, which enabled one to eavesdrop through walls & floors, but all we could distinguish were verses from Leviticus. Fru Krak was not ready to confess her secret, & if the Pastor suspected his bride-to-be was hiding something, he showed it not.

But after he had left, we had ample evidence of her state of mind. That night, courtesy of the three yellow amphetamine pills the salesman of ladies' restorative products had bade her take as a 'kick-starter' with a swig of cod-liver oil on the twenty-third day of every month, Fru Krak slept not one millisecond. All night we heard her in the house above us, kicking up an almighty shindig of self-pity: a veritable hullabaloo-fest of weeping, screaming, ranting aloud, pacing of floors, & what seemed like furniture removal, for every now & then we would hear a thundacion or a crash.

'She is packing her trunks,' assessed Professor Krak, rubbing his hands in glee. 'And preparing to leave. Mark my words, dear friends, the thing is working! How long have I waited for this!'

Then, at five o'clock, just as the first cock was crowing, the second phase of the Østerbro master-plan swings into action. This is my moment, dear reader, & I will admit to you in confidence that I feel a little nervous, if you can forgive me a moment of weakness – for to be honest, much as I find her ridiculous, Fru Krak always gives me something of the creeps. Now, however, is the time to turn the tables, so behold me there, my face ghostified with white powder, and clad in a wispy gauze apparel purchased in a horror shop near Covent Garden, as I slither out of the ventilation shaft, don roller-blades beneath my long dress, & glide in wobblesome fashion to the front of the house, where I carefully mount the steps in the sideways motion my footwear demands, make some final adjustments to my attire, & then bang thrice, slowly and threateningly, on the heavy wooden door.

Some lights come on, & I fancy I hear footsteps. I bang again, most doomily, until finally comes the sound of chains jangling, bolts being drawn, & keys turning & then, with a dark creak, the door opens a crack to reveal a slice of Fru Krak's puffed-out visage, the corners of its mouth turned down in a familiar wattled scowl. As soon as she sees me, she makes to slam the door, but I hold it open: & on seeing my face in its eerie blanchedness, her piggy eyes shoot open wide: she gives a frail, whimpering scream & steps back: at which the Ghost of the Little Cleaning Girl pushes the door open further & rolls past her down the corridor, coming to an elegant halt in the middle of the sitting-room, before turning to face her former mistress. Who now looks as if she might faint.

The Ghost of the Little Cleaning Girl has practised hard on her voice: a weak whisper, hoarse but insistent: to hear it, Fru Krak must lean closer & catch the smell of mothballs – a smell which not quite masks the stranger & altogether more butcherish odour that wafts from the innards of my dress.

'You murdered me in cold blood, Fru Krak,' whispers the Ghost of the Little Cleaning Girl.

'No!' she falters. 'No, I did not! Or at least I did not mean to!'

But ghosts, Professor Krak & I agreed back in Canary Wharf, are deaf, or at least unprepared to listen to the self-justifications of those who have wronged them in life, so the Ghost of the Little Cleaning Girl answers her not, but instead breathes, in the same slow, druzzed whisper: 'Behold your gruesome work, Fru Krak. You shall come face to face with what you have done, & beg forgiveness.' Fru Krak stands quaking & transfixed as the Ghost of the Little Cleaning Girl begins unwinding her shroud, & then unlacing her bodice, to reveal a glimpse of a prodigiously bloody, realistic & gaping gash right between her breasts – sited on the very bull's-eye at which Fru Krak aimed the blunderbuss on that night of fatal errors &, with the most alarming accuracy for one so maddened by rage, fired a single bullet. 'Come closer, Fine Lady,' now whispers the Ghost of the Little Cleaning Girl. 'Come & feel how my wound still bleeds.'

'No!' screams the desperate creature, so fearful that I wonder for a moment if she might soil her knickers. But there is no escape from holy justice, for the Ghost of the Little Cleaning Girl has now reached out with her clammy fingers (courtesy of a modern gel soap favoured by car mechanics, & known as Swarfega) & grabbed her wrist, then shoved Fru Krak's hand to her unshrouded chest, whereupon the grisly wound, thanks to a polythene bag filled with fresh blood & offal from the butcher's shop, purchased yesterday by Professor Krak, bursts forth its contents, to wit one full litre of red gore, that gushes splatteringly on to Fru Krak's hand & arm in most repulsive fashion.

O horror! So convincing is the Ghost of the Little Cleaning Girl (and I have not trod the boards for nothing) that I am almost terrified myself!

With a grating high-pitched screech, the Krakster snatches her blood-spotted hand away & staggers backward, falling on to the chaise-longue & writhing there, amid much flailing of haberdashery and *klunke*-tassels, in what I assume to be an agony of remorse. The Ghost of the Little Cleaning Girl, quickly wrapping her shawl around her to hide the now exposed artifice of her wound, but letting the blood continue to trickle down her white gauze garments to the floor, a most impressive sight, then warns Fru Krak in that same terrifying

185

whisper that she will not leave until justice has been done. No: she will continue to bleed like this, all over the Aquarian Lady's beautiful home, & follow her former mistress out through the streets, naming & shaming her, & the Ghost of the Little Cleaning Girl will also appear before Pastor Dahlberg too, & do likewise, if Fru Krak does not obey her commands, for the Little Cleaning Girl is no longer of human flesh, & now abides only by the rules of beyond, where the living hold no sway.

'You have no proof of what I did!' Fru Krak falters finally, clutching the place where a normal woman's heart would lie. But the Ghost of the Little Cleaning Girl is well into her stride now, & remains immune to her protestations, & instead motions her to follow. Fru Krak shrinks back, so the ghost makes to snatch her wrist again, at which she succumbs & follows her phantom tormentor who glides smoothly down the corridor & commands her to unlock the metal grille with which she has barred the staircase, & see for herself what lurks down there.

'No, please, I beg you,' she cries, 'do not make me go there!' but the Ghost of the Little Cleaning Girl is by now revelling in her own mercilessness, & stands there silent, menacing & immobile, until Fru Krak tremblingly fumbles for the key from the vast jangling chain that dangles from her belt & unclasps the huge padlock that affixes the grille to the stairwell entrance.

'Descend!' hisses the Ghost of the Little Cleaning Girl. And so with shaking steps Fru Krak opens the grille & makes her way down the stairs alone, while the Ghost of the Little Cleaning Girl remains where she is, on account of the somewhat inconvenient rollerblades, & there, at the bottom of that dark & dismal stairwell, unlit & stinking of toad-spore, comes Fru Krak face to face – O mercy! – with none other than the massive bulk of the righteously vengeful Fru Schleswig, bloated with rage, who fixes her former employer with a hell-scurved eye & bellows with all her might: 'You eevil wun! You merdered my pore littel babby & then lokked me in here, wer I have been livin on rattes & fungusses these past six weekes! But now I am goin strayt to Sargent Svensen to report to him this grusom killinge of my beluvvid onlie chylde!'

Which terrifying threat sends the hapless Fru Krak shooting back up the stairs & collapsing in a gibbering mush of tears & snot at my feet, which she now attempts to clutch (I swiftly roll backwards a metre to avoid her grip), & lies there glaggering & groaning.

And now the time has come for the Ghost of the Little Cleaning Girl to name her price. And it is this: that firstly, Fru Krak must empty her coffers of all the cash she possesses, & leave it on the hall table as pecuniary penance for the foul act of murder. Then she must furthermore sign this document (the Ghost of the Little Cleaning Girl proffers it in duplicate: bloodstained now, but still legally viable), revoking all her rights to the house, which she *unreservedly bequeaths hereunto & theretofore to the victim's alleged mother, Fru Fanny Schleswig, widow of this parish, & her various appointees & agents, who will from henceforth both titularly & in fact be the owners of the aforementioned property, in verisimilitude, turpitude, & for all eternity.*

'And finally,' finishes the Ghost of the Little Cleaning Girl, when Fru Krak has signed her trembly-lettered name upon the dotted line with an otherly writing-tool, namely a ball-point pen, on both copies, 'you must pack your belongings at once, & leave Copenhagen by daybreak, never to return.'

'By daybreak?' she gasps, boggle-eyed. 'Mercy, the sun is almost here!'

But ghosts are deaf. The Little Cleaning Girl glides out, leaving her former mistress snivelling in a heap to contemplate her bleak future.

What larks!

After I had made my exit & disposed of my rollerblades, Professor Krak, Fergus & I crouched in our hiding-place behind the juniper bush & watched the house. Soon dawn broke, & with the new day arrived a horse-drawn carriage, summoned by a street-urchin whom the desperate woman had flagged down shortly after my departure. Once her ten trunks had been loaded into the luggage compartment, we heard her then call weakly to the driver: 'Take me to meet Pastor Dahlberg at St Jakob's Kirke. Wait for us there half an hour, & bear us both thence non-stop to Silkeborg!'

And with the crack of a whip & a shatter-clatter of hooves, Fru Krak was gone – headed (as we later learned) for the hastiest marriage ever organized, followed by an impromptu honeymoon in a dismal out-of-season spa. With ownership of Number Nine Rosenvængets Allé & the Time Machine secured, Christmas was ours.

O *glædelig* indeed was the *Jul* that followed! Fergus had explained to Josie that the Christmas festivities in Denmark took place on the evening of the twenty-fourth, but this meant little to a child who had just been whipped out of a London summer, & was due to return there within a few days, according to the commandment of our flow-chart. Indeed the whole idea of time, for a child, is a muddled thing, as I recall: suffice it to say that upon hearing the news that Christmas was coming tonight, some five months early, Josie was over the moon, which is just where she deserved to be (have you noticed, precious one, how my loathing for children had dissipated, now that I finally knew one?), & all morning she made most hozzicky-wild running up & down throughout the house, peeking inside every cupboard, exploring every nook & cranny, & being as rowdy as she wished, now that there was no more need for secrecy & silence. Fergus & I lit all the gas-lights until the whole place was volcanically ablaze, & then we did much teenagerish snogging beneath the chandelier, before we all set about decorating the huge fir tree Professor Krak had ordered for delivery that afternoon, & for which Else, who arrived clad in a fetching outfit of pink & gold like a veritable Christmas fairy, provided the most abundant adorn-ments & baubles harvested from her shop.

'How do you do,' she said in perfect English to Fergus, who attempted an elaborate bow, while Josie in turn curtsied, for our modern visitors seemed hell-bent on practising what they deemed to be 'old-fashioned' customs. Together, Josie & I set about adding the decorations to the Christmas tree: she was in quite a turmoil of delight.

'Will we go to Legoland?' she asked, as I lifted her to hang the angel at the top. I was beginning to explain that Legoland was not yet built (for she had not quite got the hang of our journey through time, & according to Fergus believed we were 'visiting a wee theme park') when Gudrun Olsen showed up, & the child rushed to practise her curtsy again. The reunion between Gudrun Olsen & Professor Krak, who had not clapped eyes on one another in seven years, was a charming sight to behold indeed, & most poignant, for they were clearly fond of one another.

'Were they lovers before, or what?' whispered Fergus, watching them.

'No: she worked for him but it all went wrong when she accidentally murdered his orang-utan, after it attacked her face. That's how she got the scar,' I explained.

'Ah, of course,' he said, looking at me wryly, for there were many parts of my story I had merely skated over, & he was learning what he called 'Venutian' somewhat on the hoof.

The afternoon was set aside for cooking, which task Else & I began with relish, for I had much missed the traditional sweetmeats & treats of Denmark, and longed to share them with my love. Else had transformed my mourning wreath into a glorious centrepiece for the table, which by seven o'clock that same night was groaning with the most gastronomically resplendent of victuals, & the priciest wine & schnapps you ever smelled, tasted or clapped eyes on, all laid out on precious Krak crockery, with silverware & dainty napkins, & a multitude of candles & a roaring, spitting elm fire in the hearth, scented with cedarwood.

And then we all joined hands & stood around the *Juletræ*, & then began to circle it, singing Christmas songs the while: '*Hojt fra Træets Grønne Top*'; '*Glade Jul, Dejlige Jul*'; '*Dejlig er den Himmel Blå*'.

'What a joy to welcome you all here at last, in the heart of my home!' cried Professor Krak, to whom the occasion was clearly a most emotional event, as evidenced by his frequent need to dab at his eyes with a handkerchief, & blow his nose. He raised his champagne-filled glass, & we raised ours. 'Seven long years I have waited to reclaim what is rightfully mine, & I thank you all for enabling this happy moment to come about!'

We all cheered & said *skål* & drank to good fortune, & that champagne was I swear, O dearest one, the finest that I ever tasted. 'And then a second toast, this one to the miracle drug, Viagra!' beamed Professor Krak, announcing that he had made a thousand kroner selling it on the black market – enough to provide not just for tonight's feast, & the many tantalizing gifts that had suddenly materialized beneath the tree, but for many years' financial cushioning to come.

The huge steaming golden goose was so magnificent, my dear one, that I hesitate to tell you about its mouthwatering grandeur, & all that accompanied it, in too much detail lest you become so famished that you lay me aside & rush first to your fridge & then your microwave, in order to assuage your own sudden lust for food! Yet I cannot resist the account, so seductive to the taste-buds and so *hyggelig*-cosy was that stupefying meal: the goose, so golden-skinned & fragrant, bathed in its own juices & stuffed inside with seasoned apples and prunes, smothered in a fine goose-gravy & served with glistening dollops of heliotrope *ribsgelé*; boiled potatoes, white & gleaming soft, & alongside (O yum!) a huge ornamental plate of sweet *brune kartofler*; red cabbage cooked with marmalade & vinegar; & afterwards a high, toppling white mound of *ris à l'amande*, a mini-Himalaya over which we poured generous quantities of warm sweet cherry-sauce shining with fruit-lumps. Gudrun, who had most happily reverted to her role as housekeeper & insisted on serving, engineered the helpings so that it was Josie who found the whole almond in her pudding, & won the marzipan pig, much to her delight.

Glædelig Jul!

And the conversation flowed as did the wine & the laughter – though Fru Schleswig was an exception on the talking front, having transformed herself into a veritable eating machine: a napkin tucked beneath her chin & a determined glint in her eye, she was in her gluttonous element, & becoming suddenly & impressively ambidextrous in her gastronomic enthusiasm, declaring herself 'happie as a pygge in shitte'. Then, stuffed to the gills, we finished the repast with *brune-kager* and *vaniliekranse*, figs & dates, & we pulled crackers & drank wine & schnapps & made most merry, until Josie, exhausted, tore open her gifts & played for five minutes with the charming little wooden tram set that Professor Krak had bought her, before falling fast asleep with her tousled head on my lap.

The following week was Paradise. For what, pray, is bliss, but living in harmony with those you love, & having the time to kiss & hug them all you can? I speak here of Fergus & Josie, to be sure, but also of my dear Else, of whom we saw a great deal, & Gudrun too, when her duties at the laundry permitted. Fru Schleswig I leave to your imagination – suffice it to say she too was happy, in the way a house-plant might be, if well-watered & kept at the right temperature. Although the residence was now officially the property of Fru Schleswig, Professor Krak & I agreed it best to keep the tragic crone 'out of the loop' on this matter, for the time being, in case property-ownership should befuddle a brain already so dangerously overcharged with puzzling events that it might disintegrate altogether. While Josie & I played hide-and-seek and Chase throughout the house, revelling in our new-found freedom, my Fergus & Professor Krak, much in cahoots, discussed the technicalities of time-travel, & to the elder man's delight, my husband (husband in spirit, though not yet in fact) scrutinized the objects the orang-utan Pandora had brought back from her travels, and identified their probable nature & origins.

'I'd say she went to Africa on more than one occasion,' Fergus pondered, 'to judge from all these sea-shells.'

Herr Krak nodded in vehement agreement, declaring that indeed, he believed that Pandora may well have visited several countries in Africa, namely Algeria, Mali, Ghana and Togo, during a range of eras.

Fergus was fingering a most macabre handbag fashioned from the body of an armoured ratty creature, its scales like the petals of an artichoke. It was semi-curled, as if caught and skinned in a cringe of fear; its tail formed the handle. 'This armadillo artefact is likely to come from South America, very possibly Brazil,' said my dear one & I gazed with pride at him, & the more I gazed the more the wonder grew that one small head could carry all he knew. 'And I do believe that this,' he said, hefting a length of hollow bamboo with a spear-tip, 'is a blowpipe used by the tribal people of Borneo.'

Professor Krak was as surprised as he was delighted with this news, for he declared he had always suspected that the time-sucking mechanism could, in rare circumstances, catapult subjects to other locations than those situated on the Prime Meridian, but had never been able to prove it.

'To think that I hadn't a clue what that other object was,' I mused. 'The mobile phone. Remember, Professor Krak? You must then have been as discombobulated as I, when you first encountered it.'

'I was indeed,' he replied thoughtfully. 'Do you have one on you, Fergus, by any chance?' he asked suddenly. 'I have always meant to continue experimenting with communication across time, for there seems no good reason to me, epistemologically speaking, why this should not be possible, if the caller places himself correctly at the mouth of a Time-Sucker. I have not managed it before, but one never knows when one might be in luck.'

'Och, with the best will in the world, I really can't see how that would be possible,' laughed Fergus gently, handing over his device. 'It's a compelling idea, Fred, but in reality . . .'

But the older man was not to be contradicted. 'You're looking at it all wrong,' he declared, switching on the mobile & waiting for a signal with evident expectation. 'For time is actually more like space than it is like time, if you understand my drift. The fourth dimension, as it is called. I have read up a little on this matter since coming here: Hawking and Gott are the big names in your era. Clever people, but with all their talk of helixes & matter-anti-matter, they can't see the wood for the trees! If they knew how much simpler it all was than they presume to transport oneself to the lonely saline seas of the Triassic Age! Anyway, dear boy, just try to see a different time as an alternative location, merely – a philosophical shift sideways.'

This thought was already giving me vertigo, & it was clear there was no signal to be had (what a surprise!) so I left the two men discussing the importance of getting the house connected to the new electricity grid which had just been established in Østerbro, in the hope that some of the Time Machine's elaborate routines might thereby be sped up, &

went to find Josie, whom I found crouched on her mattress like a little mushroom, looking at the illustrations in the tales of Hans Christian Andersen, her eyes drooping with exhaustion. I told her it was time to sleep, then tucked her into bed & kissed her.

'The best Christmas I ever, ever had,' she said sleepily.

'Me too,' I told her. 'By a long way.'

'How long?'

'As long as a piece of string.'

'How long's that?'

'Three million, nine hundred and twenty-eight kilometres. It's the longest piece of string in the world, & it's kept in the royal curiosity cabinet, next to the pea the princess slept on.'

Satisfied with this thought, she closed her eyes, & I lay down next to her & fancied myself in Heaven. Soon I too was asleep, though I was to be woken later & carried like a big squealing parcel to another bedroom by Fergus, who wanted some fun, & what fun it was, for never have I had better rogering than with him, & never such romance to go with it: here was a man who could make me whimper with pleasure & joy all at once, & scream my head off too. But I feel blushes coming on, so I will spare you further details.

The Christmas lull was over. Armed with gift-packs of Viagra with which to bribe the men of power, I made arrangements for electricity to be connected to the household, & once the municipal workmen had installed it, & strung the relevant wires from street-poles, Fergus & Professor Krak – excited as two schoolboys – spent many hours encouraging the Time Machine to respond to electrical stimuli. Franz would visit, & make suggestions, & also take time to study Fru Schleswig's vacuum cleaner, a device now seldom dormant, for it had been revitalized by the new power system, & was being worked as never before, for the normally slothful Fru Schleswig, fired with an unusual energy, had set about sucking the dust from every flat surface, cranny, crack, or piece of upholstery she could find: the similarly re-energized Franz, behaving as though he too had been plugged into a power source, enthused about how he planned to copy its mechanism with a view to setting up shop as an inventor, for he declared himself bored with philosophy, being 'a doer not a thinker, & not cut out to ponder things in a hypothetical & crabwise manner'. It was a home quite buzzing with innovation & activity, & full of plans, for the flow-chart was to be adhered to, declared Professor Krak, which meant he must make a quick foray back to London to settle the minds of his flock, the telephoning-across-time notion having not yet borne fruit, despite his discovery of a weak signal in the garden, behind the holly tree. On his return, we would finalize our mission in Copenhagen, install Fru Schleswig as mistress of the house, & then make haste for London, where (in my scheme of things) Fergus & I would live happily ever after, amid flowers, champagne & kisses, as in all the best stories, and have many podgy little cherubs to coo over.

If Professor Krak was a little nervous about the electrical tweaks he and Fergus had made to the Time Machine, he hid it well on the morning he made ready to leave. Indeed, he had seemed as businesslike as any London Underground commuter preparing for his regular journey to work – though in the hour before he left, however, he had acted a little oddly, for he had locked himself into the Oblivion Room, & from the sounds that then emanated from it, it seemed he was pedalling most frantically upon the bicycling contraption.

'What is he thinking of?' I asked Fergus, puzzled. 'He never cared before about his health: why now?'

'Well, my theory is, hen, that he's gearing himself up for the mission,' said my love. 'I reckon that while he's pedalling, he's got the Bornean orang-utan on his mind. She's right in his line of vision there. I think it gets him all revved up, remembering what she went through. Poignant, when you think about it. But these eggheads, they're often a bit daft.'

'He loved her,' I remembered. 'When he told me how she died, he had tears in his eyes!'

When Herr Krak finally emerged, he seemed to carry a whiff of alcohol with him, & there was another smell too, more medical – but he seemed almost gay, & excited about his trip. 'Don't worry,' he assured Fergus (who was looking more than a little concerned). 'All we have done is improve both speed and accuracy. Which should mean less of a dizzifying landing, with any luck. I beg you, dear friends, fear not!' he called as he closed the door of the machine upon himself & motioned us to stand back. 'For trust me, I have done this a thousand times!'

Whereupon with a whirring & a jarring, followed by a blinding flash and a sharp sulphurous clang, he was suddenly no more, & all that remained of him, when we opened the door, was a puff of smoke & the faintest indentation of his buttocks upon the red velvet cushion of the carriage.

*　　*　　*

'Famous last words,' said Fergus at noontide two days later, when Professor Krak failed to turn up as he had been scheduled to. 'I think we accidentally did something to alter its course. But what it might be I don't know.' And he looked most grave.

'It's probably to do with getting into the Greenwich Observatory,' I replied. I did not feel too alarmed – for was I not back in my own land & time, and would it really be the end of the world if we were stranded here? Would Love not conquer all? I was drugged with happiness, replete with joy. I did not want to think about all that might go awry. But Fergus did. In the thirty-six hours that followed, he kissed me as much as before, but they were the kisses of a man who was ever more distracted, & who now spent much time inside the machine, fiddling with its innards and sighing & saying 'och' in a perturbed fashion.

Tick, tock.

Time passed disturbingly fast. Three days on, & New Year's Eve had arrived. By now we were forever looking at the clock, & calculating how long it had been since Professor Krak's departure. I was minded to turn the flow-chart to the wall, so out-of-kilter had our schedule become, & so hopelessly off the map had our communal journey wandered. I will confess to you, my precious love, that I have never much enjoyed the turning of the year: too many times the revelry has soured on me, too often, in the past, has a customer's desire 'to end the year with a bang' led me to miss the dancing, & turned the alcohol-fuelled madness of midnight too flatly into the vinegar of morn. And yet, I argued to myself, this was to be my first New Year with Fergus, & my life had changed: for that reason alone, it should be a blissful occasion, for had my life not begun afresh, thanks to the blessing of Love? But by now – if I am to be quite honest about it – a nagging worry had incontrovertibly descended, like an atmosphere, & even I, in my so far apparently infinite foolishness, had begun to have dismal thoughts about the continued absence of Professor Krak. Might he have abandoned us here, now the Time Machine was secure? Surely, surely not! When I finally voiced this thought, Fergus fell into a deeper than ever silence, while Franz, who is of a pessimistic nature, merely fuelled my anxieties further by echoing and elaborating on them, using phrases like 'ultimate betrayal' & 'human experimentation' & 'hostages to fortune'. It was only Josie, preoccupied with her toy tram set, & Fru Schleswig, now titular mistress of the home, & High Priestess of Vacuum Suction, who seemed contented & unconcerned.

So despite the best efforts to appear cheerful, it was to a somewhat muted New Year's Eve meal that we seated ourselves that night. Else, dressed in flamingo pink, & Franz, in a velvet suit, & Gudrun, in red with her scar powdered over, joined us for the *flæskesteg* I had prepared, for I did not wish my darling one to return to London without ever having tasted our national dish, & savoured the beauty of roast pork & crackling in all its Danish glory. But a sombre meal it was, & the chewing & chomping of Fru Schleswig echoed in the great hall like a bog-marsh in biological upheaval.

Josie broke the silence. 'Daddy,' she asked, her brown Fergus-eyes serious. 'When are we going home?'

More silence, & then we all spoke at once:

'But it's lovely here!' (me)

'Never!' (Franz)

'I cud eet anutha potato!' (Fru S)

'What does she say?' (Else & Gudrun).

And then we looked at Fergus. 'Daddy's working on it, hen,' he said finally. This statement was followed by more silence, with the round-eyed child wondering why we were all so agitated. Then Fergus spoke again, addressing all of us. 'My view is that if Fred hasn't returned by tomorrow, we should leave here under our own steam, without him. I'm familiar with the technology of the machine: I think we should try to make it back to London no matter what. Because something must have happened, to stop him getting back,' he argued. 'I know how this thing works now, and –'

But I cut him short. 'It's too big a risk!'

'What's he say?' asked Else, Gudrun & Fru Schleswig in unison, but I ignored them & continued in English: 'What if we land in another time & place, with no way to get back?'

By now Franz had provided translations for Gudrun & Else, who cried out, alarmed: 'Over my dead body Charlotte! You're only leaving if you've got a way of coming back. Full stop.'

'It is the most risky of initiatives,' counselled Franz, first in English, & then in Danish for the benefit of Else. 'It will end in the worst kind of doom, you mark my words. Best stay here for evermore,' he finished, eyeing Else to see her reaction. Which seemed to be one of approval.

'She iz alwiz tryin to get rid of me,' grumbled Fru Schleswig through a mouthful of *flæskesteg*. A small piece flew from her mouth & landed on a candle, where it sputtered violently, giving off a porky whiff.

'No, listen,' said Fergus, by now more agitated than I had ever seen him. 'I don't deny the risk, but –'

'*Min eneste ene*, we cannot do it!' I exclaimed, standing up, the better to stamp my foot – for this was our second ever disagreement, & it was important to give my opinion emphasis. 'We must simply stay here until there is another way of –'

But my speech was broken by an almighty crash: the double doors of the dining room flew open, and there before us, blackened with what looked like soot, his clothing hanging off his tall frame in rags, was none other than –

'Well, I'll be buggered: it's Fred!' cried Fergus, leaping up from the table. Gudrun, too, was on her feet immediately, & rushed to where the Professor stood. For a moment we were all exclaiming & laughing with relief – but any optimism we might have felt was short-lived, as Professor Krak (for it was indeed he) had clearly been through a most terrifying ordeal. He steadied himself against the door-jamb, then began sinking to the floor: Fergus caught him just before he hit the ground & Gudrun pressed a glass of red wine to his lips. Unshaven and unkempt, he looked a fright, & smelled of smoke and oil: his once noble head of hair was clotted into a single dark clump. He groaned as though in pain.

'Thank God,' he said hoarsely, his eyes closing as though to blot out a memory. 'I thought I wouldn't make it.'

Josie was watching, wide-eyed. I took her hand & squeezed it: her 'wee theme park' was turning frightening.

'What happened, pray?' I was fair jumping up & down with impatience to know what had transpired to make the Professor's voyage to London so disastrous.

'It all went wrong,' he sighed, as Fergus helped him to a

chair. Gudrun mopped his brow, & put his hip-flask to his lips for a restorative swig, then swiftly placed a plate of food before him: this he instantly began devouring greedily, like a dog at a plate of offal, employing none of his usual refinement & ceremony. Fru Schleswig watched approvingly. 'Horribly, grotesquely wrong,' he continued through a mouthful of *flæskesteg.* 'For I ended up not in London, but at the Basilica of Our Lady of Pilar in Zaragoza.'

Swiftly, I translated for Fergus. 'Zaragoza!' he cried. 'But Fred, that's a whole rotation and a half beyond where –'

'Indeed it is,' moaned Professor Krak in Danish, for he was clearly in no state to handle English syntax. 'And it was in this most unexpected place – never a favourite destination of mine (though the architecture is to be admired) – that I was vilely treated by medieval villains and hurled into a vat of fetid slime. They threw rotten goose-eggs at me, & there was then talk of a public trial, after which I would be hanged as a magician, & my gizzard fed to a species of mountain wolf known as *Lupus maximus horribilis.* Had I not managed to bribe the prison guard with my laser torch, I would not be alive to tell the tale.'

'But how did you get back?' asked Fergus, when Franz had provided the translation. It was most evident that he was thinking now of his daughter, for I knew him inside out. O, had I only insisted that he not come on such a dangerous undertaking! Had I only forbidden it! Gently, he drew Josie to him & stroked her dark mop of hair.

'The Professor stinks of poo,' she whispered.

The Professor took another gulp of wine & thence continued in English. 'The Basilica is close to the meridian. I located it, & the Time-Sucker, using my little GPS machine, which miraculously survived my dunking, & managed to trigger the Magnetic Memory Imperative just in time. That is the closest shave I think I ever had – and there have been many!'

Poor Fergus: I could see his brain working up a storm-cloud of dark thoughts. 'But Fred, can you put your finger on what exactly went wrong with the mechanism?' he asked anxiously. 'Could it be to do with the electrical element we introduced?'

'Most certainly,' replied Professor Krak, wiping his mouth and nodding his gratitude to Gudrun who was doling out more potatoes, which he attacked ravenously.

'A disaster,' murmured Franz, whom I had by now dubbed the Crown Prince of Pessimism. 'To think, that if I had not returned here before now, I would be trapped in London for ever, a slave to my own miserable fate! And now the machine has failed you, & you are trapped here, just as I was, there!'

'It has not failed us, foolish boy!' snapped Professor Krak through a mouthful of pork. 'It is simply in need of some adjustment, which I am perfectly capable of performing once I have made some rudimentary calculations. Bring me a pen,' he barked, and Franz obeyed, whereupon Professor Krak proceeded hastily to scribble a tangle of numbers and dia-grams on the white tablecloth. Fergus joined him, & soon the two men were lost in technical conversation. In subdued mood, the rest of us cleared the table; when Else, Gudrun & Franz had left, Fru Schleswig, Josie & I prepared for bed: by the time the clock struck midnight & a new year dawned, the men had repaired to the basement where they continued their discussions within the body of the machine and began what Professor Krak called the 'reconfiguration process'. And in such a manner did another New Year's Eve that did not match up to expectations draw to a close, thus confirming my theory that some festivals are never what they are cracked up to be.

The next morn, feeling no familiar male warmth next to mine, I descended to the basement to find Fergus & Professor Krak still working inside the machine. They looked exhausted, but triumphant; neither man had slept a wink, but the atmosphere had changed: Professor Krak looked relieved, & Fergus, weary-eyed & his face covered now in the most delightful stubble, folded me in his arms. 'I think we have cracked it, hen,' he smiled with pride, & I forgave him the disappointment of last night, which was none of his fault, & I fell in love with him all over again.

'Then you, Professor Krak, must have hot water, & some breakfast, & then sleep,' I insisted. 'I shall run you a bath instantly, for it's high time you got rid of that Castel Gandolfo reek from your clothes, & restored your hair to its usual glory. It's New Year: make it a day of rest after your ordeal.'

An hour later, all was peaceful again. Imagine us there, gentle reader, if you will – for it is the last time you will see us assembled in such a happy scene. Look: Fergus is dozing in front of the cedarwood fire, with a sleepy Josie tucked in his arms; Professor Krak is in the bathtub recovering from his filthy dunking in the vat; & Franz, who has returned, is reassembling the vacuum cleaner after having dissected its components – ('See here, Fru Schleswig: your intake & exhaust port, your fan, your clutch actuator, your motor, & your canisters, all working to obey Bernoulli's Principle, by which as air speed increases, pressure decreases; is it not a marvel, the way the *pressure differentials* cause the suction?') while she in turn is boasting to him (preposterously) that she taught me the alphabet when I was three, & herself once read 'an oringe-cullered booke, with one hundred & fortee payges & the wurd turnippe in the tytle'. Else is away preparing her shop for the New Year Sale & I, meanwhile, am at work with needle & olive thread, taking in one of the many robes Fru Krak had left in her wardrobe, so that it will flatter my curves & prompt my lover to grope me even more than he already does. Can such peace last? I think you know the answer to that by now.

A ring at the door. We froze.

A loud & commanding banging, and a ferocious male cry of 'Let us in or we will bash the door down!'

'Don't go!' I yelled at Fru Schleswig, who, with that bovine instinct of obedience so common among lowly creatures of her ilk, had already begun lumbering towards the hall. 'We know not who it is!'

The banging ceased, & I was glad to remember that we had triple-bolted the front door. But the respite was all too brief: within a minute, the thumping noises had started up once more, but louder this time, & with a splitting-wood timbre that hinted at alarming events on the horizon.

Fergus woke with a start & snapped instantly into action, grabbing a poker & bidding Josie to take her toy tram, descend to the basement, & hide inside the Time Machine. Alarmed, Franz quickly screwed the last component of the vacuum cleaner back in place, & Fru Schleswig clasped it passionately to her bosom, whereupon Franz went to summon Professor Krak from his bath – from which he emerged dripping &

wild-haired & clad in his wife's pink bath-robe, adorned with sea-horses.

'Right: we must now activate Plan 4b, sub-section ten!' he ordered sharply, referring to the flow-chart he had bidden us all learn by heart, but which had faded to a distant memory in my mind by then, thanks to schnapps & the passage of time. 'The Time Machine is under direct enemy threat! Deploy all defence strategies, while I hasten to prepare the catalysing liquid, which I pray is still fresh enough, after my visit to Zaragoza, to fuel the journey!'

By now Fergus, still clearly befuddled but nonetheless determined, was ascending the stairs with his poker, where from the landing window a view was to be had of the street immediately below. I followed him, my heart a-patter, for there were few things this could mean, & none of them bode well. When he reached the landing I heard him gasp.

'Lottie, quick! Is that her?' he asked, pointing to a carriage that contained a plump woman wrapped in a beige shawl, fur-hatted & hard-faced. And next to her, the pompous Pastor. I groaned in the affirmative.

'Then Fred is right, & we must act quickly,' said my love. We had changed the locks, of course, in anticipation of just such an intrusion, & there existed a blood-spattered docu-ment proving Fru Fanny Schleswig's legal ownership of the house – but what none of us could have foreseen was the speed with which events would unravel: that first of all, Fru Krak would blab about the Ghost of the Little Cleaning Girl in her sleep (a fact we later learned from an acquaintance of the Pastor's); that the Parson would interrogate his wife further; that next, the Man of God, apprised of his home's occupation by a demonic machine, would be filled with a most righteous & biblical fury, & insist on returning posthaste from Silkeborg, stopping only to awake a lawyer & hire two burly thugs to defend his rightful ownership, as Fru Krak's husband, of the property in question, & expunge Satan.

And so we did not stay to watch any further, as two monumentally big, scar-faced, stubble-jowled thugs (members of the criminal underworld, most surely, to judge by their looks!) swung their sledgehammers again, striking ever deeper into the dark oak of the front door. In that eye-blink of a moment, it became clear that there was only one course of action open to us, for we could not hold these brutish oxen off, & their destructive work might not end with the front door, but in bloodshed.

'We've got to go back to London this minute. Franz, since you are staying here, you must try to save the machine!' called Fergus as we ran down the corridor, with the young man & Josie hurtling in our wake, while Fru Schleswig rolled & pitched her way along in the rear, uttering her usual limited range of expletives. By the time we reached the basement, Professor Krak, who had sped on ahead, had already entered the machine & was preparing it for passengers.

'Right, who is leaving for London?' he cried.

'Fergus, Josie and I wish to return,' I said quickly.

'Yor not leevin me here aloan,' boomed the hippopotamic Fru Schleswig, wheezingly catching up with us. 'Do notte think u kan abandun yor pore old mutha a second tyme!'

'As you wish, Fru Schleswig,' cried Professor Krak, 'but make it snappy, for they are upon us!' (I groaned. Would I never shake this woman off?)

'But what will you do, Fred?' asked Fergus. 'Surely you can't stay here yourself?'

'Who else will guard the machine?' he replied. 'I spent years building her!'

'So build another one in London!' urged my love. 'Come along, step in quickly!' and he pushed Professor Krak through the door, & bundled the complaining Fru Schleswig after him.

'Now Franz,' called Fergus, 'you and I will fight them off for as long as we can: then I'll get inside the machine while you make your getaway through the ventilation shaft. Tell your parents some of the truth, & do your best to make sure the machine isn't destroyed. We'll be back!'

There was by now a thumping & thundering at the basement door, & the Pastor's voice boomed: 'O begone, Satan's hordes! Begone, ye foul demons of the Netherworld! For I have here Herr Bagdelsen, the best lawyer in Copenhagen, who will most rightfully attest to my wife's signature on your document being extracted under extreme duress, nay vicious torture! Ye shall have no quarter in the Lord's home, nor shall ye befoul it with thy noxious presence!'

As his speech gathers momentum, we begin to hear a louder banging at the door; hurriedly, Professor Krak pours a pinkish liquid into the quartz orb from a small vial, twiddles dials and jabs at buttons, consulting a time-sheet, a compass & a map as he does so.

'Hurry!' cries Fergus, securing the bolts. 'They're coming!'

Whereupon there is an almighty crash & the door whams open, busting the locks like matchwood. Now the two jowly men, their bodies as broad as they are tall, burst in, followed by the screeching figure of Fru Dahlberg, formerly Krak, née Bischen-Baschen, & that Servant of God, her husband, whose moment of spiritual heroism – his finest hour – has come.

Behold him, crying: 'Get thee behind me, Satan! Fie on ye, & your cursed followers likewise! Blighted are ye in the eyes of the Lord, & crushed shall ye be, as the locust is crushed beneath the rock of righteousness, & expunged for all eternity!

By now Fru Schleswig & I have squashed ourselves & Josie (whose 'wee theme park' is now a full-blown nightmare) on to the chaise-longue housed within the machine, where Professor Krak, on his knees & still wearing his wife's excruciating bath-robe, is fiddling ever more frantically with the manifold knobs of his contraption.

Yea, verily, vengeance is Pastor Dahlberg's, for the door has crashed inward & he is upon us, alongside two burly criminals who have knocked Fergus to the floor with a single blow (how I scream!), & are just preparing to heave Fru Schleswig out by the arm when –

Bing! BANG! Bong! CREAK!

Professor Krak has pulled the lever.

I scream again.

You know what happens next – for is it not the third voyage we have been on together now, you & I? So picture its mechanics, O my petal of a reader: that mighty roar, like a cracking, searing explosion, that now-familiar vivid puff of noxious light, that gasp of sulphur-gas.

WAAAAGH!

And we are reeling & gone.

I scream all the way back to London. Scream until there is no more breath in me, scream like a mad kettle, scream until I can scream no more. O woe! For just before the physics of epistemological magnetism wrenched us into flight, this is what I beheld: my precious Fergus, the love of my life, knocked sprawling to the floor by a murderous thug, a gash of crimson blood at his temple, his face dazzled by the flash, crying desperately: 'NO! NO! NO! Lottie! Josie! *Don't leave me behind!*'

Part the Fourth: Beyond Beyond

As the great poet Dante said: *Nessun maggior dolore/Che ricordarsi del tempo felice/Nella miseria!* There is no greater grief than to recall a time of happiness when in misery!

Beloved, cherished & extremely precious reader of this dog-eared, grubby journal, which at any moment risks disintegrating into a hopeless sheaf of tear-soaked jottings, the mad scrawlings of a semi-deranged woman: how I need you now! Sweet, sensitive and wise friend, help me in my hour of need, & pity my plight! O had I but known, when we embarked upon this journey together, that it would lead to such a mortifying abyss of despair, I would never have requested the pleasure of your company, for the once joyous whirligig of our adventure has now transmogrified into a veritable ghost train of grotesquerie & gloom! If ever there were a time for you to return to the municipal library, or to the bookshop where you found this sorry little tale in print, & express disgust, either by a quiet word to the librarian or asking (nay demanding!) the good man at the bookshop for your money back, then *that time has come*! Point out to those noble handlers of literature, & custodians of the written word, that there is no edification to be had in a dose of heartache, &

no bargain neither in time stolen from you thus! Do it! For your own sake!

But you are a gentle, kind one, & I know your heart is too generous for any cruelty, even to one who deserves it, & I suspect that although your resolve will begin firm, you will relent at the last moment, & instead of relieving yourself of the unwholesome burden that my confessions have become, you will find yourself forgiving their humble scribbler & instead borrow or buy yet another book, perhaps this time penned by someone more distinguished, educated & *raffiné*, & then throw a shining silver coin to the little rosy-cheeked match girl (still there, so steadfast!) on your way home. So instead I merely beg your condescension, you admirable creature – & I pray from the bottom of my heart that, should you choose to stay the course, whatever our destination be, you will remain by my side as generously, nobly & stalwartly as you have thus far, for now you are the only intimate companion in the entire universe in whom I can confide, with Fergus wrenched so cruelly from me, & Professor Krak & Fru Schleswig –

O!

Forgive me, for I must leave you for a moment, as I feel another fit of weeping coming on!

The buckets I have filled with my torrential tears, since last we met! Enough to flood the dust-plains of America & the deserts of Afric combined!

And now you, too, have a lump in your throat, you darling, sympathetic one: yes, I can sense it! Though separated physically, let our two souls now combine as one, that we may fully express our feverishly garbled emotions, & sob in one another's imaginary arms!

But hush now, for time, my increasingly bitter enemy, marches on, & we must pull ourselves together lest we fall apart entirely, & let young Josie down. So use your handkerchief, whilst I do the same, & then having excused me my moment of weakness (as I know you will, being so kind an empathizer), be patient while I reapply the full range of cosmetics, take a deep breath, & explain my new & most dreadful predicament.

It begins with a piece of heart-wrenching news, which I know will shock you to the marrow, so brace yourself for the revelation that –

I am all alone!

Alone, save for one small, five-year-old symbol of hope, namely the brave young tomboy Josie!

Yes!

And no, I cannot believe it either!

But believe it I must, & it is compulsory that you do too, for the fact is, not only are Josie & I bereft of Fergus, whom we left bloodily & heroically struggling for his survival on the floor of the Krak basement, but when we emerged from our time-travelling dizziness, the Professor had utterly vanished from the face of the earth, & Fru Schleswig along with him! Gone! Nowhere were they to be seen or found! Josie & I searched the many halls of the Greenwich Observatory high & low (I, desperately trying to make it seem merely another game of hide-and-seek for the child's sake – as if so grotesquely vast a bulk as Fru S could be secreted anywhere!), but discover them we did not, nor was there sign of them, not so much as a popped button, a whisker, an echo or a whiff. Which forced me to conclude that by some technological anomaly, our fellow-passengers had remained stuck in

Copenhagen, & that the same malfunction which flung Professor Krak to Zaragoza before New Year had once more afflicted that poor man, & done likewise to the wretched human catastrophe that is Fru Schleswig, bless her simple, vegetable soul, & stranded them in the old days, at the mercy of Fru Krak, the vengeful Pastor & their two hired thugaroos – for both were within the Time Machine when the lever was pulled: of that I would swear on my mother's life, if I had a mother. But neither were anywhere in sight when Josie & I awoke in Greenwich Observatory!

O treble woe!

And what of my current situation? I will apprise you of it swiftly, for I await the heavy footstep of my tormentor at any moment. It is now three weeks since we returned to London. I will spare you the distressing details of how Josie & I begged & cajoled our way home in our old-fashioned Danish garb, penniless, & broke into Fergus's house via the bathroom window; of the aghast & dejected reception we had from members of the Halfway Club when I informed them next morning of how our glorious mission had been so painfully & disastrously banjaxed; of the way Henrik Dogger's eyes lit up strangely when he learned that Fergus had been left behind; & of how I now actually, on occasion, find myself pining for the filthy, stinking crone that is Fru Schleswig, whom I have hitherto gone to such lengths to try & jettison! O, hark at me now: how hypocritical does my contempt of her turn out to be, how shallow the depths of my disdain! As for the fearlessly innovative & excessively brilliant Professor Krak, the man who led me to my love: how I have come to appreciate his courage, wisdom & inspiration!

But worst of all was the moment, some hours after our return, when it dawned on little Josie that her father is no longer of the world he once inhabited. How to explain to a girl of five and three-quarters that the man she knows as Dad is stranded across whole oceans of inexplicable time, when that word means nothing to her except when conjoined with another, such as 'bed', 'bath' or 'dinner'!

'Where's Dad, Lottie?' she kept asking. 'When's he coming home?'

The poor, dear little *fjord*-shrimp! Since then, it seems like every half an hour, day & night, that she has looked up at me with those sorrowful, questioning eyes. What to do then, but soothe her in my paltry English: 'Dad will come soon, *min lille skattepige*. Maybe Monday or Tuesday.' And stroke her sweet, tangle-haired head? But I know that this notion of her father's swift return is more wishful thinking than fact, & the child suspects it, & the thought of having lost our beloved man for evermore turns both our hearts to beetroot goulash. Yet I must be strong, for his child, who is a part of him & who becomes more loved & cherished by the day, with her bright little smile (now so sadly rare) & her comical way of jumping in mud-puddles, & her passion for falsified bottom-noises & gruesome grimaces. And how madly do I try & cheer her, in these miserable times: O, the handstands & cartwheels I have done! The Play-Doh dinosaurs I have shaped, the water-pistols I have filled, the gingerbread men I have manufactured, baked & burned, the bubbles I have blown, the bath-water I have sloshed, the tickling sessions I have instigated! For being the only remaining adult in Josie's much-diminished universe, apart from those three mistrustful-looking ladies in sloppy trousers who run Sunnyside Kindergarten (and perhaps there are some Scottish relatives of Fergus's? But if they appear, how to explain, for I speak no Scottish & even if I did . . . ?!), I have suddenly become – overnight – a mother. But hell's bells: what do mothers do & say? I know nothing – less than nothing – about mothering & its ways! What know I of children, except what I can remember of my own dismal childhood at the orphanage, toiling in the draughty kitchen of Fru Schleswig amid diseased rats, noxious pig-slime & green potato peelings, or taking refuge in my basement library with Baba Yaga Bonylegs? And what help was that? How to go about the task of nurturing a young life, when one has not, in reality, the foggiest clue? What mother have I ever had, save a creature who claims kinship with me, merely as a parasite claims kinship to its host? O, help me, dear one! I have never had such responsibility in my life! Never, in fact, had any responsibility at all!

But try I must, & so – much as stablemen do horses, I must muck out, exercise & feed the precious little human in my custody, & in the process create my own rituals of child-rearing – & thus it is that to the game of Crazy Frog Pillow Wars we have now added Squirt the Orange, Hunt the Toothpaste, Pick the Scab, To-Hell-With-Hairbrushing, & the Østerbro-Coquettes-Sing-You-To-Sleep, & every time I defrost & heat frozen leftovers, for every *ping* comes a pang, for it was my beloved Fergus who surely prepared this meal from his bachelor's recipe book, & a lump comes to my throat & a tear to my eye, for his spirit is with us, his little family, but his body, his flesh, his being, his self –

O!

Better to have loved & lost than never to have loved at all? O, call me a coward, but I think not.

All the sweet, tender words of Love my Fergus whispered in my ear . . . how they echo in my heart now, like lost ghosts!

He said: 'You're the love of my life, hen.' He said: 'I could drown in your eyes.' He said: 'Let's make a hundred babies, starting now.' He said: 'I love the freckles on your beautiful bottom.' And he once sung to me a beautiful song which I am sure he wrote himself, in which he insisted I must love him tender & true, & I must never let him go, because I had made his life complete and he loved me enormously, & when I feel Josie's questioning eyes settling on me in search of an explanation or an answer, I clasp her clumsily to my bosom & reassure her that all shall be well, & hope I am doing it right, my only consolation being that Josie's real mother is dead & gone, & for her therefore any mother is better than none, & this, God help me, is my humble starting-point when it comes to the upbringing & education of my lover's child. Which is just as much the upbringing & education of myself, for first of all I must become fluent in a tongue I still struggle to master, & so to this end each night when I put her to bed, I read her stories in my faulty-accented English: & thus she becomes familiar with *The Snow Queen*, & *The Ugly Duckling*, & the steadfast *Little Tin Soldier*, & *The Little Christmas Tree*, & *The Emperor's New Clothes*, & *Clumsy Hans*, & *The Princess & the Pea*, & *Thumbelina*, & *Big Claus & Little Claus*, but not *The Story of a Mother* for it is too, too sad. And though there are times when Josie cries because she misses Dad, there are times when she laughs too, & thanks to the kind intervention of Fru Jakobsen, who administers the Emergency Fund, the household bills are paid, & we are fed & clothed & furnished with a small allowance, & each morn I take Josie to kindergarten, where I have asserted to the (increasingly) sceptical ladies in sloppy trousers that I am the family's new au-pair girl, for 'Mr McCrombie, has gone away on a digging trip & I don't know when he will be back'. But they look at me reproachfully & check Josie's hair for lice & wipe the egg off her face & re-tie her laces according to their own method & ask more questions than I care to answer, & claim they cannot reach Josie's father on his phone – which is hardly a surprise, as the appliance now lives in my pocket (& O, how I have hoped against hope that he might locate the monkey Pandora's antique telephone, & ring!). Do the mistrustful ladies spot that, in my heart, I am all at sea? A sea which would be daily battered by a veritable storm, were it not for the blessed Fru Jakobsen, who fusses over us like a mother hen: how my admiration for her gracious competence & sweet, genteel nature grows hebdo-madally!

'I was just like you in the beginning,' she recalled on the second day, whilst demonstrating how Fergus's 'white goods' were to be operated. 'Quite confounded by mod-ernity, & marvelling at its ingenuity, yet critical at the same time, for do we not all come to believe that things were best "in the old days" – whenever they were? Still, *skat*, you will habituate yourself in no time. For all our complaining about this life, & our nostalgia for home, I often wonder how my husband & I will cope in the days of yore, when we return.'

There was a silence for a short while, for we both knew that it was now more 'if' than 'when'.

'We planned to settle by the sea in Gilleleje,' she sniffed, taking out her handkerchief. 'We visited it once in modern times but it is not the same, & we prefer it as it was before, even though we must cook on a wooden stove & use candle-light. Oh, Charlotte, it was just so *hyggeligt*-cosy in the old days!'

'We must get Herr Dogger working on the building of a new Time Machine,' I insisted, as Fru Jakobsen, pulling herself together, now supervised my loading of the washing machine. I poured lilac-scented powder & pearly-whirly 'fabric conditioner' into the little receptacles as instructed, & studied the controls while I continued: 'We cannot rely on Professor Krak to manage it from Copenhagen.'

She looked up sharply.

'Especially as we do not actually know that he is there,' she said.

'But —'

'Professor Krak entered the machine, did he not? Along with Fru Schleswig?'

'Yes indeed,' I answered.

'Then there is a strong chance,' she said slowly, putting a gentle hand on my arm, 'that he did not stay in Copenhagen at all, but was instead catapulted—' she lowered her voice, '*elsewhere in time & space*! I am sorry to tell you this, *min kære pige*, but I fear that Professor Krak & Fru Schleswig could be anywhere on this planet, & in Lord knows what era. The machine had been adjusted, had it not? And malfunctioned as a result?'

'But they fixed it! After Professor Krak's misadventure in Spain, they stayed up all night making sensitive adjustments to remedy the disconcerted thingummybob!'

But a chill had settled on the back of my neck, like a clammy Swarfega'd hand. I had not thought of this, but of course Fru Jakobsen was right. Professor Krak & Fru Schleswig could be anywhere on the meridian — & therefore at this very instant facing the slime-vat horrors of the Basilica of Our Lady of Pilar in Zaragoza – or dismally stranded in a warehouse full of molasses in some godforsaken Afric port, or screaming into the chilly wind on a chunk of Antarctic rock packed with squawking sea-parrots, their only missiles the very eggs that the hysterically maddened birds were protecting with their lives! I gulped.

'But in that case, it is all the more imperative that we do what we can here, lest I go mad!' I cried. 'I know Professor Krak left the plans here, & Herr Dogger is familiar with them. Meantime, Fru Jakobsen, please let us not consider the worst scenarios, for the sake of my sanity! Instead, I shall assume – nay, I *do* assume, nay I *insist on assuming* – that Professor Krak is *this very moment* (if such a thing exists in this befuddled universe) reconstructing the Time Machine in Copenhagen, & with Fergus's help, we shall all be reunited soon.' As I pressed 'Start' the washing machine's power hummed & swelled, & I felt a sudden warm surge of optimism. Yes: at the touch of a button, all would be well!

But Fru Jakobsen, folding clothes from the dryer, was not ignited by the flare of enthusiasm I had generated in myself, & instead looked all the more worried. 'My husband & I have already raised the matter of building a new Time Machine with Herr Dogger,' she said uneasily. 'And I'm afraid there are . . . awkward impediments.'

'Impediments of what nature?'

At this, she looked flummoxed, & blushed a deep scarlet. 'Well, Herr Dogger declares himself willing to construct it according to the plans, which do indeed exist (though only in partial form, he claims), but he is insisting on payment.'

'Payment?' I gasped, quite perplexed. 'Payment? After all Professor Krak has done for him, he's asking for —'

'You had better speak to him yourself,' she said, reddening further. 'For it is not a completely straightforward matter, it would seem. If it were simply a question of money, the club could raise the funds. But — well. It is . . . rather unwholesome, I fear, *min pige*. I am sure that you will be as shocked as I was by Herr Dogger's terms & conditions. I have not mentioned any of this to the club committee, and . . . well. To be frank, I am not keen to.' At which she fell into silence, & folded more clothes in a flustered fashion, while my mind turned rapidly, assessing all I had just learned. Fru Jakobsen's embarrassment hinted clearly at what Dogger meant by 'terms and conditions', for was he not a prime example of that breed of middle-aged man whose eyes cannot resist sliding greedily towards the breasts, & thence buttockwards — with a groping hand never far behind? I remembered his binoculars: it was he who had betrayed me to the club. What private intimacies had he witnessed when he spied on Fergus & myself in our stolen hours of passion — & how much had he enjoyed the view? I shuddered. So Dogger's price was sex. Something I once gave away almost for free, in days of yore, as alms to a beggar or bones to a dog — but that was before I knew the meaning of Love. Could the Charlotte of today pay such a price, now that she had learned the most vital of life's lessons? Would it lose her the one thing that mattered more than anything in the world to her, in her new existence? Would Fergus understand & forgive her, if he knew the cost of their reunion?

So join me now in my whore's garb, preparing for a session with my tormentor in an upper room of the Halfway Club, cleared for me by poor Fru Jakobsen, who still cannot hide her genteel horror at what I am prepared to do for Love and country. Out of her own ladylike decorum, she will not tell club members of the 'indignities' I face: Dogger, too, has signed the confidentiality agreement she insisted on, 'for your own sake, my dear,' she whispered to me, tears dancing in her eyes. 'I have some knowledge of legal matters & this should cover most eventualities. I will also make him agree to demonstrating steady & tangible progress on the Time Machine as he is building it, & to this end he must plan each day's work, & stick to it, & construct it on the premseis, so he can be supervised.'

The bargaining was tough, but in the end, with Fru Jakobsen acting as madam (a role she did not relish, but which she performed with much elegance, being a natural businesswoman), a settlement was hammered out: every day, with the exception of weekends, Dogger would spend six hours on the construction of the Time Machine, then share a cup of powerful Lapsang Souchong tea with Fru Jakobsen, over which he would update her on his plans & progress. After this, he would be entitled to exactly one hour (timed by Fru Jakobsen's stopwatch, & ended with a sharp toot on a profes-sional sports whistle) in my exclusive company, to use in whatever manner he wished.

As a working girl I had learned from an early age how to hide my distaste for those clients who held no physical charm, & to camouflage my amusement at those who were unwit-tingly hilarious – but as you may well imagine, sweetness, something had recently changed in me, rendering all that had gone before null & void: an internal earthquake had riven my soul apart, re-mapping my psychic contours, & (if I may abandon one family of metaphors to pursue another) the effect on my heart had been to close off certain harsh arterial routes, while letting the softer ventricles pump to a different & tender rhythm, gushing the rich blood of yearning through my whole being. Do you follow me, when I try to explain it thus? Can you begin to fathom in what subtle ways my intense feelings for Fergus had reconstituted my perception of that intimate act, which I had never before associated with Love & passion, so much as with fun (on occasion) & cash? What is more, Dogger was no ordinary client: he was the man who had taught me the full meaning of the English word 'tedium' in the classroom, & also he who had spied on my private activities & betrayed me to the club with his vile binoculars: a double villain! So now, as I enter the upstairs boudoir for the first time, I feel like a condemned prisoner bound for the scaffold, & hold but one thought in my mind: to get the wretched business over with quickly. I will close my eyes & think of Denmark.

Let us share a moment of thoughtful silence together, dear one, as we contemplate what I am about to do on the navy brushed-cotton sofa-bed made by that Swedish home-furnishing store whose full household range I have come to know so well in England! See it as a moment of mourning for an innocence long lost, then magically regained, & now about to be lost again – for no sooner have I found something that is more precious (& all the more so, for its invisibility) than diamonds & truffles conjoined, than I am about to pollute it for evermore! O, my heart is in such a state of despair that I feel close to the epicentre of madness itself! I am no expert on morality, but – well, let me ask you, my dear sugar plum, being far cleverer than I, what might *you* do, in this situation?

A foolish question, no doubt, for you would never land in such a *rémoulade*-pickle as I have. But would you – *could* you, consider handing over your lovely body (I hope that you can take a compliment!) to a lascivious tormentor, for the sake of higher things?

That, reader, is the dilemma I have faced & seemingly resolved as I await his heavy step on the stair, & the handle's turn on the door.

But O, by way of escape, let us freeze time for a moment! And in this fraction of calm before the storm, let me present you with a small poem that illustrates the dismal mood in which I find myself before my born-again virginity is defiled. A poem which I know will touch you to the core, as it has touched all Danes since the day Christian Knud Frederik Molbech penned it in his notebook. Do not be ashamed if it makes you weep, sweetest: you will not be the first, nor the last, neither! Its title is 'Rosebud', & you will quickly see why I identify with its tragic eponymous heroine.

'Ha ha!' laughed Rosebud, wild & free.
'The fountain will run full of sweet apple-juice before I blush for
    any man,
And every tree in the garden will sprout golden flowers.'
But wily Peter sat in hiding, & overheard her words.
'He who laughs last laughs loudest,' said he.
When dawn broke, he came to Rosebud.
'Come, beautiful virgin: let us stroll together.'
And so she walked with him, straight into the maw of Fate.
For there in the herb-garden, he'd hung golden rings from every
    tree.

And there in the flowered spring, dyed the waters yellow as
    apple-juice.
And Rosebud blushed deep as blood, & stared numbly at her feet.
Peter greedily kissed her lips. 'He who laughs last laughs loudest,'
    smiled he.

O, how I shudder for little Rosebud when I recall these verses, which I have translated for you here with the greatest accuracy I can muster! And how I know her pain – for can you see how similar we are? And is the wily Peter not cast from the same ugly & predatory mould as Herr Dogger? Rosebud & I – both tricked into trickery by a trickster!

Woe, woe, woe!

Bang, bang, bang. He approacheth! Tremble for me, dear one! O, you cannot know how much it means to me to know you are at my side, come Hell or high water!

And so like Bluebeard, the leering, white-bearded Dogger enters, red-faced & all a-grunt from his exertions on the stairs, bringing with him a whiff of Lapsang Souchong & an odd chemical I cannot identify.

'A deal's a deal, little girl,' he smiles, baring teeth stained with tobacco. Upon which, slowly, with the methodicalness of an executioner, he lowers his Marks & Spencer trouserware, shuffles off his greyish underpants, & bares the flaccid sausage that hangs sorrowfully between his meaty, hairy thighs.

'Meet the boss. Say hello to Big Chief Bongo,' he grins.

Weakly, feeling vomitatious, I nod my appalled greeting.

'Now pay attention, little girl, while I instruct you as to his requirements. The Big Chief is very particular, & I expect you to have learnt his ways thoroughly by the end of the lesson.'

The time had come. I draw a brief veil.

But just as in the poem, he who laughs last, laughs loudest. For now let me whip back that veil I drew a moment ago, & inform you that in the space of five minutes' huffing & puffing, Big Chief Bongo & the man attached to him have delivered me a most unexpected & happy surprise! Yes! For tra-la-la & hallelujah! Jingle bells, jingle bells, jingle all the way! I am saved by a single word, which you can look up in the dictionary, as I have done, under the letter I. You will find it somewhere between 'importune' and 'impostor'.

Have you found it yet? Well, hurry, we haven't got all day! In fact, we only have an hour – which, as we are about to discover, isn't long enough for anything. Especially if you are afflicted by –

IMPOTENCE!

Yes; Big Chief Bongo's stubborn recalcitrance soon renders my duties much less revolting & burdensome than I feared, & they even, as the days pass, become the source of some gaiety. Watch: this will be a typical session, I assure you – for apart from the costumes, there is little variety. Dogger is a man of fantasies, but limited imagination. A creature of high ambition, but negligible prowess, for praise be, it seems he is allergic to that so-called miracle drug Viagra &, much to his distress, can only maintain the feeblest of erections when visually stimulated, reaching a mere 'Niveau Un' of the would-be *Tour Eiffel* that is his member. As you may imagine, this news reassures Fru Jakobsen mightily, & she feels instantly less guilty: all the more so when I confide to her that I was actually a whore in my previous existence – information I have kept from her out of respect for her delicacy (I assure you), rather than shame at my past. And that resourceful woman in turn confides in me that she has been lacing Dogger's Lapsang Souchong with a chemical called bromide, known to have a dampening effect on the male libido.

But hark! He knocketh. Watch, sweet one, as I assume the role Dogger has assigned today with a languid, 'Come in, you naughty boy.' He enters, his piggy eyes aglint, fingers already unclasping the belt that holds his paunch in place. 'Is that a gun in your pocket, or are you just pleased to see me?' I quip in English, as American as I can make it, for today I am Mae West, of whom I had never heard until yesterday when he made his demand (the oilskin-clad Eskimo Girl having failed to adequately stimulate the Big Chief, he was after more regular fare), upon which Fru Jakobsen looked the woman up on Google & noted down some famous lines, before heading for Malarkey's Costumes on the high street, whose most regular clients we have suddenly become.

'Huhh,' he grunted. 'Sexy Hollywood star.'

Our encounters follow a pattern. Some men favour a girl's impressively upholstered upper chest, while others will naturally gravitate to the twin peaches of her bottom; some declare themselves Leg Men who eloquently fetishize the well-turned ankle, the smooth calves, or the 'nice hunk of thigh-meat' one might be endowed with, if one were me. Others, of a more risqué disposition, prefer to cut direct to the chase, savouring the most intimate flesh above all, like specialists of wine or cheese: connoisseurs who can spend hours describing textures, scents & flavours. What Dogger's predilections were in this matter I never discovered, for he grunted rather than spoke, & was a watcher rather than a doer: indeed, his new-found intimate shame prevented him from touching anything other than his own member, aka Big Chief Bongo, to my great relief. In order to speed up his self-stimulations to the maximum (which as you can guess, dear one, was very much my goal – for as much as he liked to gawp, did I prefer to turn my eyes inward), it was vital that I come over most coquettish, & awaken his fantasies.

But thanks to my costumed endeavours, the Time Machine now comes along apace, its building much speeded by the surveillance of Herr & Fru Jakobsen, those two grim custodians of hope, who supervise Dogger most unrelentingly as he works, determined that he should not slack. Insisting that whatever materials he should require, they shall supply themselves, they have ensured that he does not leave the premises, & he grumbles that he is being kept a virtual prisoner. Ha!

But yet, the faster the contraption approaches completion, the more I smell a rat in the world of the Halfway Club, but figure out what form it takes, & where it is hiding, I cannot. Even when I clap eyes on the modern version of the Time Machine that Dogger has constructed, combining (as Herr Jakobsen demonstrates) antique & modern methods & materials, & thereby securing a marriage made in technological Heaven – nay, even when I clap eyes on that, down in the community hall of the Halfway Club, where it stands, almost complete, squatly in the centre of the room, a great gleaming box with a little door of wood & glass, an unquiet murmur swells inside me, whispering: hold your horses, Charlotte-*pige*, for *something is askew*.

'Come in, you naughty boy!'

And how do I know this, in my bones? Not least because Dogger, the architect of this creation, has been acting oddly of late: he has been going through a curiously babyish phase, featuring much dog-like whimpering, & a regular demand to be slapped & spanked – the one chore which (as you may imagine) is among the few I relish, & indeed perform with alacrity, to the point of not having to be asked. But soon even the welcome infliction of much-deserved physical pain on my tormentor begins to wear thin on me, for I have dressed as a Sexy Strict Nurse for five days in a row now, & administered more 'nasty medicine', & applied more unappealing suppository treatments than I care to mention: even sadism has its limits, I find, when the torture is welcome. Yes: something is rotten in the state of Denmark-upon-Thames, & it niggles at me mightily that I cannot identify it, for the great unveiling is nigh.

And indeed, upon us. O, we Danes do love a party! We have all dressed in our finest clothes (I in my Tin City garb) for the occasion, which begins with a bubble of greetings & the consumption of fancy *pålæg* and schnapps as the Poulsen family, the Rosenvinges, Max Kong, Rigmor Schwarb, Ida Sick, the Jakobsens, & many more queue up to investigate the new Time Machine. Murmuringly, we all take turns to enter its skimpy door, & on doing so note the modernizations in its interior, where a white plastic garden bench has replaced the velvet chaise-longue, the original quartz tubes & orb are reborn in transparent Plexiglas, the clocks tick digitally, & the starting lever resembles the hand-brake of a car. Disappointed though some members of the Halfway Club may be with the functional appearance of the new machine, this is a minor matter, given the achievement of its existence, so *skål, alle sammen*! With a patriotic cheer, our red & white flag is hoisted at full mast atop the building's flagpole, & we all cry *hurra, hurra, hurra!* for king & country, even though there is now technically speaking a queen, & the size of the Danish territory has both shrunk & swollen like a dieting girl since we last lived there, since (as I learned in one of Dogger's excruciating history lessons) Denmark sold its Caribbean islands to the United States for cash, gulped back a piece of Sønderjylland as if to compensate, but then relinquished the whole of Iceland.

The schnapps having done its work & warmed the hearts of all, Herr Jakobsen, who has appointed himself Master of Ceremonies, takes to the makeshift orange-crate podium & announces that 'a new era of hope' has dawned since the distressing disappearance of our leader, Professor Krak, into the greedy stomach of time. 'Although we shall never abandon our faith that Professor Krak will one day be amongst us again, in this place & era, in the meantime we have resolved to keep the spirit of his enterprise alive, & to this end have asked the distinguished time expert & seasoned time-traveller Herr Dogger to reconstruct the original, by which means any of us who care to return to our beloved homeland can do so, just as Herr Krak hoped that we should, were that to be our wish.'

Fru Jakobsen, sitting next to me, shed a small tear which she dabbed at discreetly with her pocket handkerchief; I squeezed her arm, and whispered, 'Coming soon – Gilleleje in the springtime!' & she smiled & blinked. Meanwhile her husband continued by telling us that while Herr Dogger had been at work, he himself had not been idle. 'Since time-travel requires careful geographical planning, with regard (in this country) to the harmonization & conjunctification of both meridian and (at the receiving end, as it were) the Time-Sucker in Østerbro, I ascertained that there is indeed a suitable temporary parking-place for the machine in the grounds of the Greenwich Observatory. Herr Dogger has himself inspected the site, & has constructed an outer casing for the Time Machine, which will disguise it as an exterior prefabrication known as a Portakabin – several of which are already standing in the park in anticipation of an outdoor concert there next month. Closed to the public by a strong lock, we believe our disguised machine can sit unremarked for as long as three weeks, before anybody notices the extra facility amidst a cluster of twenty such temporary structures, which includes movable toilets known as Portaloos.'

There were murmurs of impressed approval, & Herr Jakobsen flushed with pride at his ingenuity. Herr Dogger, meanwhile, was looking most odd – on the one hand prodigously puffed-up, & on the other distinctly nervous. 'When any members of the community express the wish to undertake the (admittedly perilous) journey back to Copenhagen, as I know Charlotte here plans to do shortly, as do my wife and I, then Herr Arnbach's haulage firm will transport the machine to Greenwich Park, & return it here once it has served its purpose on the meridian. There will be room for three more passengers on the maiden voyage, but we can make a second and a third on the same day, if the first is successful. I have a book here, in which all who are keen to travel can sign their names. But I must warn you, you must see it as an irreversible decision, for we cannot guarantee any return journeys in the immediate future, the original machine having most probably been destroyed.'

There was a murmur of nervous excitement, mixed with alarm. 'But first, let me hand you over to Herr Dogger, who has agreed to say a few words to all of you about his remarkable achievement, for which we as a community are all immensely grateful, are we not?'

At which an enthusiastic cheer of approval goes up. Blessed are the pompous: he is dressed like a dog's dinner in a brown three-piece suit, & on the podium he stands rocking on his heels, as though counting the size of his captive audience. His moment has come. ('A few words'? Shall we take bets?)

'*Mine damer og herrer,*' he begins, lugubriously as a bull munching on its cud. 'It is my profound pleasure & indeed honour to be here today, at the culmination of the lengthy project I have undertaken . . .' Blah blah blah. I reach for my dictionary. Learning new English words is a habit I began when I was trying to impress Fergus, but which I have not dropped, firstly because I wish to continue impressing him, if we can but be together again, & second because how better to spend a few idle minutes (or in the present case, a good half-hour) than in the enlargement of one's vocabulary?

'Meridianic principles . . .' he is saying. 'Now known as "worm-hole" theory . . . special kind of leather to supplement the . . . delicate calibrations, whereby the merest millimetre can make a difference of twenty years or more . . . complex mathematical equations . . .' I acquaint myself with the words 'labial', 'laborious' 'Labrador', & 'laburnum', & it is just as I am investigating *lachrymose* that I sense a rustle around me – a change of mood in the audience, a restlessness – confirmed immediately by a nudge from Fru Jakobsen. I look up from my dictionary: her face is anxious, her hand raised in the air.

'I must interrupt you there, Herr Dogger,' she says sharply, '& ask you to repeat that last part, please. I am not sure we have understood.' She looks alarmed: glancing about me, it seems that she is not alone. People are shifting in their seats, & a murmur has set up. What have I missed?

'Yes,' comes another voice. 'We'd like to hear that bit again. About the catalysing liquid.'

At which my heart suddenly sets a-banging. *Catalysing liquid.* That phrase seems uncannily familiar: now where have I heard it before? Or *over* heard it? Yes! Once, in one of many dull technical discussions in Copenhagen, did Professor Krak not mention a —

'Yes. Of course,' says Herr Dogger, clearing his throat. His posture seems to change, & he wipes the side of his face with a handkerchief then clears his throat again. Do you recall that rat I smelled earlier, dear one? Well, now I smell it again, & its stench is more potent than ever! 'As I said just now, the, er, four *ingredients* of the catalysing liquid remain a, er . . .' says Herr Dogger. 'Shall we say that, er, in conclusion, Professor Krak entrusted me with the plans to make the machine, but he vowed he would never reveal the four components of the catalyser. It was a means of, er, ensuring that um . . . no one but he . . .'

All hell breaks loose. Fru Jakobsen leaps to her feet. 'And you *knew this all along*? That the machine you have made could never be activated? Herr Dogger, you led us to believe you could provide a fully operational replica of the Time Machine, not some . . . toy!' she cries, with unmistakable desperation in her voice. 'Explain yourself, please!'

A rumble in the audience turns swiftly to a roar. I feel myself go pale, & then hot, & then weak at the knees, & then a tidal wave of fury rises up in my heart. Betrayal! I charge forward towards the stage.

'Yes, Dogger, explain yourself!', I yell, grabbing him by the arm.

'Hit him!' calls a teenage voice from the audience (it is young Mattias Rosenvinge). 'You know you want to!'

Thus prompted, I slap Dogger hard on the face. This is met by a rousing cheer from the audience – to whom I now explain in explicit & shocking detail the price I have paid for us all to be so monstrously & unfairly fooled. It does not take long to acquaint the members of the Halfway Club with Dogger's sexual incapacities & creepy predilections. Parents cover the ears of their children as I expose the role that the Eastern Princess, the Nympho Nun & the lustful dildo-wielding monarch Margrethe have played in the construction of the Time Machine. But for all the jeering & indignation, there is rampaging anger too. 'So Henrik Dogger here has not only used & betrayed me,' I finish. 'He has abused the trust of every one of us here.'

'Hit him again!' calls the teenager. So I oblige, making Dogger reel back, clutching his cheek.

'I completed my part of the bargain!' Dogger protests above the fury of the throng. 'It was a fair deal!' But his shameful response is met with howls and boos, & as one, with a scrape & clatter of chairs, the members of the Halfway Club rise up & hound Herr Dogger from the hall: the Jespersens unleash their mangy mastiff Bullet on him, who bites him hard on the leg just as he reaches the door, & Mattias Rosenvinge & the Jørgensen twins pelt him with eggs from the fridge.

The last we see of him is as a limping silhouette headed for the Crown & Thistle pub on the corner of Carnegie Street.

*   *   *

But where to now? Where to indeed, when one's heart is dripping blood? What words to describe the bleakness of what faced me, now that all hope was dashed!

Love does not lie & nor does it die, when it is strong. But the world can smash to smithereens around it, & that is what happened then. And that night in the lonesomeness of Fergus's half-occupied double bed you yearn for your Copenhagen days – oh those days of innocence & cold – but instead, on the sweaty pillow, you find yourself nightmarishly alone in the Milkmaid's Uniform (complete with cowbell) thrust on you by your repugnant tormentor, your face streaked with tears, the love of your life lost to you for ever, & suddenly it is unbearable, quite unbearable, & in your garbled hallucinatory thoughts you follow the satanic fumes & speed wildly in the direction of Fru Schleswig (also gone for ever! Who would have thought that you could miss the ancient one so greatly? Indeed at all?) & you hurtle heedless & headlong to the warmth of her fat imaginary embrace & bury your head in her colossal bosom & weep, & you hear her murmur, 'Ther ther chylde. Ther ther, my littel Charlot. Ther ther my babby gurl. Ther ther,' & for the first time in your entire life you find yourself suddenly wide awake, screaming to the skies: 'O Mother, Mother! *Help!* MOTHER!'

'Did Professor Krak have travel documents forged for me?' I enquire the next morning.

'Yes, I believe my husband Georg got you a passport – along with all your other British paperwork.'

'Then we are leaving the country.'

'What?'

'Yes, Fru Jakobsen. You and I are going to visit modern Denmark. I have a plan.'

My one concern was Josie. I could not take her, for after turning the house upside-down in search of documentation, I discovered that she could travel abroad in the company of no one but Fergus. O woe: it seemed there was nothing for it but to leave the child in the care of the Halfway Club for the weekend, supervised by the snake-tattooed Rigmor Schwarb, who claimed to be 'good with children' despite having abandoned her own baby on the doorstep of a charity shop when she first arrived in London, & never seen it since!

When the time came to bid Josie goodbye the child looked anxious, nay alarmed, & I could immediately picture her thoughts: her father had disappeared; might I, her new step-mother, be about to do the same? Poor little mite! So I promised her I would come back for her, no matter what, for I was going to 'the wee theme park to look for Dad', but I would go there by proper flying-machine, & I would be gone no more than a single night, & what's more, Rigmor had offered to take her bowling, & she would have tremendous fun, & I gave her a big bag of liquorice sweets & at this she perked up, & Fru Jakobsen & I left for the airport feeling lighter, but still full of trepidation, for there was nothing to indicate this venture – conceived in desperation in the wake of Dogger's revelation – was anything other than the most doomed of wild-goose chases.

I have only a blurred memory of the airport: suffice it to say that after we had checked in (a fraught process, to my mind, but Fru Jakobsen handled it with serenity, having been through the hullabaloo before), we loaded our hand-luggage on to a moving belt of indiarubber, & watched it disappear into a small cupboard. It was only when my handbag emerged the other side that we became aware of a tinny blast of music emanating from it.

'Quick! The mobile phone!' Fru Jakobsen cried, grabbing it from my bag & pressing a button, then clamping the thing to my ear whereupon I was greeted with much crackling & interference. Good Lord, who might it be? Not the sloppy-trousered ones, at least, for I recognized their number by now & did not see it (nor indeed anybody else's) featuring on the telephone's little screen. 'Anonymous caller', it proclaimed instead.

'Hello?' I ventured. Again, the line crackled madly with interference, & I was just about to give up when –

'Iz that u, gurl?' came a loud voice. 'Cum on, speek up!'

'Fru Schleswig!' I cried. She had heard the cry of my heart after all! Telepathy! O, never had I been so delighted to hear that voice! I could have wept with relief. 'Fru Schleswig, where are you?'

Fru Schleswig thought for a moment: the line crackled more. 'Anutha place & tyme.'

'Where? When? Are you all right?'

'I am verrie well, in fact I hav got marreyed to the Sultan & I am kween of Marokwinter.'

'WHAT?' (Marroquinta?! That Afric isle now sunk beneath the waves?)

'An I got the vakume cleener here & I hav made a waye of uzin it for fermentin cokernuts for wyne, & it lives in a tempel & we all wurships it in a speshal shryne!'

Good grief! I relayed this to Fru Jakobsen & we both burst into almost hysterical laughter – a mixture of relief &

incredulity, first that Fru S was still alive, & second that she had seemingly landed on her feet, & got herself hitched to a sultan, to boot! 'What extraordinary & unexpected news!' I cried. 'Congratulations, Fru Schleswig, or should I say *Queen* Schleswig, on your happiness, & that of your vacuum cleaner – I salute you both!' The line crackled more, which brought me to my senses, for all of a sudden I realized we might at any moment be disconnected. 'But what of Professor Krak?' I asked urgently. 'Is he with you? I must speak with him!'

'Wel he iz here in a manna of speekin,' replied Fru Schleswig lethargically. 'But fakt iz, he iz at deth's dor, with feever. He said I shud trie & ring u, we iz uzin electrixitie charged up from a sweet potatoe, wot he rigged uppe with wyre & wotnotte. But power duz notte werk too wel so we hav not got much tyme. He sez to say we ar bothe alyve. But there woz a smorl erthkwayke so itz dun summink to the Tyme-Sukker, he sez, itz frakchered the connekshun, & he can notte fixxe it coz he haz this dizeez, probly *malareah*.'

'Let me speak to him!'

'Orlroit,' she mumbled, 'but u wont get much sence out of him. He iz ramblin & geezerin all sortsa nonsens. Havin nitemares & wotnotte, & blatherin bout the Tyme Masheen, wot I carnt make hedde or tayle of.' Upon which there came much crash-banging, & footsteps, & then the faint sound of muffled & rasping breathing.

'Professor Krak?' I cried. The line crackled alarmingly.

'Charlotte?' came the faint but unmistakable voice of Frederik Krak. Fru Jakobsen & I had by now found ourselves seating & she rammed her head next to mine, that we might both catch what he said.

'Professor Krak! O, Professor Krak, how we all miss you!'

'And how we now pray that you may recover, dear sir!' chimed in Fru Jakobsen.

In reply there came a faint groan. Sensing that we might be cut off at any moment, I begged Professor Krak to listen to me most urgently, & quickly apprised him of our predicament: that Fergus was stranded in Østerbro, that Josie & I were in London, that Dogger had reconstructed the machine, but we lacked the four catalysing ingredients to operate it.

In reply came another groan, most ghostly-weak, & then Professor Krak spoke. It was almost a whisper: I had to strain to hear. 'I swore I would tell no one.' He spoke liltingly, as though in a dream. 'It shall go with me to the grave.'

'But you *must* tell!' I insisted, now quite alarmed. 'You must, sir, or my life is undone! Not just my life, but many others! Your flock, Professor Krak! Think of your flock!'

'Undone,' he repeated, still seemingly in another world. 'Said I would not. To the grave. The only one. Me. Fred-Olaf Krak. Not Hawking, not Gott.' It seemed that in his fever, he was indeed hallucinating, as Fru Schleswig had said. There was nothing to do but listen. 'What they don't know is how close to the heart it all is.'

'Who don't know?'

'The others looking for the secret. Of time.'

'Close to the heart?'

'Time-travel . . . belongs in the heart. In the muscles. In the sinews. The secret is inside. The secret is pain. Exact quantities of pain. Two millilitres of each. At room temperature.'

'Pain? How can pain be a secret?'

'The three products of pain.'

'Pain?'

'You know pain. We all know pain. Human pain.'

'The three products of –' I gestured to Fru Jakobsen to make a note & she busied herself finding a pen.

'How much did you say?'

'Two millilitres is enough. Of each. Then mix with –'

He broke off, groaning. It seemed that all his talk of pain had triggered another spasm of his own agony.

'Please, Professor Krak! Speak!'

'Mix with ten parts – I am talking here of twenty millilitres, no more – of the –'

'The what?'

'The great . . .' He spoke English now: he was clearly beyond hope. 'The great –'

'Yes?'

'Human . . .' (English again. O, that he had forgot his own tongue meant that he was surely lost to us now!)

'The great human what, pray, sir? The great human *what*?' By now I was perspiring with stress. 'I beg you –'

'The great human ant—' But we were interrupted by a huge crackle on the line that broke up his voice into shards.

'Professor Krak!' I cried, when the crackle had stopped. 'You must repeat that, I did not hear it –'

'So my dear,' came his voice, most faint, but now at least he was speaking Danish again. 'I had not planned to tell you. Nay. Had not . . . but the secret of the machine is yours.'

'But I did not catch –'

'Take good care of it. You may never see me or your mother again, dear Charlotte.'

'But Professor Krak –'

'Now all the time-travellers of the world, all my pioneers, are counting on you to save our community!'

'But Professor Krak, you did not finish, or at least I did not hear the last ingred—'

But the line had gone stone dead.

'Hardly surprising,' said Fru Jakobsen, 'if all that powered the telephone was a yam. You won't get much wattage that way. It's a miracle they got through at all.'

By now we were in the departure lounge. Fru Jakobsen & I quickly agreed that given the garbled nature of what Professor Krak had divulged, it would be foolish to cancel our trip in the hope that sense would emerge from it, so we went through his words again & again, but, like a persistent fog, our bafflement would not lift. What on earth did he mean by 'the three products of pain', mixed with 'the great human something-beginning-with *ant*' that is probably an English word? Lord, our lives & happiness were at stake: fever or no fever, how dare the man speak to us in riddles! We phoned Fru Jakobsen's husband & relayed to him what we had learned: Georg said that he would call an emergency meeting at the Halfway Club to share the news, & see what the others made of Professor Krak's fever-garbled utterings – including Dogger, who might yet redeem himself. 'Georg says this all reminds him of a book he once read about a murder in the Louvre,' said Fru Jakobsen. 'Everything was a conundrum, & as soon as the hero had cracked one set of riddle-me-rees, up popped another; it went on & on apparently but you couldn't put it down because it was all about Jesus having sexual congress & squiring progeniture.'

The dry, expensive 'tapas', the foul coffee, the punishing seating, the laconic drone of Captain Morten Skagerak over the loudspeaker with information about how many metres we would hurtle deathwards from the sky if the flying-machine exploded in thin air & we were left clutching an inflatable orange life-vest & tooting pitifully on a plastic whistle: you know the routine of air travel better than I, dear one, so I will spare you the gory details of our journey, including the ingenious & original way in which Fru Jakobsen & I disposed of my sick-bag as we bore north over Amsterdam. Suffice it to say that within four hours of leaving home we were back in Denmark – though so changed it was, we might as well have landed on the moon! How flat & pallid had my homeland become, in the hundred-odd years since I last was there! How neat, clean & dull its lines, how horribly discreet its architecture, how plain its bicycles, how disconcertingly fair-haired all its women, as though an invisible celestial hair-dresser had poured a giant bottle of bleach over the whole population, but somehow missed most of the men, & some of the women's partings – & how militantly white-skinned & homogeneous everyone, after the colour & variety of exotic London! We sped through the city: though much changed, it still had some buildings intact, thank the Lord, such as Parliament & Amalienborg & the Royal Theatre on Kongens Nytor – but my, how baffling & amusing to see, everywhere in the streets, men doing the work of women, pushing perambulators & wielding heavy bags of groceries! Good Lord, if someone had told me there & then that this new breed of Danish man (so different from any I had known) could also clean & cook, in addition to (here I presumed, though maybe I was wrong) providing for his family, I swear I might almost have believed them!

*   *   *

Our taxi driver was a genial fellow, but the journey of discovery I made in his car left me fair reeling with shock at the unaesthetic nature of the 'progress' Denmark had made since last she was mine. However Østerbro proved easy enough to recognize, which gave me some solace: though the trams had gone, & the little fishermen's huts on Sortedams Lake, the swans were still there, & other birds, among them cormorants, & the sun still dazzled welcomingly on the water's surface, & – the Devil's knickerbockers! – how the once dolly-sized trees along the lake's bank had grown into hefty, flourishing specimens! Østerbrogade itself was a grey sweep of motorized vehicles & huge swarms of cyclists, male & female, with such serious expressions on their faces that you might think they were contemplating suicide, which perhaps indeed they were, & who could blame them, living in such a drab world where (according to Fru Jakobsen) they paid such monstrously high taxes, &, when crossing the road, such slavish heed to the green man? A world in which Else's once-glorious flower boutique was now part of a small supermarket, & Herr Bang's pharmacy on Trianglen a video rental store, & Herr Møller's bakery on Classensgade a 'feng shui consultancy'.

On the Internet, Fru Jakobsen had located private rooms available for Cheap Weekend Breaks on Holsteinsgade, just a few streets from the cold attic where Fru Schleswig & I once resided. 'I thought you'd like to reminisce a bit,' explained Fru Jakobsen – who probably meant it kindly: for being firmly of the belief that it is rude to dampen the spirits of others unduly, I had painted her a series of amusing vignettes which made my former life as a whore look like a most agreeable & fancy picnic.

Having paid off the taxi & deposited our belongings on the twin beds of our small, neat but bare apartment (among them my trusty dictionary, & my photograph of Fergus & Josie taken on their last 'dig', both of them buried deep in archaeological mud), I steered Fru Jakobsen – a native of Hellerup & therefore alien to this quarter – to our first port of call, a location I insisted on visiting for curiosity's sake, which was but five minutes' walk from our lodgings. Rosenvængets Allé, I was much relieved to see, had changed little in a hundred-odd years, apart from the Krak mansion itself, which had quite transmogrified: now it appeared much lighter & altogether happier in colour & appearance, & consequently less doom-laden than of yore: the creeping variegated ivy & the tall fir trees that had once fringed its parameters like prison guards had vanished, & the creaking Baba Yaga Bonylegs gate was 'a thing of the past', as the English expression goes. From the upstairs window from which Fergus & I had spied Fru Krak's two thugaroos smashing their way in came the soft thud of modern music (how contemporaneans do love their drums!), & the dark oakwood door that they had destroyed was now replaced by a new version in amnesiac white; indeed, it was as though the whole house had forgotten its former self, & those of us who had once peopled it. How thoughtless of it! A little shiver ran through me as I saw how the passage of the years erases all trace. O, how I prayed that there would nevertheless be something left of olden times, that might help us!

Having absorbed the view for a few moments, & reflected thus upon the fickle nature of time, we now set off in separate directions. Fru Jakobsen's mission, at the Municipal Library & the Public Records Office, was to investigate the property history of the Krak mansion, for clues as to what the future held, & more importantly to discover whether the records showed that a Scot by the name of Fergus McCrombie had wed (this did not bear thinking about, unless it was to me!) or died (also unbearable!) in Copenhagen, & a Charlotte Dagmar Marie Schleswig likewise – though the idea of hearing of my own death caused me to feel as though a goose was stomping across my grave. I, meanwhile, followed the trail of the Poppersen Muhl clan, which led me first to Sortedams Lake, & to the grandiose building overlooking it, that housed the huge apartment Franz's family had once inhabited. Here, luck was mine, for the first thing I spied upon the wall was a blue plaque which declared: *Franz Poppersen Muhl, inventor of the first Danish dust-sucker, lived here between 1880 & 1899.*

Hurra! So the fragile-spirited but determined young Franz had realized his dream after all: how gratifying, amusing & vindicatory all at once, that he had thus disproved the Professor's theory of 'Epistemological Impossibility'! But the dates upon the plaque puzzled me, for if they were to be believed, it seemed that Franz had quit his parents for a second time at the tender age of nineteen, only two years after his return. What circumstances can have conspired to prompt his departure, & whither might he have gone? Hoping that the answer might lie within, I studied the names next to the front door, but finding no Poppersen Muhl among them, I rang the bell of a random dweller of the fourth floor, which is where I recalled Franz's family having lived, & was presently summoned by a buzzer. On reaching the landing, it was clear at once that the original Poppersen Muhl premises (which Fergus had told me about in much detail, for he had been impressed by its grandeur) had been divided into four smaller, more shrunken dwellings. From one of the doors now came a fumbling noise, & some infant cries, & the murmur of a male voice, & finally it was flung open to reveal a youngish man with long hair in a ponytail & sporting a little goatee beard, who struggled in the door-frame to greet me amid much hubbub, for he bore a half-naked, identical baby in each arm, like two wriggling parcels, & was simultaneously attempting to open a package of disposable nappies with his teeth, with a telephone clamped between chin & shoulder. Seeing his plight, I wordlessly took the nappy-parcel from him & tore along the dotted line, while he said into the telephone, 'Tuesday five o' clock for their inoculations, then, thanks, no problem,' & finished the call looking most relieved, saying: 'You must be Gitte? With the prison canteen drawings & the surveyor's calculations?'

Deciding not to disabuse him of this notion until I was well inside the door, I followed him into a large parlour where he waved me towards a chair. Plonking the writhing twins unceremoniously on the sofa, he then pulled two nappies from the pack which the girls grabbed & clutched at, gurgling.

'Good sir, might I suggest that I be of assistance here?' I offered. 'Perhaps if I were to deal with one, & you the other, we should complete the task more promptly, for I had hoped for some discourse on a matter of concern to me.' He grunted his accord, & then, having not the faintest clue how to set about such a challenge, I observed & imitated his deft actions, & it was whilst we were thus occupied applying absorbent padding to the girls' roly-poly behinds that I told him I was not in actual fact Gitte, bearing drawings or calculations, but Charlotte, a researcher specializing in Domestic History with a particular emphasis on household cleaning, & might he have any inkling of what befell Franz Poppersen Muhl, who once lived here in the dim & distant past? At which he looked blank for a moment ('sorry, baby brain!'), & then said, 'You mean the dust-sucker guy?'

'Yes indeed,' I said. 'He whose name features on the plaque affixed outside.'

He looked at me most curiously. 'Can I ask where you're from, Charlotte? Because if you'll forgive me for saying so, your Danish sounds like it's straight out of a costume drama.'

'I hail from the Faroe Islands,' I said quickly. 'Where one of the things we like to stand on, apart from ice floes' (I was inventing frantically here) 'is ceremony. Now, good sir, please be kind enough to tell me what you know.'

'Well, the family were here for generations,' said the young man. 'I know because it was a great-great-grand-niece of the Poppersen Muhls who sold me this apartment ten years ago: she wanted to flog a lot of furniture as well but it was all very *ancien régime*: as you can see I'm much more into classical contemporary.' I glanced around briefly but frankly saw not a great deal save some bare white walls, a pot-plant, a feature-less red plastic chair, & a bleached ashwood table with a white, hedgehoggy-looking lamp suspended above it: I tried to look impressed nonetheless. 'Anyway, I can give you Fru Boisengluk's contact number, if you want,' he said. 'She might be able to put you on the right track.'

When we had finished dressing the little girls in their ornamental leggings, the man copied Lone Boisengluk's number from a notebook on to his business card (it seemed he was an accredited architect, as well as a busy father!) & I thanked him most profusely, & said I must go, & he said it was a pleasure to meet a Faroe Islander, he had no idea we were so

252

different, & he must leave too, as soon as he had e-mailed some plans to a client: he needed to shop for dinner, because his wife always expected a hot meal ready on the table when she returned.

'From work?' I asked, intrigued by this small insight into the daily life of future Denmark.

'No, it's more like a three-year part-time course in self-realization,' he said, dismally. I had heard of 'courses' in England, but never quite understood what they were for, save that women of the future hanker after them a great deal. Perhaps he saw my sympathy, for he said loyally as we shook hands: 'Vera's a busy woman. It's a huge responsibility, sharing the emotional burdens of others, & helping them take control of their lives & feelings.' But he looked oddly bemused at what had just emerged from his mouth. 'Have a good day now,' he said as I was leaving. 'You deserve it!'

Deserve it? 'Do I?' I asked, surprised.

'Of course!' he smiled encouragingly. 'You can achieve whatever you want to achieve! You've spent too long looking after other people's needs, and ignoring your own! Go for it!'

Most puzzling.

Back at our lodgings on Holsteinsgade, I telephoned Lone Boisengluk, who was more than happy to talk about her distinguished Poppersen Muhl heritage.

'My family can trace its roots back to Gorm den Gamle,' she said in a voice that made me wonder whether she might have some Bischen-Baschen ancestry. 'Is there a particular aspect of the blood-line you're exploring?'

'It's actually *Franz* I am most fascinated by,' I said, when she had finished reeling off a list of Poppersen Muhls who had dined with this or that king, princess or count, & bequeathed this or that flattering observation about them to 'the interested historian'. But at my mention of Franz there came a sudden irritated sigh from Fru Boisengluk, after which I sensed a change of atmosphere at the end of the line. 'Franz, the illustrious inventor of the dust-sucker?' I prompted.

'The *least* impressive member of the family,' she countered quickly. 'Yes: Great-great-uncle Franz, a pitiful character. The dust-sucker was his one claim to fame, but it was soon superseded by an American model.' The way she said it – for there was clear contempt in her voice – made me feel most hotly indignant on Franz's behalf: good grief, what other 'claim to fame' did anyone in this family have, apart from the fact that they had licked aristocratic arses down the genera-tions, with no sense of shame, & had chronic delusions of grandeur? None that I could see!

'And what happened to Franz, pray, madam?' I asked, attempting to put the question in a light tone that disguised my intense interest, nay anxiety: for the fact was that if Fru Boisengluk were to inform me that poor Franz had hanged himself, I would be in for a right awful shock, & was at that very moment bracing myself for the worst of tidings.

'Well, he ended up at the Sankt Hans, as you probably know,' she said sniffily.

'The Sankt Hans?' I queried, aghast. 'Are you quite sure?'

'Yes. So if you're really as "fascinated" as you claim, then that's the place to go. I have plenty of photo albums – but Franz won't be in any of them, I can assure you: he was very much the black sheep. I've also all the heirlooms & antiques, of course,' she added smugly, 'if you're interested in that side of things. You're not a dealer, by any chance? I have a

Louis Quinze dressing table that has featured in *Heritage Interiors*.'

I said goodbye as swiftly as I could after that, for the news that Franz Poppersen Muhl had been sent to the Sankt Hans, Denmark's largest & most notorious madhouse, much whizzied up my thoughts. Franz's nervous system had always been delicate, & his psychic state vulnerable at the best of times: had his displacement to London, followed by the shock of his return (conjoined, perhaps, with further conflict with his stern & snobbish parents) conspired to tip him over the edge? Or had he foolishly blabbed about his travels through time, & thus been deemed a madman by the family doctor? It was on this subject that I pondered as I followed the path along the lake's margin, dodging fanatic-faced joggers, to meet up with Fru Jakobsen, as agreed, at a café on the corner of Østerbrogade. Here, at an astrologically inflated price, we ate massive 'burgers' accompanied by mounds of unadorned raw foliage, & exchanged what information we each had gleaned. I acquainted her with Franz's dismal fate, at which she became most disconsolate, just as I had done, & in turn she revealed that her own search for 'Charlotte Dagmar Marie Schleswig' had yielded naught whatsoever (which I confess was a relief), & for Fergus McCrombie likewise. At these tidings I was inclined to be much encouraged, for (I argued) it indicated that my future husband had not been stranded in Copenhagen indefinitely – but Fru Jakobsen then pointed out that I must not be too optimistic, for Fergus might simply have left Copenhagen & travelled back to England, where he at least spoke the language, & made a life there – a possibility which could be checked by investigating the historical records in London on our return. As for my own death not being a matter of record, this might be accounted for by the fact that my birth had never been registered in the first place, due to Fru Schleswig's probable lack of acquaintanceship with civic duty. In short, as far as late nineteenth-century Denmark was concerned, I had simply never existed: a strange notion, which all of a sudden made me feel as insubstantial as a character in a novelette! Aside from that, Fru Jakobsen had learned that the Kraks' home had been sold in 1898, shortly after Pastor Dahlberg's death.

'His death?' I asked, curious. 'Shortly after his marriage, & our return to London? A hasty demise indeed!'

'And can you imagine how he passed away?' she whispered, conspiratorially.

It was not a conundrum to which I needed to apply my mind for long. 'In the arms of a whore,' I said, 'at an educated guess.'

'Correct!' she trilled. 'Dressed in his full parsonic regalia!' (That poor working girl, I thought, considering the scenario for a moment.)

'And what of Fru Krak?'

'Guess again,' challenged Fru Jakobsen, attacking her foliage.

'Well, she was a creature of habit. So I would wager she remarried. Her pattern was to kill them or drive them away, was it not? I'd bet fifty kroner that she had more than one husband, after the Pastor.'

'Three!' cried Fru Jakobsen. 'Making five in all, including Professor Krak! You genius!'

'It's not so much genius as observation, for she is of the parasitic persuasion,' I countered. 'Being a Fine Lady born & bred.'

'Well, in the end she died alone & fat at the age of sixty,' finished Fru Jakobsen, 'from a surfeit of cakes & chocolate liqueurs!' At which she blushed & crossed herself, & added guiltily: 'Bless her soul.'

That afternoon we took a train (that sold coffee! From a trolley! Where newspapers were freely available, & a little plastic rubbish bag hung beneath the table!) to the far-flung town of Roskilde. The Sankt Hans was an imposing building, within whose reception hall we were immediately hailed by a sharp little gent with a distracted air, smelling oddly enough of glue, who with some perspicacity semed to have antici-pated our unannounced arrival. He introduced himself as Ivor Winkel, & informed us that the Medical Commandant was currently on holiday in Madagascar observing wildlife 'such as hyenas, baboons and wildebeest', but as his 'right-hand man' he would be happy to assist us, whatever the nature of our business. He then led us to a large airy room with much furniture, where he gestured us to sit while he settled himself behind a plastic-topped table upon which was sprawled a large & most elaborate miniature stage-set featuring a scen-ario of chunky, viciously armed warriors, odd-shaped attack tanks, & tiny models of trees, hills & boulders, with a spear-bristling fortress behind. He explained that this all consisted of 'Dark Elf, from the Fantasy range'. Were we familiar with Warhammer?

We apologized for our ignorance on the subject, & he sighed that it was of no matter, as many members of the institution were into it, 'especially those who tune in to voices'.

'Might we conduct some research into a former inmate,

Doktor Winkel?' I asked tentatively. 'If you have records going back as far as the turn of the nineteenth century?'

Yes, he supposed we might investigate the archives & indeed if he was clever & pulled some strings (for he had friends in high places if we knew what he meant) he could probably get hold of a key to the archive room, but he warned that once in there, we had best keep a low profile & avoid the nurses, or they'd medicate us or worse, ask questions about how we were feeling 'in ourselves'.

Although this was most maddeningly puzzling in a way quite typical of the future, the Doktor proved as good in deed as he was in word. He left us 'in the capable hands', as he put it, of the television, & for ten minutes we were transfixed by a children's programme in which a venomous snake dislocated its jawbone & – gorily fascinating! – swallowed an entire white mouse in one slow & wriggling gulp, before the Doktor returned, having procured the requisite key. He then led us through a labyrinth of corridors, in which we passed many intense-faced people of all shapes & sizes, none of whom gave either us or the Doktor a second glance, until we came to a door marked Archives. 'If you're looking for early records, it will probably be on paper rather than CD-ROM,' Doktor Winkel said knowledgeably. 'But forgive my haziness about the precise filing system. Would you like to sleep in here tonight, even though there may be the odd rat?'

'Er, I think not,' said Fru Jakobsen delicately, nudging me in the ribs & shooting me a wide-eyed look. 'Just leave us the key, if you would be so kind, Doktor. We'll lock ourselves in instead, & that way we won't be disturbed.'

This seemed to satisfy the Doktor, & so without further

ado, Helle Jakobsen & I set about hunting for the name Poppersen Muhl in the long narrow musty room that housed the hospital's archives.

'Our Franz is lurking in here somewhere, you can be certain of it!' cried Fru Jakobsen, expertly sliding open the drawers in which documents were kept. 'Under P!' Swiftly, she ran her fingers through, throwing up clouds of dust, then stopped & whipped out a yellowed piece of paper. 'Franz Poppersen Muhl!' she cried in delight. 'Good grief,' she said, tapping the sheet, 'it says he was a patient here from 1899 until his death in 1980! Do you realize, that means he lived to be a hundred! *Private funeral . . . buried in the tomb of the Poppersen Muhl family . . . invented & patented the dust-sucker whilst a patient* . . . Ah! Look here, it seems that he left all his scrapbooks & diaries! Twenty volumes of them!'

'But look at this place: they could be anywhere!' I cried, for the room was stuffed to the gills with archival memorabilia. 'Where to start?'

'Try row twenty-five, shelf ten,' smiled Helle Jakobsen, consulting the paper again (how clever she was!), & sure enough, high up (stepladder required & found), squatted a row of bulky volumes bound in grey leather. Wobbling on my perch, with Helle Jakobsen keeping the ladder stable below, I pulled one out & coughed as the particles flew: it was dated 1897–8, & labelled in red ink: *To London & Back*. Did I not recall Franz working on just such a scrapbook in London, in which he made spidery notes & glued in ephemera such as cinema tickets, flyers for pizza deliveries, photographs of historic monuments, & cards from phone booths advertising HOT LESBO CHICKS GO WILD? But Satan's underwear: twenty volumes! We could never smuggle them all out of here, &

even if we could, reading our contraband would take an eternity!

Flustered by this thought I opened one at random, dated 1923, & read an entry.

June 25th. My bowels have been giving me gyp again, & I am queased. Heigh ho sweetcorn! I played four rounds of gin rummy with Herr Lagerfeld, then spent one hour & twenty minutes working on the design of my 'rat suicide' device. The trapping mechanism still has me stumped. Nettle soup for tea: this will do nothing to improve matters gastric. Mama visited & left a packet of geranium tea, which I threw in the rubbish as soon as she had gone. Papa has sold some more stocks & shares, she says, & they have a new pianoforte upon which she plays 'Für Elise' despite her arthritic fingers. We discussed Brahms, & I speculated that science might one day come up with a way of modifying nature, so that crops might glow in the dark, the sea become boiling hot, pigs grow wings, etc. 'O dear Franz, not that conversation again,' she pleaded finally, after I had aired my thoughts & predictions on these & other matters futuristic, so we then sat in silence, punctuated by Herr Gunn's monstrous burping, until she left. Weather mildish. Saw a starling, & fed it some crumbs. In the night Frøken Jette Sørensen died writhing in agony like Madame Bovary after taking an overdose of toilet cleaner, & we all had to say a special prayer for her, even those of us who, like me, do not believe in God, & were not quite sure who Frøken Sørensen was or what she was for. Oh well: another day, another dollar, as they say in the US of A!

Lord, trawling through pages & pages of such self-absorbed nonsense in the hope of a clue concerning my Scottishman's fate could take for ever!

'We shall have to settle for taking four or five scrapbooks,' I decided. 'From the first few years solely. We will simply walk out of here with them, behaving as though we own the world: that is the way to do it.'

'You mean *steal* them?' asked Fru Jakobsen, looking mildly aghast, but I could see she recognized we had little choice. 'But Charlotte *skat*, how can we be sure to get away with it?'

'Experience,' I said. 'For in my Østerbro days, Fru Jakobsen, I am sorry to tell you that as well as plying my trade as a harlot, I was also a dab hand at shoplifting.'

While my refined friend absorbed this shameful fact, I, all a-cough with dust, selected what I judged to be the most relevant volumes, then went in search of a vessel in which to smuggle them out, leaving Fru Jakobsen to riffle through the pages of a scrapbook from 1970 entitled *Important Things Life Has Taught Me & Other Reflections*. Eventually I unearthed a box in a storage cupboard housing supplies of toilet paper & tampons, & when I returned, found Fru Jakobsen smiling to herself in a most contented & dreamy way.

'You know, I think Franz had rather a good life here after all,' she said. 'For the thoughts expressed here are not the conclusions of an abject creature who felt that his life had failed. On the contrary. I would say that in the Sankt Hans, our delicate young friend transmogrified into a wise & fulfilled man, with much to live for.'

Glad though I was to hear this, & keen to see the evidence for myself (for I will admit to some surprise at this notion!), the reasons for Fru Jakobsen's assessment would have to wait for a later juncture, it now being urgent to make away forthwith. It was with some relief that we discovered Doktor Winkel nowhere to be found, so we left the key dangling from a warrior's spear atop a Dark Elfin tower with an anonymous note of thanks, & made a speedy exit, returning to Roskilde train station & thence to Østerbro, stopping only to purchase a mushroom & pepperoni pizza with extra olives from the Turkish gentleman on Nordrefrihavnsgade, that we might set to work on our researches straightway, without the distraction of hunger-pangs.

Once at our lodgings, we settled down with diaries & victuals. 'No rest for the wicked!' smiled Fru Jakobsen, still bearing vestiges of that earlier, dreamy look on her face. Quite unlike me (for I was all agog to learn what had befallen my Fergus), my elegant friend seemed in a state of quite mystifying unhurriedness, & resolutely determined to 'enjoy her evening', as she put it, & to this end she drew from her handbag two small bottles of flying-machine Rioja & poured us each a glass, raising hers in the air with a jaunty '*skål*', & declaring that all was for the best in the best of all possible worlds. What spirit of lassitude had suddenly possessed her, *for helvede?*

Stifling my annoyance at my companion's inexplicable nonchalance, I devoured my half of the pizza (Fru Jakobsen, meanwhile, took her ladylike time) & began to read furiously, skipping & jumping my way through Franz's aches, pains, hopes, passions & disappointments, past drawings of suction mechanisms & sketches of the Time Machine & lists of favourite meals, most of which seemed to involve white comfort food such as tapioca, potatoes, whipped cream & cauliflower, all the while keeping my eyes skinned for a single name: Fergus. At last, I found an entry.

'Ha!' I cried. Fru Jakobsen languidly set aside her pizza & sat on the bed next to me. 'Listen to this!' I said, & read aloud.

4 January 1898, Østerbro:

Calamity! Did I not predict that things would go most horribly awry? Yes indeed I did! And now they have, & I know not what to do, & Mama has gone to see Herr Bang to ask for some special soothing potion for my nerves, for I have not been myself since my return from London, & now this, this … Words cannot describe the psychic turmoil that has been engendered in me! Anyway, Charlotte's beau Fergus McCrombie, who should have returned to London, materialized on the family doorstep at a MOST inauspicious time, right in the middle of luncheon (a flæskesteg, my favourite). Fortunately it was I who answered the bell, it being the servants' afternoon off. He was quite unkempt, his face injured & scarred & his arm in a sling, & he insisted most vociferously that I must come to his aid. It seems that after I had escaped via the ventilation shaft as instructed, Mr McCrombie had been assaulted by thugs whilst the others – namely Professor Krak, Charlotte and her mother & the child Josie – had time-travelled back to London, leaving him becalmed in what he (rather insultingly, to my mind) referred to as 'history'. He is most determined to return, but the Mother Time Machine is now smithereened, & the house in Rosenvængets Allé permanently occupied by the Pastor & his bride.

Lord, what a jinxy palaver! I had him clean up, then begged Mama to let Mr McCrombie stay with us, & came up with a story of sorts about how he had missed a ferry-boat to Harwich & sold his daughter to a travelling circus, at which Mama looked most concerned & sceptical so I flew into a rage, & remained in that state until she said, 'Please, anything you like, dear Franz, so long as you calm down,' & so we gave Mr McCrombie one of the spare rooms, & I asked Father the next morn to let our English friend, who is in fact apparently Scottish, teach me more of his most agreeable if vocabulary-laden language, as my fluency had fallen away since my coming home, & he looked doubtful but then I started to blub. Papa, having a low tolerance for unmanly men, said hastily, 'Very well, whatever you want, my boy, take it easy now, *remember your nerves.' But I was by then in a genuine state of anxiety, & my stomach could barely stand it & my bowels became disturbed in a diarrhoeic fashion. Is there no end to my troubles?*

'So Fergus had his wits about him enough to escape, & make it to the home of the Poppersen Muhls, thank Heaven!' cried Fru Jakobsen, adding in a lower voice: 'But Lord above, that young Franz never ceases to whine, does he?'

'My greatest concern is that the Time Machine has indeed been destroyed,' I said, feeling my heart sink even lower, 'thus confirming our worst fears!'

'Read on!' commanded Fru Jakobsen. 'Let us see what your young man does next!'

So I whizzed & flipped through many more pages of complaints about mysterious & possible life-threatening aches, & pains, & bacteria, & vacuum-cleaner sketches, in search of my future husband's name, but did not see it until I spotted that he was now called 'our Scottish friend'.

January 5th. Our Scottish friend has insisted that I take him to visit Else, for he is convinced she has information that might assist him in devising a means by which to return to London. Until now he always seemed to me quite a sane man but now he has started to talk about rebuilding the Time Machine himself –

(O, my brave & ingenious sweetheart, I thought: I remember cursing your interest in the Time Machine's innards, but now do I thank Heaven indeed that you paid it the attention you did!)

– & will not listen to my protestations, which are well-founded enough, but tells me by way of reply that Charlotte always called me the Crown Prince of Pessimism, & now he understands why! I was somewhat insulted but agreed to walk him to Else's flower shop, & besides I could not say no, for he was in quite a state of anxiety & I

feared that if I did not obey him I might suffer, the Scottish race having a well-known propensity for violence. At the florist's, where I played the part of translator, we apprised Else of Fergus's plight & the loss of Charlotte, at which she was much horrified & pained, & she said we must instantly call on the services of Gudrun Olsen, for it was she who had supplied most of the materials for the Time Machine.

(O my fellow Østerbro Coquette, how bright you are!)

So we all went to the laundry where, surrounded by steam, as in a sauna, Fergus, with myself interpreting, once more explained the situation, & begged Gudrun Olsen to recall what manner of materials Professor Krak had bade her supply for him. Seeing our Scottish friend's desperation, she began to write a list, which heartened him greatly, though she said she feared she could not remember it all, but he claimed to have had a good look at the machine before it was smashed. What had him stumped, however, were the four mysterious ingredients of the secret catalysing liquid: could Gudrun remember purchasing any bottles?

'Aha, the catalysing ingredients! He has thought of them already, creature of genius that he is!'

The next few entries did not mention Fergus at all, & indeed there followed a section consisting merely of calculations concerning the physics of dust-sucking. Then:

January 21st. O, fantabulosa: my cherished project, the Original Poppersen Muhl Dust-Sucker, has come closer to reality today! These good tidings come via our Scottish friend, with whom I have finally (after some wrangling, I assure you: they can be tough bargainers these futuristic types) struck a deal. Being far more mechanically-minded than I, he has agreed to share his expertise & assist me in constructing a prototype (see diagram, & note in particular the placement of the outer clutch actuator in relation to the exhaust port – a touch of brilliance if I say so myself): I in turn have undertaken to help him

procure the various materials he needs with which to construct a new
Time Machine, & thereby return to London, a subject on which he
speaks with increasing frequency & desperation. He at first wished to
build the thing in parts, in his bedroom at Mama & Papa's, then
assemble it on site. But when I had explained my parents' opposition to
anything they deem 'eccentric', we settled for a side-room at Gudrun's
laundry, until such time as the structure can be moved & fully
assembled beneath the holly tree in Fru Krak's garden on Rosenvængets
Allé – this being the one location apart from the cellar that is straddled
by the Time-Sucker, or 'worm-hole', as our Scottish friend calls it.
When I questioned him about how he hoped to keep such a thing
hidden, he revealed that he had gathered together a host of old
Christmas trees which had been left in the street for collection, &
thus added fifteen fir trees to the garden on Rosenvængets Allé – which
the couple never seemed to enter – in the space of a week. As soon as he
was ready to move the Time Machine there in sections, Fergus said he
would circle the contraption with them, thus camouflaging it from view.

'What ingeniousness!' I cried. 'Are men not wonderfully
brainy creatures, Fru Jakobsen? Why, this ruse is similar to
dear Georg's inspiration with the bogus travelling toilet: how
the masculine mind runs along such nifty tracks! Now all
Fergus has to do is assemble the machine, & find the liquid
catalysing ingredients! How touching, that we are both at a
parallel stage!'

'But both seemingly stuck,' said Fru Jakobsen, pragmati-
cally. 'Due to the fact that the four mystery ingredients
remain – well, four *mystery ingredients*,' which brought me
galumphingly back down to earth. My wise friend was quite
right of course, & it was with a somewhat heavier heart that I
read on. The next diary entry merely engendered more
confusion, & did nothing to encourage optimism, for it

recorded that Gudrun Olsen, interrogated by Fergus through the medium of Franz, had recalled that Professor Krak had often bade her listen while he read aloud Hans Christian Andersen's *The Story of a Mother*, about a woman whose child dies, & who will do anything to get him back. Anyone who knows this tale will be aware of how gruesome heart-breaking it is, but what was the Professor's purpose, in depressing poor Gudrun so? Apparently whenever he had finished reading this sad, sad tale, Professor Krak would treat Gudrun most kindly, and dry her tears with his handkerchief, & pay her an extra ten kroner on top of her wages. *Our Scottish friend & I discussed this at length with Gudrun, who was most keen to help – but none of us could work out what the significance was*, wrote Franz.

'What on earth might that all mean?' I queried, baffled. Fru Jakobsen merely shook her head. I read on, & learned that Fergus did indeed begin his project of building a new Time Machine in the garden of the Krak house, & disguised it successfully with fir trees.

The structure being complete, & corresponding in most ways to the original Time Machine (though more chaotic & less refined in appearance), all that now remains, wrote Franz on January 21st, *is to identify the four secret ingredients of the catalysing agent. Last night our Scottish friend & I held a lengthy conversation on the subject, but the truth is we know not where to begin, & we emerged none the wiser; the list of possibilities being seemingly endless. Over a glass of schnapps our Scottish friend declared himself puzzled as to the baffling contents of the Oblivion Room: did I remember what was in it?*

A stuffed orang-utan, I recalled. And there was a box with a scalpel in it, & some books, & perhaps some pieces of old carpet, & a table with a medicine bottle upon it. At this he became animated: what kind of medicine, he wanted to know? I replied that I believed it was a clear liquid, perhaps antiseptic – which, we agreed, could well be one ingredient of the mixture. But what on earth were the others? And what was that scalpel for, & did the catalysing liquid have to be 'freshly made', & why was it designed to last a few days?

I yawned: it was by now midnight.

'Shall we put the light out now, *skat*, & get some rest?' asked Fru Jakobsen. 'I'm most exhausted, after such a hectic day. We still have the best part of tomorrow, for our plane does not depart until the afternoon. And if there's any more to be done after that, why I can remain here a few more days & you can direct my researches from London, if it seems imperative.'

'But I need to find out if Fergus discovered –'

'Best sleep on it,' Fru Jakobsen interrupted me in a kindly but firm manner. 'I really do have the most enthusiastic premonition about the way events will turn. Rest, I have always noted, is quite a problem-solver. Here, have a sleeping pill,' & she handed me a violet-coloured capsule. Overcome by a sudden yearning for oblivion, I swallowed it obediently & was gone.

But where to? Well, to my mind it seemed the strangest place I had ever clapped eyes on: it appeared to be a jungle. Perhaps Borneo? Yes; I was in Borneo, I knew it from the vegetation, & the way the wind shuddered high in the forest canopy above us. Us? Yes: for there above me, high high high, I spotted Pandora swinging from branch to branch on suspended lianas, like a trapeze artist at the circus! My O my, how beautiful & free she looked: how different from that stuffed creature, so tragic-faced, in the glass case!

'Fergus, come & look!' I cried, & there all at once my love materialized at my side, his daughter clamped to his back like a baby ape, & we were waving to Pandora, & she was flipping somersaults to show off, & flinging down bunches of bananas. And then Gudrun arrived, & her scar was gone, & she carried a book from which she began to read: it was *The Story of a Mother* by Hans Christian Andersen, but it became too, too sad, & she had to stop, & Pandora descended from her tree & put a comforting arm around her & the two of them wept together, & Josie looked on amazed, then cried: 'O, look! There's Uncle Fred riding the bicycle that doesn't go anywhere!' & we all followed him to a clearing where – O joy! – there indeed was Professor Krak, bare-chested & sweaty, pedalling furiously with a happy smile on his face. 'Toil, toil, toil, pain, pain, pain!' he cried, then drew from the box on the small table beside him a gleaming scalpel, with which –

O!

I woke with a start & sat upright in bed. Of course! There was the answer! It was all there, in my dream: the three products of human pain: blood, sweat & tears! The scalpel was for the blood. The sweat came from the exercise. And the tears: first, from *The Story of a Mother*, which is too, too sad – & after the death of Pandora – why, her memory! That was why her stuffed body, in its glass case, had been placed so strategically within sight of the exercise bicycle! One drop of each, mixed with ten parts of . . . & here he had spoken English, had he not? 'The great human ant—'

Eureka! For what had Franz & Fergus discussed in the last diary entry but the bottle of medicine which appeared to contain –

'Antiseptic!' I cried aloud, & leaped out of bed & shook Fru Jakobsen awake.

'I have it! I have the answer! Blood, sweat, tears & anti-septic!'

'Very good, dear,' she sighed sleepily. 'I am delighted for you! Most gratifying. Now can we go back to sleep & talk about it in the morning?'

The next day, Fru Jakobsen claimed there was a last-gasp *slut-spurt* sale at the department store Magasin, & she would like more than anything else to take a peek, despite the monstrous modern prices: would I mind? I was quite baffled. Here we were, having finally made a discovery that might secure our happiness & our futures, & she was contemplating a shopping trip! But she seemed quite resolute, in her genteel way, & as I am a fast reader, I estimated I could work my way through Franz's diaries just as well on my own, & the pressure was somewhat off, now that I had cracked the pestilential catalyser riddle, so off Fru Jakobsen went, & on I read. But as I did so, my emotions were soon helter-skeltering floorwards. I will let Franz's diary speak.

January 25th. Fergus came to me most excited this morning, & said he had been thinking about the catalysing ingredients, & believed he had the answer. He went on to talk in a complicated manner about the deductions he had made through trying to analyse the significance of the items in the Oblivion Room, to wit the stuffed monkey, the exercise bicycle, the scalpel & the medicine bottle. On & on he went on this track, & not wishing to arouse his Scottish wrath I gave the appearance of listening politely whilst mentally sketching a device for coiling electrical cords, & trying to remember whether I had warned Mama that my system was still feeling most sensitive. I have heard that boiled rice & bananas are an excellent cure for an upset stomach, while in the future (about which I must never speak for fear of seeming like a lunatic — though Lord, it is hard!) they swear by 7UP for all intestinal misfortunes. Just as I was pondering how one might set about reproducing such a carbonized beverage in my own era, I noticed that our Scottish friend had stopped talking, & was looking at me expectantly, as though I should supply an answer.

'Sorry, can you repeat what you just said?' I asked — then added hurriedly, 'Just the last bit, of course, which I didn't quite catch. Not the whole story, I beg you.'

'Blood, sweat, tears & antiseptic!' he cried. 'Those are the secret catalysing ingredients, I am sure of it! It all makes sense! Three of them easily extracted from the human body, but subject to decay — which is why it cannot be stored for more than two days. The fourth liquid — well, it was in that bottle on the table in the Oblivion Room all the time! Antiseptic: what else?'

O joy! My clever man! I read on, greedily.

'What else indeed,' I replied, still not quite there. It sounded quite addle-brained to me, yet somehow not uncharacteristic of Professor Krak's way of thinking. Yes: it had a kind of logic.

'So now we must put it to the test!' he cried happily. 'The blood and sweat are easily come by. I will cut myself, & take a jog around the lake. The antiseptic, your mother can supply us with.'

But what of the tears? Although of a sensitive nature, & not ashamed to cry when something moves me, I suddenly (& most frustratingly) found myself quite unable to coax the necessary muscles on this occasion, & nor could our Scottish friend, however sad the thoughts he summoned, such as the sale of his daughter to the 'circus', & the loss of Charlotte to modern London.

'What about Else?' said Fergus. 'Is she the tearful type?'

'Well, she used to be a performer, so maybe she could muster some,' I said.

As it turned out Else needed scarcely any prompting to cry, for she missed her friend Charlotte terribly, & thought Fergus's attempts to be reunited with her a moving & romantic & inspiring story, so when she had fully blubbed, & we had squeezed a drop from her handkerchief into Fergus's blood & sweat, off we set with a vial of the precious liquid to Number Nine Rosenvængets Allé, full of hope.

Would that I had stopped reading there, & kept my optimism! But I could not desist from turning the pages, I simply could not! O woe!

When Fru Jakobsen returned an hour later laden with shopping bags & packages, she found me weeping on the bed, the last volume of Franz's diaries having led me into a state of unconsolable despair.

'What on earth has happened, *skat*?' she asked, looking most concerned.

'I do not know! I do not know what fate has befallen my love, & it seems our whole reunion is in jeopardy! Without more of Franz's scrapbooks from the Sankt Hans, I can discover no more! For the formula I came up with in my dream – well, it seems that Fergus came to the same conclusion about its ingredients!'

'So why do you weep?'

Unable to speak, I merely moaned & pointed to the relevant excerpt of Franz's diary.

February 11th. Today our Scottish friend appeared especially in the doldrums, as he had once again tried the antiseptic solution, & nothing positive had come of it. 'If I have got it all wrong, then how?' he cried, as we sat by the fireside pursuing our 'English lesson'. 'And in what way? It must be to do with the quantities. I'll just have to keep mixing & trying – but I could be stuck out there in the Time Machine in the Kraks' garden for ever, experimenting! And in the meantime, the Christmas trees have gone brown, & are dropping needles, & I don't know how much longer I can keep the Time Machine hidden!'

Things are getting most desperate, & all the while Mama & Papa send our Scottish friend unfriendly glances, & they want to know how he spends his time, & I can tell they disapprove mightily of what he did to his daughter. I can see I made a mistake in telling them about the circus, but I was thinking on my feet! When does he intend to travel back to Scotland, they want to know. It is most stressful & wearying. Tomorrow I shall visit Herr Bang & order some pink medicine.

February 17th. 'Why the hell doesn't it work?' our Scottish friend asked me today. 'Is it possible, Franz, that Professor Krak kept a bottle of antiseptic in the Oblivion Room purely for – well – antiseptic purposes? To treat the cut made by the scalpel when he was extracting blood?'

This was the conclusion Fergus wearily & most reluctantly reached, & relayed to Franz: that he thought he had figured out three of the ingredients but the fourth remained a mystery wrapped inside an enigma, & – O God! – in any case he knew not the proportions of the mixture, or at what temperature it should be introduced into the sphere, & . . . O, how my poor love was in deep, deep despair! Tears in my eyes, I conveyed this to Fru Jakobsen.

'And then what happened?' she asked. It was with gratitude that I observed she seemed finally to be paying the matter the attention it warranted.

'He began trying various other liquids as the fourth component, in varying quantities,' I told her. 'Dissolved pig-fat, paraffin, vinegar, milk, lemon juice, elderflower wine, diluted soda crystals & many others, in all manner of combinations. But then came two calamities: first Pastor Dahlberg & Fru Krak – who I suppose we now call Fru Dahlberg – took it upon themselves one night to venture out in order to observe the full moon, & surprised Fergus in the garden, where they presumed him to be a burglar, & the next day they procured themselves an Alsatian guard-dog – attached by a long chain to its kennel by the front gate – that barked at the slightest disturbance. Next the Poppersen Muhls warned Franz that Fergus must leave by the end of the week, for they considered him a "hectic influence" on Franz, & O, Fru Jakobsen, we are quite, quite undone!'

'And then?'

'And then the diary comes to an end, & we cannot find out what befell them unless we return to the Sankt Hans & procure more volumes!' I cried, by now quite distraught.

'Come now, I'm sure it's not as bad as all that,' proclaimed Fru Jakobsen matter-of-factly. 'I think you must simply abandon hope of Fergus coming to London under his own steam, & instead concentrate on what you can do to reach him. Your lively imagination will rustle something up, I am sure of it. Come now, apply your mind to those ingredients again. Blood, sweat and tears go together, don't they – but I'd say antiseptic is the misfit, for it is not something one would normally carry about one's person. Think of how practical Professor Krak is, dear. What might he always be able to come by? I know! Why not try looking in your dictionary for an English word beginning with *ant*?'

Upon which, without further ceremony, she announced that she was going to take a stroll around the botanical gardens, & thence to the cinema, & she would leave me with the bottle of schnapps she now produced.

'Abandon me here, in this state?' I wailed. 'Doing all the investigating myself?'

'Well, two of us can't read a dictionary at once,' she argued. 'And you seem to enjoy looking up words; indeed, it's quite a hobby, is it not?'

In the seemingly militant absence of support from my companion, I had to admit that my choices were limited at this point, for regaining access to the Sankt Hans archive in the wake of our theft seemed an impossibility, given that our flying-machine departed in a mere four hours. So I reached for my red English dictionary, with its wafer-thin pages bearing thousands of definitions & sub-definitions, my first & only gift from Fergus, & how the tears came to my eyes when I reread the inscription inside, written in his plain Scottish writing, so different from my own loopy & curlicued hand: 'For Lottie, with love beyond words.'

O! Feel my fevered brow, dear reader! Does your heart swoon with mine?

'But look at all these pages!' I cried despondently, urging Fru Jakobsen to at least measure the weight of the volume in her hand, for it seemed to me heavier than a whole bag of flour. 'So many words! And when you consider it, does not *every single noun* have an "anti" version of itself? Where to begin?' But Fru Jakobsen had donned her jacket & headed for the door, leaving me, I shall confess to you, with a sharp nudge of disappointment at her laconic attitude, which seemed uncharacteristically ruthless under the circumstances. Had I misjudged her?

'Have a stiff drink,' she counselled, waving an airy goodbye. 'Then begin at the beginning, go on until you come to the end, & then stop.'

Upon which she took her merry leave, seeming quite determined to enjoy her time in Copenhagen, so there was naught to do but follow her advice & reach for the schnapps bottle, at which a warm glow instantly spread through my chest, bringing with it a tiny flicker of hope. Bottle in hand, I sprawled on the bed, working my way patiently through the nouns, trying out each with the prefix 'the great human', & considering what might be classified as a liquid, or produce same.

The great human antic. (*'Antic: fantastic action or trick.'* Yes, I had been tricked all right, but not fantastically!) The great human anticathode. (Krak was certainly a man for blinding one with science!) I swigged some more, & felt the warmth expand further through my chest. My face felt a blood-rush & I realized I had very swiftly made myself somewhat drunk. Good: maybe it will help, I thought, as I took another swig & contracted an immediate bout of hiccups. The great human antichrist (ectoplasmic? But how to catch him?). *Hic.* The great human anticlimax. (Exactly what I had just suffered!) A further swig & I began to feel quite dizzy. The great human anticonvulsant. (Aha! Hic. Possible). Might a 'great human anti-devolutionist', if chopped into small enough pieces, be successfully liquidized in a modern food processor? Soon the words were dancing before my eyes &, before I knew it, I had fallen into a queasy slumber . . .

It was afternoon when I was awakened by a knock at the door. I staggered to my feet. Fru Jakobsen had returned from her trip to the cinema, & she was now sniffing the air. She spotted the schnapps bottle. 'Charlotte-*pige*!' she exclaimed. 'I suggested, I think, a small pick-me-up, rather than —'

'O Fru Jakobsen!' I cried, & burst into tears. 'How plunged into gloom I am, & how mightily drunk, & what a headache I am in for! How I curse Professor Krak, for making life so difficult!'

'You did not solve it, then? I'm going to pack your bag for you now, Charlotte, while you try to concentrate on how the Professor's mind works, for there I am sure lies the key to your riddle.'

But how did his mind work, exactly? As Fru Jakobsen tutted & mother-henned around me, I groggily tried to picture the Professor as I most clearly remembered him. That man is surely paying the price for being so secretive now, I thought, stuck with a malarial fever on Marroquinta! My first sight of him had been in the Observatory: a tall gangling man with a flapping jacket & waistcoat, windmilling his arms, & twitching all over with neurotic intensity. And then his telephone call, so recently: 'the three products of human pain'. Blood, sweat & tears: all ingredients that came from the human body under duress. Pain had been the key, he had said. Human pain. Then dilute in ten parts of '*the great human ant*—'. I pictured Professor Krak again, that first time we travelled on the underground. Attempting to calm me, he had offered me a swig from his hip-flask: I remember refusing, but he himself had taken a vast gulp & I recognized the distinctive smell of schnapps. What had he called it, then? A wonderful restorative? Thereafter I noted that the surreptitious quaffing of alcohol was quite a habit of the Professor's, especially when his nerves were on edge . . .

Suddenly I sat up so fast that my head spun. Good grief! What if, when the Professor first offered me a swig from his hip-flask, he had called it 'the great human antidote'? Surely that was possible? It fitted, too, for had I not just used it as an

277

antidote to my own pain, a means of numbing my own agony, & drowning my sorrows?

'EUREKA! I have it! I have it by the nose!' I scream, & am just in the process of gabbling the details of my discovery to Fru Jakobsen – ('you clever girl, I knew you would solve the conundrum!') – when a tinny blast of music sounds from my handbag.

'Quick, Charlotte, the telephone!' she cries. 'Someone is calling you!'

I delve into the bag, fish out the device & snap, 'Yes, who is this?' into the receiver. My brain is quite fizzing.

'It is Rigmor Schwarb, in London. There is terrible news, Charlotte: I am so sorry.'

O no! Josie! My heart was gripped with woozy panic. Rigmor Schwarb was a woman who had abandoned her own baby in front of an Oxfam shop: what madness had I committed, to entrust her with my lover's precious babe!

'The authorities. They came round,' she said. 'A police-woman & a social worker, who have been following you. The teachers at Josie's kindergarten became suspicious some time ago, & contacted them. They interrogated Josie about you, & then they took her away!'

'No!'

'Yes!'

O, woe! The one thing that my lover had counted on, surely, when we were riven asunder, was that I would take care of his darling child – & I had failed him! O fool that I was! I burst into tears: the contrite Rigmor, too, was sobbing.

'And they said that unless Fergus himself comes to get her, Josie will be fostered by someone on the list!' she went on, when she had blown her nose noisily. 'Georg Jakobsen has been trying to make them see reason, & has barely been off the telephone, giving assurances that Fergus will return, & that you are Josie's official au pair, but they say that without written evidence to back it up, their hands are tied, & they have to follow protocol!'

Oh, *for Sataan.* If I did not immediately soberize enough to conjure up a solution to this new predicament then we were quite undone!

'Quick, let me speak to Georg,' I tell the now bawling Rigmor.

'Hello?' comes Georg Jakobsen's oddly calm voice.

'Now listen carefully, Georg,' I tell him. 'If this doesn't work, we will lose both Fergus & his daughter so I am counting on you!'

'I'm all ears, Charlotte-*pige*,' replies the good Georg.

'Can you have the Time Machine set up in Greenwich, on the meridian, tonight?'

'It's feasible,' he said slowly. 'Yes, I believe it can be accomplished.'

'It has to be! Please do it, dear Herr Jakobsen, for my happiness depends on it, as does the future of all of us!'

'Don't worry yourself so much, my dear. I have spoken to my wife & she assures me all will be well.'

What presumption! I thought, but said nothing for there was no time to lose: our flying-machine awaited us at the airport.

'The other thing you must do,' I told him (my thoughts now assembling themselves under one roof), 'is to procure some rather particular ingredients, & have them all ready for me in a jar. Take note: two millilitres of human blood, another two of human tears, & another two of sweat, mixed with ten parts of schnapps. Trust me, Herr Jakobsen, but unlikely as it sounds, this is the secret catalysing liquid which will trigger the starting mechanism of the Time Machine. Please pack all that you & Helle wish to bring back to Denmark, for you are going home sooner than you think – but now I must bid you farewell as we must hasten to Kastrup Airport!'

'Might you procure us some pickled herring on your way?' he asked, still sounding calm. 'We do miss good Danish *sild* over here: the English are quite ignorant of the subtleties of marinade. Oh, & some *remoulade*? The departure lounge is one of the most sophisticated in Europe.'

I had long suspected that, like his wife, Georg Jakobsen was in possession of a very cool head, but this was taking insouciance to extremes, it seemed: our futures hung in the balance, & he was thinking of herring & savoury dressings!

Fru Jakobsen, equally nonchalant, buffed her nails all the way home on the flying-machine, while reading a magazine containing many photographs of caviare. Georg Jakobsen met us at the airport, most enthusiastic & full of pep, with a free flow of assurances that the new Time Machine was all poised & ready for activation, & their suitcases were in the boot: all that we need do now, before setting off once more for Denmark (O vertiginous thought!), was to convince an organization by the name of 'Greenwich Social Services' that I was indeed Josie's legal guardian. And by the way, had we remembered his pickled herring?

In the car heading for Greenwich Herr Jakobsen, who drove the vehicle with impressive assurance, began elaborating on the legal process of regaining custody of Josie which would involve providing proof of my identity & my employment as Josie's au pair, & documentation which certified that

Fergus was planning to return from his 'business trip' on a given date. 'I'm afraid you may have been a little optimistic in hoping to secure Josie today, for we are likely to be looking at a long wrangle,' he concluded, adjusting his seatbelt.

'There will be no wrangling at all, dear Herr Jakobsen, if you & your wife will be good enough to humour me by doing precisely as I ask you,' I countered. 'For I have devised a plan.'

Once we had arrived in Greenwich, Georg followed a set of side-streets until we came upon a squat red-brick barrack-like building with a high fence & security cameras at three different levels.

'Georg, please be so good as to stay in our vehicle & keep on the alert, with the engine running,' I instructed. 'And when Helle & I come out with Josie be prepared for a quick getaway.'

In the leaflet-strewn entrance hall, Helle Jakobsen & I noted a device by which one triggered a fire alarm, whose simple instructions indicated that one should 'in case of emergency, break glass'. This, we whisperingly agreed, could be put to use in the latter stages of our rescue mission, but for now each had her own task – hurriedly agreed upon – to perform. What the chubby bespectacled girl at Reception made of Fru Jakobsen's declaration – expressed in the most ornately polite Danish you could wish to hear – that we were planning to kidnap a child from the premises, & would appreciate her remaining as incompetent & flustered as possible for the duration of the operation, I do not know, for while Fru Jakobsen was thus fulfilling her role as decoy, I was surreptitiously slipping past the desk & embarking upon a frantic search of the building. Many of the empty rooms I happened upon were designated as quiet areas, conference rooms & places of worship but in a side-wing I was in luck, for hearing the sound of children's voices, I followed a corridor that led me to a spacious dining hall in which I spied, through the door's small window-pane, a tableful of twenty or so little ragamuffins of all colours, sexes & ages, fighting, throwing balled-up napkins at one another, & munching on a British snack of breadcrumbed meat shaped into dinosaurs, under the supervision of an immensely fat woman clad in tracksuit & trainers, whose main focus of interest seemed to be securing the children's Jurassic left-overs by sliding them on to her own plate, where she snaffled them down as though she were dying of starvation. And there amongst the excitable throng of children, clad just as she was when I first clapped eyes on her, complete with mask, cape & gloves, was little Spiderman! Mentally, & with all the psychic energy I could muster, I exhorted her to look up, but she was too busy screwing her napkin into a small ball, ready to hurl at any child who attacked her, for it seemed there was a game going on that involved hair-tugging & missile-throwing, in which she was an active participant, if not a ringleader. I waved through the glass-paned door, but I could see no human eyes through the mask. I was just giving up hope when a flying napkin grazed the child's head, causing her to swivel in my direction, whereupon I caught her attention at last. Quickly, I gestured 'silence', & that she must try to slip out & join me. Cottoning on immediately (for had not gesture been our very first means of communication?), she stood up & addressed the fat lady who, still munching, then noticed that Spiderman was clutching her little *tissekone* & suddenly looking most piteous. The toilet! Our ingenious superhero had asked to be excused! The fat lady nodded her accord & continued her ruminant chewing, while Spiderman left the hall, closed the door behind her, & hurtled straight into my arms.

Silently, we hugged one another until it hurt. Pulling off her mask & mussing her thick tangle of hair, I saw that her darling little face (so grown-up she seemed, all of a sudden!) was alight with relief.

'Lottie!' she cried. 'I knew you or Dad would come and rescue me! Get me out of here! They make us sing "If You're Happy and You Know It Clap Your Hands" five times a day, & they tell you off if you won't join in!'

Upon which I impressed on her the need for concentration on the task ahead, if we wished to be reunited with her dad, who had become stuck in 'the wee theme park' & needed our help at once. She became most rigorously attentive, so I outlined the plan of action, confident that she would absorb it in all its detail, & follow my instructions without hesitation, for Miss Josefina Prudence Rosenberg McCrombie, much like her indomitable hero Spiderman, lacked not in courage, & could be counted upon to keep all her senses about her in a tight spot.

Next I made use of the mobile telephone to send Fru Jakobsen a text signal, as we had agreed, indicating that she could terminate her one-sided Danish conversation with the receptionist & make a dignified exit, pausing only to set off the building's alarm by breaking the safety glass in the entrance hall.

Pandemonium!

'Run!' I cried, & Josie & I set off at high speed.

The broken glass not only set several sirens a-wailing but also triggered an indoor rain-shower device that drenched us most thoroughly, but in the panic that ensued, we were able to make a most pleasingly nifty dash to freedom via a side-exit which led directly, as luck would have it, into the very car park where Georg & Helle Jakobsen now anxiously awaited us, whereupon I bade Georg *apply the pedal to the metal*, as the English expression goes.

'*For Fanden*, Charlotte-*pige*, how did you manage that?' he asked, dumbfounded.

'Are you quite certain you want to know, *skat*?' asked Helle Jakobsen, offering us all *saltlakrids* pastilles.

'Perhaps not,' he said, looking at his wife with a doubtful expression, 'because one thing I do know about bureaucrats, be they in the past, the present or the future, is that they like their forms filled in, & their paperwork triple-stamped. Yet you emerged from that building, good ladies, without so much as an advice leaflet!'

'*Uha*,' said Fru Jakobsen a moment later, for there were now sirens to be heard in the distance, 'it seems that the authorities have been quicker off the mark than we bargained for.' As we drove through the wrought-iron gateway of Greenwich Park & headed up the hill towards the Observatory through the dusk, the siren noise intensified behind us. Above us, darkness was falling, & seagulls slewed across the sky like shooting stars.

'The Portakabins are round the back: I'm going to drive right up there & park in that woodland, as we've no time to lose,' said Georg as he expertly turned the wheel & we began heading across the grass.

'This is surely not allowed!' cried Fru Jakobsen – to which Georg replied that indeed, it most certainly was not, but why should not *both* of them become criminals at the end of their stay in England, & in any case, where we were headed, no one could reach us with an on-the-spot fine. The car crawled steeply uphill towards a collection of white box-like structures in the shadow of the lit-up Observatory, its satellite apparatus & its spherical ball now starkly silhouetted against the darkening sky.

'Look!' cried Josie. For there, high above us, hummed the laser line, pulsating its eerie green light. Herr Jakobsen parked & we bundled out of our vehicle, each carrying a bulky Jakobsen suitcase, & rushed pell-mell towards the row of temporary cabins & toilets. Recognising our own bespoke one by virtue of the discreetly painted Danish flag it sported on its roof, Georg Jakobsen unpadlocked the door, & we all squashed tight inside Herr Dogger's version of the Time Machine, ready for take-off.

The sirens were growing ever louder as Herr Jakobsen shakily removed a jar from his pocket & filled the orb with the pinkish mixture it contained.

'I hope I have mixed the quantities aright,' he murmured, 'and that Rigmor's tears of penitence are of a sufficient standard. For if not, God help us! Now hold tight, everyone!' he cried.

And pulled the lever.

Say what I might about Herr Dogger, I must grant him that he had improved on the original Time Machine, for our journey was swifter & smoother than any before, & it was almost pleasant to see the blurring images of rocks, stones, savannah, forests, deserts, waves, moon, stars, sun, & sea that whizzied around us like assorted clothes inside a tumble dryer as we hurtled through time.

We landed softly enough, for the ground was clad in a thick eiderdown of white, white snow that sparkled in the sunshine. But O, the chill! In our haste, we had quite forgot the season, & Josie & I were wet to boot, after our encounter with the sprinkler system. *For Fanden*, we would freeze to death in minutes!

'Take my jacket, Miss McCrombie!' cried Herr Jakobsen, shedding it in a most gentlemanly manner & wrapping it tight over Josie's little Spiderman cape – but I noted that her lips had already turned blue.

'We must find warmth & shelter immediately, or we shall perish from frostbite!' I cried, picturing our photographs on the front page of *Politiken*: four inexplicable corpses, one a child dressed as the Devil, frozen rigid as statues, discovered by Pastor Dahlberg & his new bride, in their snowy garden – if that was indeed where we found ourselves, for in principle this was where the Time-Sucker was located. Sure enough, there now came confirmation in the form of a loud & angry barking from a snow-clad kennel that stood by what I now recognized to be Fru Krak's front porch.

'The Alsatian guard-dog!' I cried, remembering Franz's journal. 'The creature is attached by a chain, but he will alert them to our presence: we must swiftly away!'

By now Georg had furnished himself with a sturdy beech-wood stick with which he bravely insisted he would keep the madly barking brute at bay while we 'ladies' ran past its kennel & out into the safety of the road.

'Are you ready?' cried Georg, upon which the dog – a huge brute with dangling testicles – reared into view, brandishing yellow teeth & a fanatical glare. 'Then prepare to run for all you are worth, and do not look back until you are beyond the reach of its chain!'

The dog had by now smelled conflict, & was leaping about, tugging vigorously at its leash, so it was with shivering trepidation that we all set forth towards it – knowing, too, that at any moment the righteous Pastor & his invisible companion, the Holy Lord, along with his fine lady wife Fru Dahlberg/Krak/Bischen-Baschen, might appear at the doorway.

The dog had been well coached in violence, for it did not hesitate to leap for Georg's throat the very instant he approached to distract it, but Georg was quick on his feet, stepping jauntily out of the animal's reach & waving his stick at it in a taunting fashion; snarling, the infuriated creature sank on its haunches & then proceeded to circle him threateningly, its chain pulled to the maximum, while Fru Jakobsen, Josie & I ran helter-skelter for safety. Once at the gate, & out of the dog's reach, we turned – only to see that events had taken a frightening cast, for Georg, having had the upper hand, had lost it & was now struggling with the creature, which had grabbed one end of the stick in its teeth & was tugging at it madly, growling all the while! The valiant Georg looked momentarily hopeless, for it was evident that if he released his grip he would be weaponless, & the animal upon him, tearing his flesh & crunching his poor bones. Yet he could not ward the creature off for ever!

'Georg, let go of the stick & run!' shrieked Helle, but he shouted back that he could not, & we should press ahead & he would catch up with us!

'No!' Helle & I yelled in unison, but just as we did so, Georg, struggling desperately against the strength of the vicious canine, lost his footing & slipped on the icy path. No! The end was now nigh, for with a single mighty leap the maddened animal had hurled its whole weight at Georg & smacked into him, landing with a thud upon his torso. Helle screamed, & I gulped, & Spiderman prepared to attack, but then there fell a strange silence: it seemed that the impact of the two bodies had stunned both man & beast, for neither of them now moved. With a cry I ran towards Georg to drag the slumped creature off him, but just as I did so, two strong arms came from nowhere & grabbed me from behind.

I screamed, & so did Spiderman.

I swung around & there he was.

'Dad!' yelled Josie. For it was he. Those manly, pirate good looks, that heart-melting smile: I swear I did fall in love with Mr Fergus McCrombie all anew in that split second, & counted myself the luckiest girl in all of Galileo's galaxies!

'Got you, hen,' he murmured, hugging me tight, & Josie ripped off her Spiderman mask & hurtled to join us, & Helle embraced Georg who had now come to, & emerged from beneath the lifeless dog.

'I stunned Gnasher here with a dart dipped in a tranquillizer I bought from Mr Bang's pharmacy,' explained Fergus smilingly. 'I shot it from the blowpipe the orang-utan brought back from Borneo.'

'Is he going to be OK?' enquired Josie, all of a sudden going over to stroke its fur, a look of deep concern on her face.

'Sure, hen. He'll wake up in fifteen minutes with a bad headache.'

But Josie, tipped over the edge by the plight of the dog, was no longer able to contain the tears she had been so bravely holding back all this while, & she clung to her beloved father like a small monkey, & the three of us remained locked in one another's arms most *hyggeligt*-cosy for many minutes, babbling incoherently all the while, & squeezing tight enough to kill. O & I cannot tell you, my precious one, what bliss it was for all of us to be so reunited, after our differing ordeals apart.

'Lottie, hen,' Fergus said in my ear. 'And Josie. Listen carefully, you two: I swear we'll never lose each other again.' And he whipped off his coat & wrapped it round us both for warmth, & then greeted the Jakobsens – who were cheering aloud for joy at being home again – most effusively.

'Let's get some shelter,' Fergus then said, & led us into a corner of the garden where, behind the skeletons of some fifteen Christmas trees, lurked his version of the Time Machine. 'It's a scaled-down model,' he said modestly, revealing to us a charming, if a little haphazard construction that tilted somewhat. 'With fewer specifications, and it's not as fancy, but the basic mechanics are all there. If I'd only been able to find the ingredients to the catalysing –' he began, but I hushed him.

'I know how hard you tried,' I said, and quickly explained about our lightning voyage to modern Denmark – born, I told him, of sheer desperation – & its happy result.

'*Schnapps?* Schnapps! Of course, *of course!*' he cried, slapping his forehead. 'I should have guessed: that hip-flask Fred always carries on him! Christ, schnapps is practically a fourth body fluid, as far as the Professor's concerned!' Then he stopped & took a step back, scrutinizing me with a sudden, almost scientific interest. 'You've put on weight, hen,' he said at last. 'Were you aware of that?'

'I hear that English food makes you swell,' I said, feeling

not a little flustered & defensive, for I had not noticed any changes in my body, save that my breasts seemed even plumper. A soft & most happy smile spread across Fergus's face. 'It suits you. Even sexier than ever.'

'And you are even more like a hero,' I replied, stroking his stubbled jaw & kissing that adorable cheekbone which I had so missed & longed for. 'But tell me, where is Franz now?' I queried, coming to my senses. 'For he ended up in the Sankt Hans.'

Fergus looked troubled. 'Well, I've been wondering. I had to move out, because I was in the doghouse with the Poppersen Muhls, because Franz told them I sold Josie to a circus. I can't blame them for giving me the cold shoulder, but it got hell of a difficult, so Gudrun let me crash in the drying-room at the laundry. I took Else with me a week ago to visit Franz's parents and they were even more edgy than before. Said Franz wasn't home, and was "taking a cure". He'd been getting more & more outspoken about the time-travelling, & they weren't keen on the vacuum-cleaner stuff either.'

Resolving to visit Franz as soon as we might, our most immediate task was now to find lodgings for the night. Half an hour later Georg was proudly unpadlocking the massive wooden gates of the Authentic Hair Emporium in Christianshavn. Oil lanterns in hand, we ventured into the main warehouse, where we beheld a bewildering assortment of mannequins, stacked in rows, all sporting elaborate wigs, amid multitudinous sacks of human hair ('from nuns & the dead', explained Helle reverently) & bundles of mesh & other accoutrements.

'We are planning to transform the premises into the headquarters of a chain of beauty salons,' declared Georg proudly, as he gathered wigs & mannequin-limbs & threw them into the huge wood-burning stove to make a fire. Soon we had lit it, & it blazed fiercely, & our makeshift lodgings soon felt most *hyggeligt*. 'Our business is going to be a success this time,' said Herr Jakobsen proudly – but how he was able to evoke an image of future wealth with such confidence was a bafflement to me, until Helle asked, 'Remember my trip to the public library, Charlotte?' I replied that I did indeed, her visit there having taken place only two days ago, give or take a century. 'Well, I did a little investigating on my own account. It seems that we will have opened three new premises by September 1898, & a fourth before the year is out.'

'So is that why you were so relaxed on our trip to modern Copenhagen?' I asked her, warming my hands by the fire, where my two McCrombies were now attempting to grill waffles. 'Tell me, is that why you went to the cinema, & filed your nails, & shopped in Magasin, when I was going out of my mind with anxiety?'

She smiled benignly.

'In part. But mostly it was because I had already looked into *your* future, *min skat*, & seen that it was good. That you & this dear gentleman here would be reunited, & have all those things you dreamed of.'

'But how?'

'Do you remember a volume of Franz's entitled *Important Things Life Has Taught Me & Other Reflections*?'

'Yes! In the Sankt Hans.'

'Well, it was clear from that. It seems you & Fergus came to visit him in his old age, & many times before that, as did Georg & I.'

I did not know what to say for a moment, for I felt quite

dumbstruck. Fergus took my hand & squeezed it reassuringly, but I could not be restrained.

'Fru Jakobsen, I am glad indeed to hear this, but none-theless perplexed! Do you mean to say that you learned I would *not* be parted from Fergus for ever, as I so feared, & yet you uttered not a word to me on the matter, to set my heart at rest? You calmly allowed me to endure all that suffering & anxiety?'

'Well, I thought it best,' said Fru Jakobsen with finality. To my surprise, I saw that Fergus was nodding in approval, clearly having fathomed something I had not.

'Well, kindly explain yourself then, madam!' I cried, feeling suddenly quite overheated. Helle patted my hand.

'Well, *skat*,' she said. 'The fact is that being no expert on philosophical matters, I was merely applying a measure of prudence. Might you not have behaved differently, had you not experienced the sense of urgency, & gone to the lengths you did to discover the ingredients of the catalysing liquid? Might things then not have transpired otherwise than they did?'

'The Grandmother Paradox,' said my future husband knowledgeably. 'Professor Krak talked about it. It's never been resolved.'

'But if Franz says in his diary that we visited him –'

'Franz was a madman, according to his doctors,' said Helle Jakobsen gently, adjusting her shawl around her shoulders. 'He could have imagined everything I read there. Your visits could have been but wishful thinking.'

I considered for a moment.

'And was there more? About what will happen?'

'Yes,' she said, smiling. 'Much more.'

'Then I beg you, tell us nothing of it!' I said quickly, for I had become most averse to anything horoscopic.

'I'm in agreement on that one,' said Fergus. 'Who wants to open their Christmas presents early?'

'Me!' said Josie.

'You already did, last time we came to Denmark!' I said, poking her with my toe & making her squeal.

'Personally, I want to see for myself what the future holds in store,' said my beloved man, kissing me & placing his outspread hand on my belly, where – *Satan's knickerbockers!* – I now felt a sudden & distinct kick.

Some months later, back in London, I was occupying the sofa in a state of advanced fecundity with a tangled cobweb of yellow wool across what used once to be my lap (for I was learning to knit), when the telephone rang.

'I know you can barely move, but can you get that, hen?' asked Fergus. 'I'm up to my elbows in plaster of Paris here,' & he was indeed, for he was fabricating a cast of a Greek button, circa AD 800, so I picked up the receiver & said in my now fluent English that this was Mrs Charlotte McCrombie, who did not wish to purchase a new kitchen, sample a cable package, win a free trip to Disneyland, or answer any kind of questionnaire about her spending habits.

'*For Fanden*, can this actually be little Frøken Charlotte?' came a voice in Danish on the other end of the line. A voice I had feared I should never hear again!

'Professor Krak! You are alive! What joy! And I am married to Fergus, & very soon to be a mother!'

'Congratulations,' he said. 'I hope to meet the new addition to the family very soon!'

'O, Professor! *Hurra!* Can this really mean that you are finally returning to us, sir?'

'That is indeed my plan,' he replied. 'But I still have no means by which to leave Marroquinta – delightful though it is – with the Mother Machine destroyed. Have you & your clever husband an alternative, my dear?'

Quickly, I apprised Fergus of the situation, & in an instant he had wiped the plaster from his hands, procured a pen, & was deep in technical conversation with the Professor, clearly as overjoyed as I to discover our friend still so emphatically in the land of the living.

'Right, Fred,' Fergus finished, after much excitable jibber-jabber about stellar schedules, fault-matrices & exotic matter. 'I've got your exact co-ordinates noted, so just stay put on the island. I'm glad to hear Mrs Schleswig has landed on her feet with the Sultan. Though I'm delighted to have her as a mother-in-law, of course, don't get me wrong, she's always welcome here. Oh, horror there on Lottie's face . . . yes, I'll be happy to bring some spare parts for the vacuum cleaner, no problem. The baby's due next month, so we'll be with you –' Here he broke off, & enquired of me, 'When shall we say, commandant?'

'As soon as I've got my figure back.'

'You heard that, Fred? Yes, still the same lassie. Anyway, once that's achieved, we'll get the fake Portakabin transported back to Greenwich Park, & we'll be with you faster than you can say quantum physics.'

If you have never visited the Afric isle of Marroquinta in the year 1000 AD, dear reader (and I'll wager that you have not, as it features in none of the holiday brochures that regularly thud upon your doormat, with titles such as Top Destinations or Paradise Breaks), let me acquaint you with a few of its curious & most exotic delights, as witnessed by the McCrombie family on its first foray to that tropical Nirvana. The entire 'nuclear' clan, now numbering four – for yes, I had by now given birth to a marvellous child (though O, the pain! Have you passed that female rite of passage yet, dear one? If not, do not hurry yourself, for nothing in this life can prepare you for the physical agony of passing a three-kilogram infant through an orifice designed for quite happier purposes!), & was looking quite marvellous on it, if I may make that brief boast – arrived at eventide, landing softly & without undue nausea upon a deliciously warm & sandy shore, where a full moon, a deep golden yellow, hung above the rim of the horizon & the sky shone with stars so dazzling they seemed to come from a sky quite other than any we had known.

Within moments of sighting water, Josie was busy a-splashing on the shoreline & hunting for shells while I, with the sleeping heir in my arms (be impressed, for young Hamish now weighed fifteen kilograms), breathed in the soft & salty breeze & marvelled at the liveliness of the waves, so different from the home life of our own dear Baltic, while Fergus consulted his compass, & established our bearings. 'South by south-west,' he pronounced, 'which means we head in that direction, hen – hey, hang on a moment – *look*!' He was pointing to the middle distance where all at once, beyond a fuzz of trees, a huge & most magical-looking palace appeared before us, shimmering white in the moonlight.

'Hell's bells, it's twice the size of Harrods!' I cried, erecting the three-wheeled buggy, & strapping the babe within – whereupon he awoke & began a cheerful burble which –

our child being a genius – featured syllables from a multitude of languages including Danish, English, Italian, Farsi & Chinese, though as yet conjoined in no particular order. Excitedly, we followed the line of the beach until we came upon a pebbled road which led into a steamy & most succulent jungle, where night-birds hooted & a glorious smell assailed our nostrils. 'Frangipani,' declared my knowledgeable Fergus, inhaling deeply, then plucking two white flowers from the tree above us, one for me & one for Josie. (O, Mr Romantic!) Thus perfumically decorated, we reached a clearing from which there spread an empty road as wide as Strandboulevarden: here (good gracious!) a troupe of camels wandered in swaying fashion along its glittering white cobbles in the direction of the palace. We followed them: colonnades of high pillars materialized alongside the highway, with small shiny-leaved trees from which hung ripe pomegranates, & there now drifted towards us, mingling with the frangipani blossom, a smell like cinnamon, or opium, but sweeter. After some ten minutes we arrived at a pair of carved wooden gates, where stood several huge black-skinned sentry-men in cowrie-shell armour, some of whom set about tethering the camels while two others opened up the great doorway, & waved us in with their long palm-fronds in the direction of a courtyard, where –

'Fred!' yelled Fergus. For who had appeared before us but the tall, gangling, unmistakable figure of Professor Krak! Josie at once flew towards him & hugged his legs, & I could not but laugh aloud, for how very altered he was, with his bushy beard & his vividly red & blue tunic of zig-zaggy stripes & polka dots – quite different from any former garb he had sported, including Fru Krak's pink sea-horse gown! His skin looked weather-beaten, bronzed by the sun to a darker shade, but he seemed in vibrant good health & much rested, & had more flesh on his bones than in olden times, which suited him greatly.

'Dear friends, what a delightful reunion!' he beamed, ruffling Josie's hair & shaking our hands heartily, & then praising the babe who (his lungs being most forceful) now roared his delight & kicked out lustily in an enthusiastic greeting. 'Come, let us present you to the Sultan, who has been my saviour here,' said the Professor, '& you can also be reunited with his delightful queen, Fru Schleswig – who, as you will see, has quite found her element!'

We followed him along cool stone hallways & corridors, through courtyards & enclosed orchards of oranges, lemons and kumquats, past fountains & pools littered with sweet-scented rose-petals of sunset pink & yellow. Good grief, our eyes were fair a-pop! Finally we came upon the throne room where the great black Sultan sat, dignified as a sculpture hewn from granite: he stood upright as we en-tered, & I gasped to see him in all his two-metre immensity, then gasped again, for there, beside him, was enthroned a similarly imposing humanoid creature, who looked mightily familiar! It was only in that moment that I realized it was but scale that had hampered Fru Schleswig's chances of romance in the past, for next to the Sultan she looked quite an acceptable size, & even seemed to take on what might be construed as a version of femininity, clad as she was in a diaphanous garment of scarlet silk encrusted with sequins & festooned with jewellery.

'O Fru Schleswig, what a strange new world!' I cried, as she waved a ring-bedecked hand to greet us.

'What a strange new world!'

'Tiz new to u,' she said. The smell of marzipan wafted from her gigantic bosom. 'But I bin here mor than a twelvmunth. Oi lykes it, & oi am stayin.'

'Dear madam, meet your grandson, Hamish Georg Schleswig McCrombie,' I said with a curtsy, quite unable to hide my delight at my mother's transmogrification – for did I not always tell you, dear reader, that aristocratic blood flowed in my veins? The good woman who begat me being now a veritable queen, does that not entitle me, as the offspring of royalty, to call myself Princess Charlotte? Yes, dear one, it does indeed, & you may now kiss my hand! Ah, how one's deepest aspirations have the knack of coming true, if one but looks the other way!

Upon which happy thought I thrust the infant Prince Hamish at the mountain of silk & jewellery-clad flesh that was the monarchess, where he soon disappeared into her many pillowy layers, gurgling most happily. While the Queen of Marroquinta sat back in her throne & jiggled the babe on her knee, with Josie leaping about in excitement next to her, the Sultan welcomed us most warmly in his clicking Afric tongue, & then impressed us by uttering some Danish.

'*Min kone*,' he said, pointing to Queen Schleswig. ('My wife,' I translated for Fergus & Josie.) '*Meget tyk*.' ('Very fat.') '*Spise mere, bliver tykkere*.' ('Eat more, get fatter.') '*Det er godt*.' ('That's good.') Queen Schleswig beamed. 'See?' she said, reaching for a chicken leg proffered her on a platter by a servant. '*Thatz* the manne for me.'

Not just the man, but the life, too, dear reader – and a life she very much enjoys to this day, for the royal Queen of Marroquinta, aka Fru Fanny Schleswig, opted to stay contentedly put on her distantly doomed Afric isle, & who can blame her, when instead of making do with a chilly annual dog-bath on Classensgade, she can sprawl naked on a chaise-longue by the Sultan's turquoise-encrusted lily-pond, licked slowly by camels tempted by the marzipan she has smeared liberally all over? It seems that at long last Fru Schleswig has finally found her niche in the universe, & it is a life that well suits her, for the Marroquinns appreciate her in a manner no Dane would ever do, this being a land where fat is highly prized, not least by the adoring Sultan who showers his fleshy white queen with jewels ('roobiez, saffyrez & emrelds, I'll hav u no, & no skimpin on the golde settinges, neither'), & once every full moon, in the temple where the sacred vacuum cleaner is housed, she performs certain intimate & ancient rites (to the music of 'Tragic Johanna', as chanted by the Grand Marroquinta Choir), for Queen S, being partial to getting drunk, has profited from some of Franz's ideas & devised a means of converting its pipe & canister system for distilling purposes, thereby producing a most tasty alcoholic spirit not dissimilar to our native *akvavit*. And every night the royal couple feast on delicacies such as Stuck Roast Pig, Fricassee of Flying Fish, Persimmon Roulade & Jellyfish Pie, & though communication is minimal between them, are words not superfluous, when you are tucking into such fare, & drinking yourself into happy oblivion by the light of the silvery moon?

We spent a gaudy & delicious hullabaloo of a week on Marroquinta, with much eating, drinking, dancing & singing: while Fergus & I canoodled lovingly beneath the palms, our babe Prince Hamish learned to crawl, shoving fistfuls of tropical sand into his mouth & frolicking on the beach with his sister, who had brought her Spiderman costume with her & was most happily engaged both in entertaining him, & in devising games to play with the other children who emerged from the shade of the pomegranate trees, full of wonder at the mysterious white foreigners who had landed in their midst.

These things I reflected on, beloved one, in that time, & I impart them to you in the belief that they will one day, if not now, make sense to you, if you have not already discovered them, which you probably have, being far cleverer than I, & much quicker on the uptake! I reflected that accidents will happen, & oft those accidents may turn out to be happy ones, despite initial appearances to the contrary. That however ill appears the hand that Fate has dealt you, such as being burdened with a creature such as Fru S, a sprinkle of imagination can transform pumpkins into carriages & pellets of cat-litter to precious stones, & lavatory-cleaners into Afric queens. That wishing upon a star is not the most foolish thing a girl can do in life. And that there is nothing on this wide earth, & in all time, as important as Love. It is worth dying for. But better, it is worth living for, too. And how I plan to live!

'Where did you go for your holidays, then?' asked the good ladies of the Sunnyside Kindergarten when we returned to London. 'You all look fantastic.'

'Somewhere way, way, way off the map,' said Fergus with a smile.

And now you are dying to know what became of us all. Well, Professor Krak still resides in Greenwich, & makes regular forays in the Time Machine to distant times & places, often accompanied by Fergus, who – just like the monkey Pandora – cannot resist the temptation of bringing back souvenirs to add to his unstoppable collection of ancient artefacts. With the frequent international exhibition of such wares (about which he writes most eloquently in academic journals – and O, did I tell you, reader, about that marvellous brain of his, the size of a pumpkin!) his career has flourished mightily, for reasons I am sure you can surmise – though I beg you, tell no one, for some of his fellow-archaeologists, being somewhat narrow-minded, might consider his visits to the cultures of yesteryear a form of 'cheating', & misprize him.

For my own part, having so much to learn about twenty-first-century Britain, I am loath to take up any more joy-riding, but once a year we enter the Portakabin & make speed for Copenhagen, where Franz remains eccentric but contented in the Sankt Hans, the tentacles of Helle & Georg's beauty empire spread further & wider by the week (even reaching the godforsaken city of Aalborg!), & Else is in a permanent state of pregnancy, for ever since her union with a Russian count (who one day came in to purchase mimosa for his fiancée but, taking one look at Else, decided to switch brides), she is happily breeding a second generation of Østerbro Coquettes. Meanwhile would it surprise you to learn that on the first of such annual visits, the Professor managed to persuade a certain Frøken Gudrun Olsen to accompany us back to London, where she might have plastic surgery to remedy the disfigurement wreaked by Pandora? And that within a few months, her scarred face had become as flawless as her English, & she was seriously considering the Professor's proposal of a partnership, whereby she might mastermind his various endeavours, & become his wife?

'Fru Krak the Second!' she smiled happily, whilst checking the fluctuations of the stock market on her mobile. 'Well, what make you of that?!'

And the Time Machine? I hear you cry. Can I, too, go for a ride?

Well, here I must disappoint you, reader, for much as I wish you could, Professor Krak – with the sensible Gudrun very much in accordance – has been quite adamant that after all our troubles, the machine, and all the possibilities it offers to the Romantic Travelling Soul, shall not be replicated. 'There are plenty of unscrupulous characters about,' he warns, 'who would not hesitate to abuse my discoveries for financial gain – and worse.' Indeed, when he employed a private investigator to track down Henrik Dogger, he learned that the dastardly man had already tried to disseminate his time-travel theories – first in letters to famous astrophysicists &, when they failed to reply, by preaching to the converted at Psychic Fayres! Concerned that it was only a matter of time before a rich individual or venturesome organization took Dogger seriously, on Gudrun's advice Professor Krak had a member of the British underclass break into his lodgings in the distant suburb of Surbiton & erase the thinking parts of his 'software'. Then, as a further precautionary measure, the Professor jiggled & juggled the co-ordinates of the Time-Suckers by means of 'digital re-encryptment' (please ask me not what that entails, dear one, for you should realize by now that I have not the foggiest clue), in such a way that they might remain permanently undiscoverable. 'When Fru Schleswig & I found ourselves stranded in Marroquinta, I made an exception to the confidentiality principle, what with being delirious, & the situation constituting an emergency,' the Professor declared. 'But henceforth, the secret of time-travel dies with me.' Gudrun nodded sagely, & patted his arm.

From dust we came, & to dust must we return.

O, precious one, you know what looms now, & so do I, for the final page is upon us, & thus as all stories must, mine now draws to a close – even though in real life it shall continue, as shall yours, beyond these covers & spin like gossamer through the thin air, dancing up & down & whither knows where!

And what is there left to say of myself? Naught. Naught, dear one, for you see before you a happy woman, who possesses all that the human heart could wish for, & more. More! For I have my cherished-for-ever Fergus, the love of my life, & our dear Josie, & Prince Hamish with his chubby fists & ear-splitting yell, & as I write I am swelled up anew, this time with a set of twins, the first of many dozens of rowdy & undisciplined children we shall surely have, my love & I, in this bright shining place that is neither past nor future, nor before nor beyond, nor the back of beyond, but here and now, where Love dwells, and you too have dwelled a while, listening patiently to this tale, in the time before we parted ways, & O, I shall miss you so, sweet companion, so loyal & true! (And how beautiful you are today! How sweetly flushed your cheek!) But now let us blow a kiss &, as each of us disappears further into the distance, wave our handkerchiefs to one another (O, wipe away that tear, Lottie McCrombie, you sentimental fool!), & from a story which began with real dust, it is to fairy dust that I return, bidding you a fond and tender farewell, with a smile on my lips & a song in my heart, wishing you & those you love a life as joyous as the one I am planning for myself.

But last of all I thank you, thank you, thank you, dear one, for stealing time to spend with me, for you know in your heart, do you not, that my story, for all its apparent unlikeliness, is true, just as a fairy-tale is true, if its listener wishes it so to be! And was it not worth it that you did?

Ah, the power of the heart, beloved reader.

The power of the heart.

O say yes!

ACKNOWLEDGEMENTS

I am grateful to Clare Alexander, Michael Arditti, Polly
Coles, Gina de Ferrer, Humphrey Hawksley and Kate
O'Riordan for their perceptive readings of the manuscript.
And to Carsten, for the real-life love story.

A NOTE ON THE AUTHOR

Liz Jensen is the acclaimed author of *Egg Dancing, Ark Baby* (shortlisted for the *Guardian* Fiction Prize), *The Paper Eater, War Crimes for the Home* and, most recently, *The Ninth Life of Louis Drax*, which is to be made into a film by Anthony Minghella. She lives in London.

A NOTE ON THE TYPE

The text of this book is set in Linotype Janson. The original types were cut in about 1690 by Nicholas Kis, a Hungarian working in Amsterdam. The face was misnamed after Anton Janson, a Dutchman who worked at the Ehrhardt Foundry in Leipzig, where the original Kis types were kept in the early eighteenth century. Monotype Ehrhardt is based on Janson. The original matrices survived in Germany and were acquired in 1919 by the Stempel Foundry. Hermann Zapf used these originals to redesign some of the weights and sizes for Stempel. This Linotype version was designed to follow the original types under the direction of C. H. Griffith.